She begged for two promises

CANARIES IN THE COAL MINE

The first was to save a life.
The second was to take one.

ROSS GREENWOOD

CANARIES IN THE COALMINE
Copyright © Ross Greenwood 2022
All rights reserved

No part of this book may be reproduced in any form by photocopying or any electronic or mechanical means, including information storage or retrieval systems, without permission in writing from both the copyright owner and the publisher of the book.

All characters are fictional.
Any similarity to any actual person is purely coincidental.

The right of Ross Greenwood to be identified as the author of this work has been asserted by him in accordance with the Copyright, Designs and Patents Act 1988 and any subsequent amendments thereto.

A catalogue record for this book is available from the British Library

In memory of Abby Eddings
2001-2019

Forever eighteen years old.

Forever in our hearts.

For V. Thompson, T. Hudson, J. Swift and J. Eatough.
Canaries, one and all.

Trigger warning

From the beginning of this novel there are numerous themes that some may find distressing. If any of these issues affect you, www.bbc.co.uk/actionline can direct you to a whole host of support services. Take care, be safe, Ross.

I was sand, when I should have been concrete.

Trevor

CHAPTER 1

Present day

I watched Samantha traipse around the wing today. It reminded me of a film where a prisoner was forced to carry a wooden cross towards their place of execution. The man repeatedly tripped or collapsed, but, ultimately, he struggled up the hill to his death. I have a feeling Samantha's story will end comparably.

Angelica and I were at the gates when they first brought Samantha onto the wing. The look of primeval fear that was on her face is familiar now after seeing so many others arrive looking the same. Her wild eyes caught mine for a moment. I suspect in hope, but there is little of that here. Certainly, too little to share.

They do what's called first night observations when you arrive. The first night is so hard, but the second night isn't that different. Samantha has been locked up for three nights now. People avoid her. As crazy as it seems, we can sense something is very wrong with her. Once you recognise that, in here at least, it pays to keep your distance. Collateral damage is a regular occurrence.

Samantha trudges up the stairs. Her hair is lank, and her face is blotchy. The baggy, grey tracksuit bottoms swing loosely above her ankles. Her T-shirt is large and misshapen. She doesn't wear a bra.

I've tried to talk to Samantha. Her journey was mine. Those steps belonged to me, what seems long ago.

I even tried to have a chat in her cell. There was nothing in that room other than a change of prison tracksuit, which she'd dropped on the dusty floor, and a TV with wires out of the back. No pictures, no soap, no toothbrush that I could see. Not even any spare underwear.

You have to fight for things in here or you go without. Whether that's verbally with the staff, or physically with the other cons, they are the rules.

When I spoke to her that time, I knocked on her cell door even though she'd left it open. She was slumped on the bed, head in hands. Drool hung from her mouth. Even dignity had left the room.

'I'm Robbie,' I said, after double checking her door card for her name. 'Do you like to be called Sam?'

She looked up after what seemed a long time, then stared right through me. It was as if I was a harmless, shimmering ghost. As though she had already moved to another realm, and I could do her no harm.

Her voice was little more than a squeak.

'I prefer Samantha.'

'Samantha Mainwaring. It's a nice name.'

She blinked, then her head went down again, and she would say no more.

Angelica tried as well, but Samantha just cried in front of her.

It's late afternoon now and Samantha hauls herself along the landing, past judging stares. She reaches her cell and goes inside. Her door gently closes. What can I do? We all have heavy crosses to bear. Few have the strength to help others with theirs.

I'm about to return to my cell when Samantha's door opens. She appears with a blue scarf around her neck. Her face is blank. I watch her tie the other end of the scarf around the railing. The washed-out blue cover of the material reminds me of my bedsheets.

She puts one foot up on the railing and slowly rolls her body over the side.

CHAPTER 2

For a few seconds, I don't react. Her tongue is immediately forced out of her mouth as she violently jerks. She keeps her eyes shut, but her neck muscles strain under the burden. Whatever caused her to perform this act isn't enough for her body not to try to survive.

I hear a long, loud scream. It's coming from my throat. I rush forwards but only her feet are within touching distance from down here. I try to push her soles up, but she kicks my hands away as she struggles.

'Bloody hell,' says Angelica behind me.

We turn to the office, where a young officer appears having heard my cry. His ashen face pales further as he takes in the sight. It's Angelica who acts the fastest.

'Help me, Robbie.'

She runs around to the other side of the table tennis table. I follow and we and shove it under the now gently swinging Samantha. Angelica leaps up onto it. The table sways perilously under her considerable weight. She puts her arms around Samantha's upper thighs and roars as she lifts Samantha up. Angelica's biceps bulge with the effort. Samantha's exposed belly rests on her would be saviour's shoulder. Angelica widens her stance, tips her head back, and lets out a deep growl.

Samantha's eyes open. They are red and furious. She looks down and starts to beat the top of Angelica's head with her fists as though it's a drum.

'Undo the knot,' shouts Angelica.

I sprint across to the landing steps and leap up them

three at a time. I race through the gawking prisoners who are leaning over the railing to watch the show. More officers arrive at the wing gates.

The young lad on duty today has recovered his wits and races up the stairs after me. I reach the ligature point and try to undo the knot. I know at once I have no chance. It is seized solid by the weight it bears. The officer shoves me out of the way and removes a small red tool from his belt. He hooks the blue material inside it and with a quick sawing technique, cuts straight through. There's a crash below. I look over the railings and see Samantha on top of Angelica on the floor. The broken table sits beside them.

Us prisoners are soon hustled towards our cells, like sheep herded by angry farmers. Samantha walks off the wing with a uniformed escort on each side. Incredibly, neither she nor Angelica are seriously injured. Samantha departs with the slightly embarrassed look of someone who tripped over a carelessly placed handbag. Angelica shrugs off the nurse's interest and returns to her cell without saying anything. I sit on the little plastic seat in my room afterwards, stunned, but not surprised.

I suspect I'll never know exactly what happened in Samantha's life to lead her to this point, but I can hazard a guess. The cause will be other people. It usually is. There are anywhere from fifty to a hundred suicides a year in UK prisons, according to Angelica. That's at least one a week. That doesn't even come close to describing the horror of these places, because thousands of attempts are thankfully unsuccessful.

Regardless, approaching sirens are a regular occurrence. People stagger out of their cells, dripping with blood, victims of their own demons. Even when I'm gone from this place, I will never forget what I've seen here. Each act is a nail driven into my memory.

Samantha's nightmare will become part of my own.

CHAPTER 3

The next evening, the prison is calm, but my heart is not. It's strange because I've seen nothing unusual to make me feel this way. I moisten my lips and wipe my palms down my tracksuit bottoms. It's close to bang up time, so I've returned to the relative safety of the doorway of my cell to watch the wing.

The eating area is vacant, and the phones are free. Perhaps I'm not the only one to pick up on the tension that fills the air. It won't be because of what Samantha did yesterday. She's already been forgotten.

That's how it goes inside. People make plans behind locked doors, then their lives change in seconds. The rest of us are forced to carry on. I wonder who the victim will be tonight.

I watch Angelica as she meanders past the deserted pool tables below me. She exudes an innate strength climbing the stairs. At the top, she shouts goodnight to the other inmates. There's an easy confidence to her that was lacking when we first arrived.

In three weeks, it will have been an entire year. At the beginning, it felt as if the world outside and everything in it was frozen. That only *we* continued to live. I've since realised it's the other way around.

Angelica, chosen I think because she is no angel, is not her real name. She hasn't changed it officially yet, but Alex Hemming is dead to her. After what we did, that name will forever be associated with the most terrible of sins.

Angelica high-fives the sneaky Andrews twins when she passes their cell on the way back to her own. They bullied her the most at the beginning, but they're wary now. Everyone is. At first, Angelica denied her crime, but she quickly realised normal rules don't apply behind bars. Fear is power. She soon told people that she committed that devastating crime on purpose.

As our trial date approached, I shrank and wilted further. Angelica changed, too, but in the opposite way. I suppose she knew her likely fate. As the curtain dropped on our old lives, she swiftly accepted the harsh truth of her situation. She called it her destiny. There was even a small smile when the judge's sentence was ten years.

The officers begin locking up. One starts at the bottom landing, the other on ours. Some of the prisoners wait like me in their doorways for a final glimpse of relative freedom before they are locked away. Others have already closed their doors, probably to save them from being slammed shut. Usually, I put my TV on loud or it makes me jump even though I know it's coming. Over eleven months, and I'm still not used to it.

Angelica has reached her cell now. She stops next to the railing and looks around as though admiring the view. Her smile is wide and high. It's odd. I can't understand this latest change. She catches me staring at her and gives me the two-fingered sign for peace, which I return. The hairs rise on my arms and the back of my neck. Something's not right.

I turn to McNulty in the cell next to me. Seventy-nine-years-old, double the time behind bars than in front of them, and proud of it. There's a downturned mouth this evening and real concern in those tired eyes.

'What is it?' I ask.

McNulty has a tell for nervousness: a fist jiggles like when you shake dice before rolling. Right now, both McNulty's hands are going like the clappers.

'Bad news, Little Mouse.'

'What's the matter?' I ask.

'I seen it before.'

McNulty's and Angelica's gazes are locked. Angelica nods at McNulty, with a look that I can't discern. I spot a slight nod in reply, before McNulty slowly shuffles around to stare at me.

'Seen what?' I have to shout over a roaring din as two inmates fly out of the showers at the end of the wing, naked, towels swinging up high like they're riding rodeo bulls.

'She's going to make a statement,' says McNulty, who then disappears from view and closes the cell door.

I look back to Angelica who returns her focus to me. She hooks her thumbs together and flaps her hands. The gesture of a bird. Even across the drop to the floor below, I detect another change in her demeanour. Her anger, which has recently been clear to us all, has vanished. She smiles because I understand her message.

Angelica is a canary. She wants to know if I'll be one, too.

CHAPTER 4

The sound of slamming doors becomes deafening as the officers near my cell. Hardwick is on duty. He's a fair man, but overworked like the rest of them. I stand in the doorway, but I'm not sure what to say. I must say something.

'In,' he orders me.

I step back, the door slams and the heavy locking mechanism clunks into place. Too late, he's gone. My skin tingles all over my body. Returning to the back of my single cell, I shout out of the window vent.

'McNulty.'

It's likely McNulty can hear me. We've conversed this way ever since I got a single cell. That was down to Angelica. I was happy to share with her, but a month ago, she asked for a meeting with one of the governors and we were soon split up. Time has slowed since then. The nights in here draw out on your own. Concerns and worries fester and grow without distraction.

Angelica was vague when I asked why she wanted her own pad. All she said, cryptically, was that she needed to be alone.

'McNulty!'

'What is it, Little Mouse?'

McNulty has called me that ever since I left my cell on my first morning here. I was on the other side of the landing then. McNulty and a few of the other old folk on here watched as I came out for breakfast. Scurried was the word they used. They said it was like seeing a mouse stick its nose out of its hole to check for danger, before scampering along while sticking close to the skirting board. Not stopping for more than a second, constantly on edge, eyes searching, checking, then racing back to safety with its food and vanishing from sight.

I've never minded the nickname because that's how I am here. In fact, if I'm honest, it's the way I've lived my whole life. Since that terrifying first morning here, my behaviour hasn't changed. I soon discovered there are cats here to my mouse.

Thank God I'm getting released before Angelica is and not the other way around.

I shout out to McNulty.

'What have you seen before? What's wrong with Angelica?'

'I told you. She's going to make a statement.'

'What kind of statement? What do you mean?'

'I don't know, but she's behaving like her mind is set. Maybe she's going to piss in a cup and throw it at the officers at roll count. Angry inmates often do that if they aren't happy about getting transferred.'

I think back to her behaviour today, but Angelica's been at the workshop both shifts, and only nodded at me when she returned. She looked a bit washed-out, but we all do inside. Turns out she has a talent for constructing things, like her father. I was busy mopping the wing all day. My mum used to joke I'd end up as a cleaner. I swore blind that I never would.

'Angelica never told me she was being transferred,' I shout.

I strain to make out the reply but the distorted chat from cheap TV speakers is all I can hear. It's McNulty's way of telling me the conversation is over. I return to my door and stare through the crack at the side where the hinges are. Angelica's closed cell door is just in view. What will happen when it's opened for roll count? She didn't seem out of control. Might she attack the staff?

Prison is routine. The only different thing of any note recently is the conversation we had just before we were locked in two days ago on Saturday night. She asked, no begged, for two favours. We'd been watching a Harry Potter film and I didn't take what she asked too seriously. She mentioned it again when the screws told me to get out of her room for lock up. I stopped at the door, and impulsively agreed with a smile.

I wasn't getting released for three weeks, so I knew I'd have time to clarify what she meant. But maybe I didn't have that time because she'd already heard about her transfer.

What occurs to me now is that she's planning to leave in a way that shocks. I'll be walking from this prison in three weeks' time. It looks like they might have to drag her out. Hopefully still kicking and screaming.

CHAPTER 5

My spinning mind forces me to sit on my bed. At times, I forget the horror of our situation. The shock and unnaturalness of this place fades after a few weeks and you rub along. We humans are nothing but adaptable. We seek out little pleasures to survive. Angelica and I can usually find humour even at the darkest of times.

Sleeping in a barred, concrete, rectangular box where a jailer locks you in at night becomes your normality. A thin blue mattress, compressed by many more before you, on a metal tray bolted to the wall, is your bed. You simply get used to it. If someone steals your pillow, rest your head on a jumper instead. Wait until someone else's head is turned, then take their pillow.

The only thing that you don't get used to is the worry. A constant hum of anxiety surrounds everyone. I'm surprised the prison doesn't vibrate with all the fear within its high walls. At least the violence is tangible and exact. Afterwards, you can usually put those events to bed, whereas your thoughts never sleep. I often wonder if I were to die in here, would anyone apart from my mother really know or care.

The kind of life you are going to have when you leave prison is also an energy-sapping concern that never goes away. Looking forwards is only positive if you have something good waiting for you. Here, only the foolish are in denial about the challenges that lie ahead.

I hear the first metal click of the heavy locks as the officers begin roll count and open the first door. There's a shout of 'cell one, two', the bang of the door shutting, then the loud scraping from the long bolt as it's drawn across with finality into the metal frame. That means there are two inmates in the first cell. The next shout is 'cell two, one' for the second cell, which has one occupant.

I get up and squint through the gap at the side of the door again. I find myself flinching at each jarring sound. When the bottom landing has been counted, the officers thud up the stairs in their heavy work boots. I hold my breath as they open Angelica's cell. One! The door bangs shut. Nothing happened.

Instead of feeling peace, my mouth dries and my knees buckle. I know what she's going to do. I shout but McNulty removes both hearing aids at night to read. The TV is often left on loud to irritate the rest of us. The shouts of the officers as they approach my cell becomes clearer as they get closer. They open McNulty's door.

'One,' bellows Hardwick. 'Turn that down or off, McNulty.'

The blaring chat of what I'd guess is a quiz show loudens, but then cuts to silence. There's a pause of a few seconds. I imagine Hardwick staring hard at McNulty before the door is closed. When they open my cell, I'm ready.

'Sir, I need to speak to you.'

'Tomorrow,' says Hardwick, pulling the door to.

'Please, one minute. It's life or death.'

The door stops moving. His right eye squints as his resolve weakens. He's one of the good guys, after all.

'I'll come back.'

I hear a tut from the other officer next to him before my door is closed and the bolt is rammed home. I try to calm my breathing, but blood pounds through my veins like a high-speed train in a tight mountain tunnel. I pick my plastic chair up off the floor where I knocked it in my haste to talk to Hardwick. Grabbing a brush, I sit and run it through my thick, long, black hair. I've been doing this to relax ever since I was little. Only today, it doesn't work. My ears ring and my heart races. Angelica's serious face appears in my mind.

I've never known anyone like her. She's certainly one of a kind. I met her the day I started my first job in a burger restaurant. It's hard to believe that was just two years ago.

CHAPTER 6
Two years ago

My mother grabs her coat and pulls on her Peruvian chullo hat, complete with pompoms even though it's April. She's never got used to the weather here, having spent virtually her whole life in the humid tropical climate of the Ecuadorian lowlands. She once ventured to Quito for six months to work, but apart from meeting my father, hated every moment.

'*Estoy lista. ¡Vamos!*' she shouts with a stern nod, which means she's ready to leave.

I've told her three times that I'm more than happy to go on my own, but she insists on coming. My first evening shift starts today at 4 p.m. and finishes at 11 p.m. I haven't been able to sit still since I got offered the job yesterday. It will be my first.

My mother finishes her cleaning jobs by midday. She has a school at the crack of dawn, then a dry cleaner after that, before finally a pub, all before they open. She's been self-employed for years and no stranger to hard work, perhaps even thriving on it. I'm not sure why I'm so different.

All three places affectionately call her Tiger. My mum, Maria, had never learned English before we arrived. Most rural Ecuadorians don't bother studying it at home. There's a phrase we use. You come to Ecuador; you speak Spanish! She can follow a movie, but that's about it.

She cleaned for other companies at first but reckoned they were getting wealthy off her hard work. One day, she walked around the shops and pubs in the city centre and pitched to clean for them. My father wrote her sales line down for her, "You pay me ten pounds one hour. I am cleaning *tigre*", which is Spanish for tiger. Then she got out her big cleaning bag and started to show them, polishing the counter at the adult-learning school, the bars at the five pubs she went in, and even wiping down the one-armed bandits at a betting shop.

Three places took her on and they love her. She's funny, sweet, even smaller than me, and a relentless cleaner. It helps that she is a little *loca*, too. She has a huge family back home and they're all pretty crazy.

It's nice that she wants to escort me today, but there are two real reasons why she wants to come. The first is because she's lonely. England is a strange place for her. Peterborough feels like a big city at two-hundred thousand people when you're used to no more than a thousand. She can't get her head around how modern it is. She won't even contemplate visiting London, thinking it's full of people madder than her. I've explained many times that EastEnders isn't a documentary. She's still not convinced.

The second reason is what's currently arriving at the bus stop outside our house. It's a double decker Stagecoach bus this time. My mum has a look of uncontrolled glee on her face, waving madly at the driver who smiles back. They all know her because she catches them for work. For my mum, the fact you can pay about £50 per month and get unlimited travel to work and back on these tall, growling, steaming, space-age vehicles is almost too amazing for her to comprehend. It's a long way from the broken-down, noisy chicken buses in our villages.

I pay my fare and can't help grinning at my mother as she presses her pass against the glass of the driver's cab like a police detective showing their warrant. She gives him the same stern nod she gave me. We take a seat, letting her be next to the window. As always, she squeezes my knee hard as we 'take off', then sits in silence like everyone else. She's usually the only one grinning.

Since my father's gone, we lead a quiet life. Pointless, I would say. School was hard for me arriving aged fourteen. My mum is mestizo; mixed race from Amerindian and European ancestry. I'm not sure what that makes me with a black British father, but I found it hard to fit in here. Not that anyone was especially rude. They all knew I was different and kept their distance, having mostly made their friendships long before I arrived. Whenever I tried to make friends, it felt like I was trying to prise them away from another person, which would make them lonely instead.

My mum needs hotter, more consistent weather than Peterborough can provide. The fact she hasn't bothered to learn the language properly tells me she doesn't plan to stay. Maybe there's a third reason why she's coming now. She wants to make sure I actually turn up at Gordonsburger. I've choked numerous times in the past on the way to jobs.

The bus cruises swiftly through the streets and out onto the parkways heading towards Serpentine Green Shopping Centre. We get off, link arms and head into the entrance. It's a busy Friday afternoon. The sign at the door tells us Serpentine Green is the leading Peterborough shopping destination with over thirty-five high street and top branded fashion stores.

I love it here. It's all glass and marble and full of a wide range of people. The checkout person on my last visit had shaved half her head and dyed the remaining half green to match her lipstick and eyeshadow. I wish I could be so modern. Sometimes I fool myself that I'm going to go to the Notting Hill carnival, Pride in London or Glastonbury and just be who I am, but I never do. I lie on my bed and watch other people having fun on YouTube, pretending that my mother likes it when I stay home.

I passed my GCSEs at sixteen with good grades, but found the jump to A-levels a real struggle with the language barrier. My English was excellent when I first arrived. My father spoke it all the time, so I'm full of his strange British phrases. It improved fast to a higher level, but not quickly enough. I was always a few seconds behind, especially with technical terms, which might not seem a lot, but the confidence oozed from me. My brain would freeze whenever I was asked a question in front of the class.

Perhaps I'm fooling myself there too, because I'm no genius, that's for sure. I wasted half a year trying to improve my grades, then dropped out. That was a year ago. To my shame, I can't think of anything much that I've done since. It's easy to blame Covid, but there were jobs out there.

Sometimes I help my mum with her cleaning if she's tired, but I don't want any commitment to that line of work. I receive universal credit which I can exist on. Most days I look at 'stuff' on the internet. Recently I've been researching what happened to my father, but suspect I'll never do anything about it. What a life! The few friends I made all went to university. We catch up on holidays but other than that I'm as solitary as my mum.

The owners of Gordonsburger are a handsome couple not much younger than her. Keith is from Gordon, he told me with a big grin at the interview, hence the name. I assumed from his almost impenetrable accent, that Gordon is somewhere in Scotland. His wife, Laura, is Argentinian and the main reason I got the job was because she could speak Spanish to me. After all, my CV was a badly concealed web of lies. When we arrive, she is outside cleaning the restaurant windows in the same fervent manner my mum wipes down the desks at the school.

'Roberta,' says Laura, holding out her hand.

'Robbie,' I reply, shaking it with a smile.

Laura and my mother stare at each other for a nanosecond before deciding that they are going to be great friends. They hug and kiss and chat about me at twenty to the dozen as though I'm not right in front of them. Finally, my mum looks like she's about to leave.

'Robertiti,' shouts my mum. '*Fuerte!*'

Robertiti or Robertina are Spanish terms of affection for my middle name, which is what I go by. Laura will no doubt become Lauriti. My mother scowls at me, then clenches her fist, then she and Laura laugh their heads off. Must be a middle-aged South American mother thing. Not feeling at all *Fuerte*—strong—I push open the door and leave them to their chuckles. I find Keith taking payment from the only customer in the place. Keith smiles a lot behind his bird's nest beard.

'Roberta, welcome. If you go over there with Angelica, I'll be right over. She's starting tonight too.'

I glance across to where he's pointing. Staring back at me is a big woman, and she looks glum. I walk over and stand next to her. She's nearly a foot taller. Angelica stares down at me for at least five long seconds, all thick, black eyeshadow and glaring blue eyes.

'You look a bit like a skinny Mexican Rihanna, with sexy eyes. Lucky you.'

Then she gives me a wink. Straight away, like the two of them outside, I know I'm meeting someone special.

CHAPTER 7

The shift is nearly over. It was chaos. The waiter who was supposed to teach us the ropes didn't show. That left Angelica, Laura and me servicing twenty tables. I made many mistakes. I made a bad choice with my footwear. Angelica trod on my foot twice, so maybe steel caps are in order, or at least trainers like she's wearing.

Yet, I love it. The pace is fast. I revel in being the centre of attention for the first time in my life, even if it is only when I'm taking an order. Angelica stops too suddenly in the kitchen and a steak she's carrying slides off the plate and hits the deck. She picks it up, says five seconds under her breath, and pops it back on the plate. When they pay, the customer says it was the best steak he'd had in years. He must like them with the additional flavours acquired from the floor.

The atmosphere in the place isn't quite right, though. It's large and gloomy inside, so even though there are plenty of customers, everyone seems to whisper at their tables. They've only been open a few months, so they have time. The menu seems to combine Scottish food with Argentinian steaks. Well, I don't know much about running a restaurant, but I suspect at these prices, the novelty of this place will soon wear off.

I'm nicely tired when Laura leaves us to the last few diners so she can cash up the tills. My final table is a couple. They're both short, white and ginger. They'd clearly had a row before they came in. He was rude to me and her when he ordered. I kept noticing Angelica look over as I tolerated it and remained professional. It will be nice to get rid of them though, so as I take over the dessert menu, I'm hoping they'll decline. I hand it over with a smile.

'We'll be needing a free dessert,' says the bloke.

'Why is that?' I reply.

'Our meals were horrible.'

I glance at their plates. His is so clean I should check under the table to see if he brought his dog in with him. Hers has about a third of her huge chicken pie left. She looks as though she would like to crawl under the remains of her crust.

'Not that horrible,' I say, gesturing to the plates.

'The customer is always right. I'll pay for the starters, that's it. Fetch the manager.'

I'm not sure what to say. Glancing over, I catch Angelica's eye who's letting out the final other two clients. She strides over. I open my mouth to explain, but she cuts me off.

'It's okay, darling. I heard.'

She stands next to the table, leans across the woman, and places her fists on the table in the same way a gorilla would. It's the most unladylike gesture I've ever seen in my life. She leans into the man's personal space so far, that he's forced to lean back in his seat.

'Get ya fucking credit card out, or you'll never forget my boat race.'

And, just like that, Angelica and I are friends.

CHAPTER 8
Present day

She explained after that boat race was slang for face. I'm just recalling how much I liked Angelica from the start, when the flap on the observation panel to my cell creaks open. Hardwick's eye appears in it.

'What is it?'

'Open the door, please.'

'I can't open the door now we're in night state.'

'Rubbish. You have to when you let the court returns back in.'

'That's different.'

'Please, sir.'

I hear him growl. Then the bolt is yanked back, and my door is unlocked. Hardwick opens the door all the way. He's a big man and he fills the doorway.

'Make it quick before the roll clears. I've got a date tonight.'

I realise I have only one shot at this. People learn swiftly in prison, and I'm no different.

'Angelica's going to kill herself.'

Hardwick doesn't hide his disappointment at hearing that. His eyes close. If he takes my word as gospel, then he'll need to open an observation book on Angelica. That will take him hours. I've had a few opened on myself.

'What makes you say that?' he asks.

'She told someone she was checking out. That can only mean one thing.'

I observe Hardwick's struggle on his face. He curses

and closes my door. I stare through the gap. I can hear the tinny echo as he taps his keys on the railing while he stamps around the landing. He comes into view just before he reaches Angelica's cell, which he opens up. He's outside it for a good minute, but all I can hear is rap music that's coming from a few cells along from me. Another minute or so later, Hardwick shuts Angelica's door, walks away, then opens my door again.

'I've just had a good chat with her,' he says. 'She's checking out because she must. Her transfer papers have come through.'

'Did you ask her if she felt suicidal?'

'Yes, and she said to tell you she's fine.'

I can't help a little smile. Not much gets past Angelica.

'She's lying. I know she is. Put her on observations throughout the night.'

'I'm not opening a book on her just because you've got a funny feeling in your stomach. I eat the food here too, so that's not unusual.'

His attempt at lightening the tone isn't appreciated.

'It's on you, then. I've told you, so if she takes her life tonight, they'll want to know why you didn't do anything about it.'

The small smile slips off his face. There will be no little favours from him in the future.

His radio springs to life.

'The roll is clear, both sides of the prison.'

Hardwick lets out a deep breath.

'I'll speak to the night staff. It's Donna, and she's already in.'

'Thank you, sir. She can always look in tonight when she's doing her other checks.'

Hardwick softens his stern look.

'Tonight's shift was my last on this wing. I said I'd do a year, but I'm going back to the intensive drug landings. Funny how I'm looking forward to the old-fashioned dishonesty of shoplifters and burglars. This wing drags you down after a while.'

I nod.

'Okay, good luck, sir. You've always been fair to me.'

Hardwick's lazy smile is back.

'I hear you're away yourself. Good luck to you, too. I never thought someone your size would last five minutes with all these weird types.'

I give him a rueful smile. My survival on here is very much down to my guardian Angelica. This time he locks the door so quietly, I can't even hear the lock clicking into place.

I shout out to Seidu to turn the volume down, but there's little chance I'll be heard over the drill music that's now blaring out. Seidu is one of the larger overfriendly ones on the wing who you wouldn't want to bump into when you were alone. So instead, I stand and stare through the door, knowing that every time the night shift starts, they look in all the cells to make sure the handover roll count is correct. That's my chance to catch Donna.

Donna is the opposite of Hardwick. She is heavily overweight and seems to struggle with the constant walking which her role requires. I imagine her knees creaking on the stairs. Her inspections of the cells are dutiful at best. It's forty minutes later and nearly eight p.m. when I finally hear her plodding around the landings. She's got an irritating way of snapping the observation panels back into place which is just an unnecessary annoyance for us inside. When she reaches my panel, I'm staring out of it. She jerks backwards.

'A word, miss, please.'

She plods to the next door and their panel squeaks open. I slap my palm against the door, then knock five times on it, hurting my knuckle.

'What is it?' hisses a returning Donna through the gap in the door.

The night staff aren't usually fully trained officers, so they only have a key for absolute emergencies.

'Did Mr Hardwick pass on the message about checking

on Ms Hemming?'

'Yes, he did. I said I'd look in every hour. Happy?'

'No, once an hour is not enough. It needs to be much more than that.'

'I'll be the one who decides what's appropriate.'

'That's correct. After all, it will be you they question if anything happens.'

We eyeball each other for a moment, then she's gone.

Lazy cow, I think, then stop myself and take three deep breaths. I'd be as cruel as nearly everyone else in here if I started judging people on looks. I, of all people, should know better.

My cool lasts an hour. Donna comes back on the wing, plods up to Angelica's door, has a quick look in, then leaves. She ignores my attempts to get her to come to my cell. I give her a minute, then stab the emergency call button.

'State your medical emergency,' comes out of the intercom. It's Donna's Yorkshire accent.

'If she'd cut her wrists half an hour ago, she'd already be dead.'

'Oh, it's you. I've just spoken to Alex. She's fine. Said she's looking forward to getting out of here.'

'Her name's Angelica now.'

'Yeah, whatever. Don't press this buzzer again unless you have a medical emergency.'

I feel so helpless. It's the worst feeling and a very common one in prison. One of the folks on this wing rang home and a stranger answered the phone. It sounded like a party was going on in the background. They lost their mind afterwards. Your brain plays cruel tricks on you here, letting you think the worst is occurring, and there's not a damn thing you can do about it.

I wait another forty-five minutes and can't stand it any longer. The call button gets pressed again. I can just make out the sound of it ringing in the hub area at the centre office where the night auxiliaries sit.

I check the time on the TV and five minutes pass. I press the call button again and again. Finally, she answers.

'I told you earlier. Do not abuse your in-cell call button. Someone with a real emergency could be trying to get through.'

'Do your fucking job,' I holler into the speaker, which is stupid, really, but I feel better for a few seconds afterwards.

I stand quietly at the door to listen to her coming onto the wing. Still nothing. I press the buzzer again. This time I can't hear it ringing, so she must have turned the ringer off or put it on mute. That's not uncommon. I kick my door hard five times. Bad-natured abuse is yelled from a variety of directions. Most of it mentions what's going to happen to my arse when we're unlocked in the morning.

Then I hear Donna plodding onto the wing. She checks Angelica's cell for three seconds, then vanishes. I again boot my door, but she ignores it.

I've had some long nights in here, but nothing like this. Each second is like a poke in the eye. Another hour passes, and Donna doesn't complete any more checks. Maybe I'm being stupid. No, something's not right. Every part of my body is tingling with worry. I press the call button. After another minute of nothing, I put my TV volume on full. This upsets numerous other inmates around me.

Donna returns to the wing. She once more, checks on Angelica, then I hear her approaching my cell. I turn the TV off.

'Last chance,' she snarls through the door. 'If I hear one more peep from you, I'll turn off the power to your cell and place you on report. You'll lose your TV tonight and probably for two weeks after. It's not worth it. Alex says she's going to sleep now. She wanted me to pass a message on. Don't forget what she said and keep the noise down. Don't forget what I've said, either. Last chance.'

An hour later, after I repeat the behaviour she warned against, my TV dies and the lights go out except for the emergency panel. A notice that I've been put on report will no doubt slide under my door shortly. I hear the hollow sound of McNulty tapping in between the window bars with what sounds like a plastic mug. It's how McNulty gets my attention.

'Go to sleep, Little Mouse. You've done all you can.'

I'm about to protest, but what more can I do? It's gone midnight now. I put my pyjamas on, which are one of the few little luxuries I spend my money on, then slip under the thin duvet. It's as impossible as trying to sleep before Santa comes. I manage to listen to three more visits from Donna by two a.m., which I suppose is better than nothing. My eyes begin to close, and I feel myself nodding off.

But what will they find in Angelica's cell in the morning?

CHAPTER 9

I wake up to the prison coming to life. It's cold in my room, being on the wrong side of the building for the morning sun. I reach out of the bed and drag my duvet off the floor and re-cover myself with it. My TV is on but silent, so they must have put the power back on in my cell.

There are too many coughs and footsteps for them just to be getting out the kitchen workers, so they must be unlocking everyone's doors.

I remember Angelica! I roll off the mattress, numb and stiff, pull my black pumps on and stagger towards my door. I note that a piece of paper hasn't been slid under it, so maybe I haven't been placed on report. The unlocking officer has finished Angelica's side of the landing, although he's seriously taking his time. Some officers swing the door wide open and say, "Morning, breakfast!". Today's officer has just cracked each door open a few inches. It looks dark inside Angelica's cell. Nothing appears to stir within.

Right now, I understand the real horror of prison. It's the waiting. Too much of which is a terrible thing. Waiting for court, waiting for sentencing, waiting to be unlocked, waiting for meals, waiting to be assaulted, waiting to leave, or waiting to die. It's a breathless, claustrophobic feeling knowing your life is ticking away and all you can do is wait.

My mind flashes through the millions of moments Angelica and I shared stuck together for the many months we shared a tiny cell. Swapping make-up and dreams. Confessing to worries and sins. Building bonds that will never be broken. She would brush my hair as my mum used to do. I would patch up her scratches and bruises from the fights that came along like the buses my mum used to ride. This cannot be the end.

I surprise the officer opening my door by yanking it out of his hands as soon as the lock is turned. It's an older, grey-haired guy, who is usually only in the central control area. I don't need to look at his name badge to know he is Senior Officer Exton.

'Is Angelica okay, sir?'

'I'm just covering for someone running late, Robbie. Speak to the other officer, or go and see for yourself.'

I slip past him and edge through the sluggish bodies coming out of their pads. This morning smell never gets old either. Many on here don't ever use the showers. I weave around some of the bigger inmates as I hasten to Angelica's cell. One attempts a swat at me as though I'm an irritating fly. Angelica's door is still only marginally open, so she has not yet shown her face. When I get outside it, I take a deep breath, then push at the door with my index finger. It swings open with an unoiled squeak.

'Angelica?' I ask the lump in the bed.

The lump moves slightly and makes a bit of a groan. Smiling, I stride to the windows and pull open the curtains to let the light and warmth stream in. There's an odd aroma in the room, kind of musty and sweet. Similar to when people are making hooch, but this smells less organic. It's not like Angelica to let her room get like this. She's always wasting her hard-earned wages on joss sticks.

'Angelica, come on, get up. You had me worried.'

The bedsheet has been pulled over her head, but she's breathing, because I can see the material moving up and down. The sheet is damp though, where it rests on her forehead. I step closer to the bed where the smell is stronger. Angelica's breathing catches in her throat. It reminds me of my father's death rattle.

I move my hand to the top of the sheet, pinch the edge of it, then pull it slowly from her face. The sun casts a yellow glow over her blotchy skin. I rest the back of my hand on her forehead. It's cold and clammy.

Angelica's eyes flick open, and I scream.

CHAPTER 10

Her left hand reaches out from under the sheet and lightly holds my arm, pulling me towards her.

'Promises,' she gasps. Her rancid breath is the source of the fetid smell.

I can't help myself from recoiling. With her yellow eyes, and pallid skin, she can only have overdosed. I lurch out of the room. One of the officers is looking up at me from the landing below, the other, Exton, is slowly making his way along the landing towards me. He's shouting for everyone to get out of his way. I tip my head back and this time I really shriek.

Exton arrives and roughly moves me to the side. I watch him wrinkle his nose when he steps through the doorway. His radio sparks into life.

'Personal alarm, personal alarm. Senior Officer Exton, last known location, Yankee One wing. First response, please attend.'

Exton walks straight out again, pressing the talk button on his radio.

'QV, this is officer Exton. We have a code blue on Yankee wing. I repeat, code blue on houseblock three. Ambulance required. Hotel Three required.'

Exton shouts over the railing to his colleague.

'Bang 'em up. Ambulance on the way.'

Exton turns to me.

'What's she taken?'

'I don't know.'

He scowls at me.

'Get back to your cell, then. Move!'

I step backwards, but don't want to leave. The first responders arrive. Officers in white shirts flood the wing, shouting as they push inmates into their cells. I watch the nurse with her big bag slung over her shoulder cautiously following behind them, keeping one eye on the prisoners who still haven't returned to their cells. It's the same nurse who came when it was my turn to completely lose control.

A tall Asian officer races towards me, pointing to the other side of the wing.

'Behind your door,' he snarls.

'I need to know…'

'Go, last chance,' he prods his heavy keys at my chest.

Before I know it, he's hustled me around the landing and into my cell. He slams the door and locks it before I have chance to get my mind in gear. Oh, Angelica. What have you done? How could I have not noticed?

I rest my back against the door and slump to the floor. My mind is filled by images of my father. His eyes were the same colour.

CHAPTER 11

Six years ago

The school bus drops me two hundred metres up the road from our house. I can tell something is wrong because my mother watches me from our doorway. My mother is rarely still. We live at the edge of the village, so I have to travel for an hour to a bigger town for my education. Even though we have electricity and inside toilets now, there's no internet except whatever signal you might get from your mobile.

'*Robertiti, venga!*'

My mother beckons me into the house, where my father sits at the battered wooden table in the kitchen. He's removed the sunglasses that he's been wearing a lot lately. We are close in a way that children should be with their fathers. He's a comforting presence who provides for us, makes me laugh at mealtimes and keeps my mother very happy. They smile all the time around each other, or they did until my father became poorly. I sit next to my dad. My smile slips when I notice his odd eyes.

There's a watery corona around his irises and a faint yellow hue to what should be the white parts. Even his normally glowing tan skin looks dulled. He always speaks in English to me even though he now speaks Spanish like a local.

'You know I haven't been feeling right, Robbie. Well, today we got the results. I'm afraid it's cancer.'

While cancer is still a scary word, it's not an uncommon subject out here in the banana growing regions of Ecuador. It's well known that those who work in the industry have a much higher chance of suffering from it due to the pesticides.

'What kind of cancer?'

'It's a blood one, and reasonably rare. The only good thing is that it's a fairly slow-growing cancer and with access to modern medicines the prognosis is good.'

I picture our local hospital, which is far from modern. From what I've heard, even the big ones in Quito and Guayaquil don't fill you full of confidence, either. Few who visit them seem to come home.

'Right,' is all I can think of. 'Now what?'

My mother, who has been wringing her hands next to my father, can't control herself. She blurts a reply in rapid Spanish.

'Your father is going back to England. The chances of a cure are much higher there. We suspected something like this, so plans have been made. We leave next week.'

'We? You and him? What about me?'

'You can come too if you like, or finish your schooling here. You'll have to stay with my sister because once we've paid for plane tickets and other costs, we won't have enough left to keep this place on.'

'Where will we sleep in England?'

'Your father has a school friend in a place called Peterborough with a big spare room. We can stay for free until your father is better and we find work.'

My mother talks with confidence, but her bottom lip quivers when she stops speaking. She's barely been out of the province since I was born. She doesn't speak English and all her family are here.

'What do you think?' my dad asks me.

'What will help? Me being here, or coming with you.'

'I want you both with me,' he replies without missing a beat.

I answer by throwing my arms around his neck.

I feel guilty afterwards because I'm excited. I've known forever that I don't belong in a small town. I've always imagined living somewhere big and flash, despite the fact that few locals move away. I want to be at the centre of things but not be the centre of things, if that makes sense. This is my chance to let the world know I exist.

I hope I'm ready.

CHAPTER 12
Present day

I'm given my breakfast at my cell door, long after Angelica has been stretchered away. The female officer who delivers my sandwich, crisps and yoghurt doesn't even open her mouth once despite all my questions.

They keep us locked down until it gets close to lunchtime. When my door opens, the female officer who fed me earlier is there with an older woman in a suit who I met for the first time on the day I arrived here.

'Come with us, please,' says Ms Parkin.

They walk away down the landing, giving me little choice but to follow. The officer who rang for the ambulance is on the gate. He looks over my head when I pass, making me feel invisible. Ms Parkin is the prison deputy, or something like that. It was her who told us which part of the prison we would be in when we arrived. I follow them off the wing into an office immediately on the left of the gates. They both sit on the other side of a desk, leaving me with a seat opposite. Parkin was okay then, and by the kind expression on her face now, that's going to continue.

'Robbie, can you shed some light on what happened to Angelica?'

'Is she okay? I've got no idea. I think she was being transferred, and it all got to her.'

'Hasn't she only just been sentenced?' asks Parkin.

I nod. They exchange glances.

'She would need to have her sentence plan completed before she was transferred out,' said Parkin. 'They usually take at least three months. Why did you think she was being transferred?'

I shrug, not wanting to say that Angelica told me she was. It seems she lied to me because she planned to leave for good.

'Is she going to be okay?'

Parkin maintains eye contact.

'She's taken an overdose, but she was unable to tell us of what. She slipped into a coma shortly before arriving at the hospital. There are issues with her major organs, in particular her liver and kidneys.'

'That doesn't sound good.'

'They pumped her stomach, but it was empty. Too much time has passed, so whatever she took is in her system.'

'Will she die?'

'I suspect it's going to be touch and go. It'd help if we knew what she'd taken.'

'I'm sorry. I'll see if I can find out on the wing. Someone will know something.'

'Okay, Robbie. Time's ticking. You've got twenty minutes until everyone gets locked up again. Anything you find out could save your friend's life.'

CHAPTER 13

The officer lets me back on my wing just as another wing are returning from the gym. I get verbally abused from the usual suspects, like I often do. They all cheer when I give them the finger, but I haven't got time for fun. I race upstairs to the first-floor landing.

McNulty is the person to ask about wing rumours. Despite being old and cantankerous, and feigning indifference to others' problems, McNulty knows everyone's business. The cell is empty. I ask the officer if he's seen McNulty or Banks, the other busybody on here.

'In Banks' cell,' he replies.

They prefer to chat in Banks' cell. It's right down the bottom, the last cell. Banks was put there, apparently, because of incredible snoring. I find them both sitting on the bed looking very worried.

'What is it?' I ask.

'Banks lost three paracetamol last week. Wilko just came in to say that others have discovered missing pills recently. I've just checked mine and six of them are gone too, along with some other heart medication.'

'A few of my diabetic tablets also vanished over the last week,' said Banks.

'Why didn't you say something?'

'We're old. I often can't remember whether I've taken them, so I'm always running out.'

'Can you overdose on paracetamol?'

Banks and McNulty nod in tandem. I'm just about to sprint from their cell to tell Parkin, when I remember about the transfer story.

'McNulty, did Angelica say the word transfer, or did she say the word leaving, or something else?'

McNulty looks devastated on realising the implications, but manages to comment.

'Thinking on it, she just said checking out.'

I race back to the wing gates, but the screw won't let me through them.

'It's to tell Parkin something,' I shout at him.

'It's bang up. You don't have time to leave the wing.'

My patience snaps again. I'm about to display some of the anger that got me here in the first place when I notice Parkin stand up in the hub. She has a phone to her ear. I watch her nod twice, swallow, then slowly put the phone down.

She looks over in my direction, white-faced, and shakes her head.

CHAPTER 14
Two weeks later

It's mid-morning when the priest comes to see me. He's the only one who's been of any help. Parkin visited my cell a few days after Angelica died, but only seemed intent on brushing it under the carpet. I had a stirring of anger that people hadn't done their jobs that night, but she was very placating. In the end, complaining wasn't going to bring Angelica back, so I let it go.

Without her here, I'm adrift. Instead of sleeping, I float along for hours on the edge of sleep, leaving me exhausted and listless. I was tempted to buy some weed to put me under, but I don't want to be any more vulnerable to dark thoughts than I already am. At first, I was prepared for the attacks of bullying to start, but I've been left alone.

In fact, quite the opposite has happened. Banks gave me a chocolate bar when I've barely received a smile before. Officers, including Exton, check in on me. There are sometimes three officers working on the wing now, instead of two, which makes a big difference. Daily cell checks are thorough. Any signs of dissent from the more argumentative prisoners are quickly nipped in the bud. One bully, Penny, got dragged to the block for spitting in Hardwick's face. There was a line of blood twenty metres long, until McNulty mopped it up.

The priest is dressed casually in dark-blue trousers and a light-grey shirt. Even his dog collar seems looser than normal.

'Thank you for coming in to do this for me, Father,' I say.

'No problem. I don't live far away, and funerals are only short services. Rare for them to be on a Saturday, though. Are her parents religious in any way?'

I think of Trevor.

'No, her mum has died since we came in here. Her father never visited, so I'm not sure what's happening. Did you find out if there was a live stream?'

The priest smiles and rests a hand on my shoulder.

'No, it won't be recorded. I had a quick chat with the celebrant at the crematorium. It's a small private service which starts at midday.'

'What do we do?' I ask.

'You and I sit together at the same time. We will remember her in your cell as you requested. I can say a few prayers if you'd like, but mostly it's contemplation. Do you have a picture of Angelica?'

I point at the picture which my mother sent in for me not long after we arrived. My mother thought it would remind us that good times would come again. In the photograph, Angelica and I are outside a nightclub in town in matching red jumpsuits. We laugh like we don't have a care in the world. Hard to imagine that it's not been much over a year since then. So much has changed. Seemingly, none of it for the good.

Being with Angelica made life better. I felt like I wasn't missing out anymore. She didn't care what anyone thought, or she at least pretended she didn't. I now wish I'd done all the mad things she suggested, like going mountain climbing, instead of talking her out of them and living safely.

'Father, why wasn't I allowed to go? She was my best friend.'

'It's close family only who are permitted at funerals when you're doing time. Parents, grandparents, children. You'll be able to pay your respects in a week when you get out. Assuming there is a plaque or headstone somewhere for you to visit.'

Something about the way he said the last comment makes me look up. The priest checks his watch. 'Five minutes,' he says, avoiding my gaze.

I have visited the worship room in the prison before. I suppose each room has to be neutral so they can celebrate all faiths there, but it felt cold and impersonal. It's hard to imagine any God spending much time behind these walls. We're all forsaken. Angelica spent a lot of time in my cell. I can sense her presence here.

I think Angelica wanted to make a statement to the world, but if she's looking down, she'll be disappointed. The suicide made the national news but her name wasn't mentioned, saying they were yet to contact relatives. She made it onto the local news, by name as well, when the post-mortem results showed that she must have begun poisoning herself with paracetamol and miscellaneous drugs for days beforehand. The last sixteen she took were merely nails for the coffin she had already lain in.

At twelve, the priest says a small prayer, then sits quietly next to me, and we stare at the photograph in front of us which I have rested against my TV.

'Would you like to say the Lord's Prayer together?' he asks.

'No, thank you. I just want to picture her happy in my mind.'

'Perhaps you would like to talk to her. It's a way of saying goodbye that some find helpful.'

My instinct is to ask him to leave because I feel stupid. It seems like more bullshit, but for some reason, I give it a go.

'Angelica, I'm so sorry that you felt that what you did was your only way out. I tried to be a good friend for you. I'm sorry I wasn't enough. You won't be forgotten. I'll make sure of that.'

I recall her asking for those two favours before she died. I don't say the words aloud for obvious reasons, but I do make a promise of my own. I picture Angelica's laughing face and commit right now to saving a life for her. And, if necessary, I will consider taking one.

CHAPTER 15
A week later

It's the day of my release. Obviously, I haven't slept, but it's been the best night of my life. I've studied and absorbed every single detail of my cell. Stroked the metal frame of the bed, the thinness of the curtains, and tasted the metallic water from the tap. I won't forget.

In a few days, I will have been on this planet for a total of twenty-two years. I've lost an entire year of that existence decomposing behind these bars, but the real tragedy is that I was wasting my time long before I got sent down. No more.

I brush my black hair and tie it into a long ponytail. It's taken me two hours to fix my make-up. I want to look a million dollars the moment I step out of here. Coming back isn't an option, regardless of what I promised Angelica. I pull my favourite jeans on, the pair that my mum sent in. They're loose and hang on my hips now. I suppose prison stops you binge eating because you soon run out of food.

It's almost time. I place my hands around the window bars and watch the sun as its reflection creeps down the long wall of windows opposite. It's easy to imagine someone else staring across at me. For a second, I imagine they would see Angelica's tall ghost behind me. Well, if she's still here, she's leaving now, too.

My door opens at six-thirty. The female officer steps inside my cell.

'Reception. Ready?'

'Yes, do you have a trolley?'

'You can carry those two bags.'

'This one's heavy. I don't want to sweat.'

She shakes her head, then gives in.

'Okay, I've got a cage to go back for the kitchens. I can drop you off on the way. Come on, I'll take you down now before the mainstream prisoners are unlocked.'

I drag my two plastic bags out. The bigger one holds all my clothes. Bless my mum. She regularly dropped new stuff in for me at the beginning, knowing it would help. The second bag has all my toiletries and a PlayStation inside it. Angelica managed to blag the console from a prisoner who was leaving. I think they were having a little thing together. It's ironic that Angelica struggled with her sexuality until she came to prison.

A few nights before she took that final overdose, Angelica returned all of the things I'd lent her. It was mostly shampoo and clothes. She said she was spring cleaning. I now know otherwise. Perhaps I should have been more on the ball like she was. When someone dies in here, which is a surprisingly common occurrence, they bag the contents of their cell up and return it to their relatives. If you've left anything you own in their cell, it's generally your bad luck.

I should give the PlayStation to someone else, but it reminds me so much of our time here. I don't even like video games that much, but for burning time, it's proven unbeatable. Angelica used to shake her head at the games where you could shoot the cops, then play them with enthusiasm.

The officer opens the wing gate and points to a cage near the housechblock doors. It reminds me of the ones they had at the burger restaurant. I never realised how much I loved that job until the business folded. It had become part of my identity. It made everything seem normal, including myself. I was a waitress. It's surprising what a reassuring thing that can be, but Angelica was part of my normal. How can I make life work again without her?

The officer unlocks the double housechblock doors and helps to steer the cage through them. The prison is waking up and staff are arriving. Various officers walk past. Many have worked on my wing. It feels weird to say goodbye to your jailer, but most of them have been kind and thoughtful. I imagined the prison would be staffed by huge troll-like men wandering the landings with thick fists full of large keys, but there were only a few of them.

Many of the better ones were even younger than me. Perhaps they are able to view the world differently from older generations. Maybe you gather baggage as you move through life.

'Bye, Robbie,' shouts a really young-looking black woman who told me once that this was her first job.

'Bye, Robbie,' says Senior Officer Bradshaw. He was the one who once saw me hovering at the railings on the first floor near the visits hall. All it took to bring me back was a touch of human contact.

'Bye, Roberta,' says Officer Halstead. He was kind and friendly every time I saw him. Angelica called him The Sponge of Death because he made her cry so often by being understanding. A few of the other officers walking in don't even acknowledge my presence, though. One shakes his head in disgust.

At the gates to Reception, which is where they return our phones and personal belongings of value, the officer escorting me pauses.

'Look, I'm sorry about what happened to Angelica. I liked her. We all did. You've shown decent character after all that's happened. I hope things work out for you.'

I smile, but don't comment. Her kind words are appreciated. I can't help thinking of the first time Angelica and I walked down this corridor. It felt like we were being led down to the bowels of the earth.

CHAPTER 16
A year ago

It's nearly six p.m. when we're finally taken off the court transport van to be processed in the prison. They are ready for us. The rest of the reception area is empty of inmates. I'm not sure if they cleared the place before we got off the bus or it's merely a slow night. I get the feeling, though, that people have come down to have a look at us. Our holding cell might as well be a goldfish bowl with the huge plastic window allowing passing rubberneckers a long unsubtle glance.

Angelica does a little dance when a sharp-suited woman stares at us for at least ten seconds. It feels a bit like she's selecting one of us for special treatment.

The same woman reappears a few minutes later with a male colleague who opens the door, says his name is Allan, and asks us to follow them to a different room. This also has a large plastic window. Allan stays outside while the woman in the suit sits down at a desk with nothing on it except a computer, which she ignores. She spreads her hands out on the desk and gestures for us to sit down.

'Evening, ladies. I am Ms Parkin, or Ma'am.'

We nod, then take our seats.

'Terrible events brought you here. You were on the news earlier. Prisoners thrive on drama and any entertainment is a reprieve from considering their own existence. No one has any love for the police, neither are your crimes unique, but they will make you targets. I'm here to discuss the safest place for you.'

None of the options seem safe when they are given to us.

We both state that we want to share a cell.

My right leg begins to jitter of its own accord when she tells us it's time to go.

'Maybe Parkin has given you Parkinson's,' whispers Angelica.

'You're a sick woman. The only thing this experience has given me is a weak bladder.'

Allan has collected our meagre belongings. Ms Parkin smiles.

'Here are your things. Officer Allan will escort you.'

We have very little in the way of 'things', having spent two days at the police station. We each have a bag of basic toiletries. Our clothes were taken as evidence.

'I can't believe we get to walk onto a busy wing dressed like a pair of chavs,' I comment to Angelica with a false bravado I don't feel.

'I'm rocking this tracksuit,' she says. 'Light grey doesn't suit you, though.'

Angelica reaches over and squeezes my hand. She has to yank her hand away afterwards because I don't let go.

Angelica's mousey hair sits heavy and greasy on her head. With no make-up, I can see every freckle and blemish on her face. There are plenty of both. She raises her chin, preparing for the inevitable abuse which will descend on us.

'As she said, I'm Mr Allan. You can call me that, sir, or guv.'

He gestures for us to follow him down the corridor. I feel unkempt and tired next to his brisk, sharp manner, with his clean white shirt at odds with my crumpled unironed clothes. He opens another door, and we walk into a huge gloomy warehouse-type building. Yet it's empty. It's like a cavern with many metal doors leading off it. I look up half expecting to see stalactites hanging down.

'Can you push that for me, please?' says the officer.

He points to a small trolley which is full of faded blue towels, bedsheets and fraying dishcloths. Angelica shrugs and pushes it, cursing lightly at one of the wheels being stuck sideways. I follow next to her, putting my hand on the side of the trolley to keep it straight.

It's a dark night. Even though the lights are on in the big space we're walking through, it feels like they are fading as we approach the door at the end. I really need a wee. This is the moment that's been stopping me sleeping ever since we discovered we were going to be placed in prison until our court case was heard. The officer removes his radio from his belt and talks into it.

'QB, this is Romeo Four, please confirm there is a freeze on houseblock three hub area, over.'

There's a brief pause. He waits with his key in the lock of the big green metal door.

'Officer Allan. Freeze confirmed, make your move, over.'

Angelica doesn't look at me as the officer opens both doors to let the trolley through, but I see the sheen of sweat on her forehead. It matches the one on mine. All of a sudden, the trolley seems heavier as we continue outside between two barbed wire topped fences. The pitted gravel path drags the trolley from side to side. I can't help staring up at the rows and aisles of barred windows in the gigantic building ahead of me.

Spitting rain flickers as it falls past the piercing bright floodlights.

'Keep moving, please,' says the officer.

'No one rushes to enter hell,' grumbles Angelica, but she carries on pushing.

The next set of doors open before we arrive. A female officer in a large waterproof coat holds the doors open.

'Straight to Yankee One wing. You can leave that trolley there,' she says.

We walk in.

There's a big Y above one of the wings. We step towards it, my nostrils twitching at the strange stench which seems to surround me like a sick fog. It's how I would have imagined a mortuary to smell. I glance down another wing with a Z above it. The row of grey cell doors seems to stretch out of sight down the landing. A person with colouring like mine is leaning against the gates. Our eyes meet and hold, until the officer with us shouts at them.

'Away from the gates.'

The prisoner scrapes a fingernail across their throat and vanishes into the throng who haven't noticed that we've arrived yet

At Y gate, an emaciated creature starts laughing, then turns around and strides down the wing. The shouted words are clear to hear.

'Killer, killer, killer. We have a killer.'

When I imagined this moment, I saw myself staggering past row upon row of jeering hardened cons, but in some ways the reality is worse. People slump against railings or lean lifelessly against cell doorways. Most look away if I stare in their direction.

The frazzled inmate from the gate has reached the far end of the wing and mounts the stairs to stand at the top with arms wide like the messiah.

'Cop killer. Cop Killer. Welcome to your reward.'

The officer brushes past us.

'Ignore that crazy fucker. Everyone else does.'

He heads to the office, leaving us standing in front of the gate. People stare at us mostly with disinterest. A few have keener eyes. It reminds me of films I've seen where slaves are being sold.

Some of the looks that come my way are hungry. One athletic runner-type in ridiculous tight green shorts smiles at me. My skin crawls. Sweat runs into my eyes, making the faces hazy and more demonic. The runner waggles a little finger and thumb at me, the *give-us-a-call-on-the-phone* sign.

Angelica chuckles next to me.

'You'd need to be pretty desperate to ring that one,' she says.

But we are desperate. In here, we are nothing. We have

labels on our backs, and I don't know the rules.

A wolf-whistle comes from upstairs. Up on the left is a person so massively overweight their facial features are distorted. A hand cups a big boob while a small red tongue pops in and out of a toothless mouth.

Allan comes out of the office and looks up at the pervert.

'Back in your cell, Smeg, or you'll get no canteen.'

Strangely, Smeg's face falls drastically. There's real panic in the big watery eyes which blink. Smeg hustles away down the landing surprisingly quickly, causing everyone else who was enjoying the view to quickly retreat back into their cells. They reappear at the railings when Smeg has passed. I catch the eye of a couple of them, but they look away, almost bashfully, before I do.

Someone young with a weird, limp, black Mohican hairstyle is shouting into one of the phones at the bottom of the wing while looking in our direction. There's a big circular damp patch spreading on the front of their grey tracksuit bottoms. A wheelchair user with no legs bashes the furthest phone handset against the wall. After a shake of the head, the phone is dropped and left to dangle.

'Follow me,' orders Allan.

We walk down the centre of the wing.

I keep expecting stuff to be thrown down from the top landing.

The officer stops outside a closed door.

'We're here. Cell eighteen. You're in together, so that should make things easier.'

He pushes the door open without having to unlock it. A stooped inmate with straggly grey hair sweeps the floor.

'That's enough, McNulty. On your way.'

'Just making it nice for these youngsters, guv. If you gals need anything, I'm in cell forty.'

'Don't push your luck,' says Allan with a scowl.

I want to say thank you as McNulty shuffles away, but there's an undercurrent I don't quite get. Angelica has more balls than I have.

'Do you have to be so rude, sir. It doesn't cost anything to be polite.'

The officer's expression doesn't change.

'McNulty propositions children, drugs them, and attacks them. As far as I'm concerned, people like McNulty should be tortured, then executed.'

He ushers us into the small room but stays at the door. It smells strongly of bleach

'I'll lock you in for the night. That's for your safety and the wing staff's convenience. You're innocent at this point, but the people on this wing will have tried you in their heads already from watching the news, and found you guilty. Some will try to help you. Others will try to fuck you. Both of those things will likely be forced on you.'

I swallow, but can't think of anything to say.

'Learn the rules, stick together.' he pauses and looks over Angelica's frame. 'You might need to fight.'

Then he's gone, and we're locked in.

I sidle towards the door, ears straining for sounds from outside our cell. There's a slit in the centre of the metal door at eye level which is about ten centimetres wide. I look through the glass which reveals a blurred image of the wing. A distorted face appears in my view, and an eye stares in. It moves and is replaced by a red tongue which presses against the window and proceeds to lick upwards in a flickering sexual way. I slam my hands over the flap to conceal it.

We have arrived in society's darkest hole.

CHAPTER 17
Present day

It's a bright spring morning when I step from the prison. I expect the air outside the prison to smell different, fresher maybe, but the dominant scent is car fumes, which I'm not used to. It's hard to believe that my ordeal is over, although I have a year of probation to complete. If I disappear without telling them, for example by fleeing to Ecuador, then I will be arrested the next time I return.

It's an oddly weightless experience to step away from the gatehouse. Part of me wants to run screaming through the carpark opposite, but there's nobody waiting for me. I half-expect my mum to appear even though she flew back home. They left me until last to be released. I feel foolish now, worrying if there would be reporters waiting outside. I suppose Angelica was always the main event.

I look down at my boyish attire. My black jeans have a hole in the knee, and my checked shirt feels shapeless and dated. I set off towards the industrial estate, which is the fastest route to my new home.

'Hey, you dropped this.'

I turn around to find a young girl running towards me. She hands me back the small envelope that the prison gave me as leaving expenses. It's only £46, but the girl's eyes linger on it as though she's handing back a fortune.

'You just left the nick, didn't you?' she says.

'Yes. How did you know?'

She taps the back pocket of her washed-out blue jeans.

'They gave me one too.'

Even outside the gates, prison surprises me. How many people would have returned it in these circumstances?

'Okay, I really appreciate it.'

I place the envelope back in the pocket of my jacket and this time zip it up.

'No problem,' she laughs. 'Your accent. You're Spanish, aren't you? I did a bit at school.'

'Close, Ecuador, but we speak Spanish.'

'Okay, good guess, though.'

We stand in silence for a few moments, smiling, but both struggling to remember how to carry on a normal conversation. She looks anywhere but my face when she next talks.

'I was hoping my sister was going to pick me up, but I've been waiting a while.'

'Sorry.'

'Don't. It's not a surprise. I'm going for a drink. Do you fancy one?'

'Will the pubs be open at ten?'

'No, silly. I've only got that £46, so we can go to Netherton shops, get a four-pack for a fiver. There's a park at Buckland Close.'

It's not the most tempting of dates. Although, if I'm honest, I haven't received many decent offers over the years. A couple of guys asked me out when I was doing my A-levels, but one of them was weird, and the guy who took me to the cinema barely said ten words the whole night. I had a date with a girl just after I left school, just to see if I was missing anything, but it was a disappointment. She was terrible at ten-pin bowling, too.

This girl looks like she could do with some company, and she did give me my money back.

'Okay, sure. I'm not much of a drinker, but I'll have a couple.'

We stroll for a few minutes in pained silence. She has a nice walk, but a habit of squeezing her right hand into a tight fist. The coat hides a slim figure. There's a touch of Kate Moss about her blonde bob and full lips, but her eyes never stop moving and analysing.

'I don't remember seeing you in the prison. I would've remembered someone so pretty,' she says.

'Were you upstairs?'

'Yes. I only served six weeks on the junkie wing, and I was clucking when I went in, so I didn't leave my cell much.'

'I was downstairs.' I pause but have to ask. 'Clucking?'

'Yeah, you know, withdrawal. I'd been trying to quit the brown, and I was hungry, so I pinched some food. Security was watching me.'

'What did you steal?'

'Bacon. I really fancied some.'

We chuckle.

'I'm Robbie.'

'Addison.'

'Addison is a nice name.'

'Thanks, it sounds sexy with your accent. It sounds like a type of glue or fence paint when most people say it.'

I laugh which sets her off. It's getting quite warm by the time we reach the shopping parade. Addison has a big coat on, but she manages to look cold. We stroll into the off-licence. I notice the woman behind the counter rise from her seat as we wander around to the fridges at the side of the shop.

'What do you want to drink?'

'*Cerveza, frio.*'

'Ah ha, yeah, cold beer for me, too. Trick is to get them from the back.'

'I like Brahma, it's Brazilian, occasionally we have it in our village.'

'It's pricey here,' says Addison, 'Must be the transport costs.'

'Whatever. I'm easy.'

'These will sort us out.'

She grabs two four-packs of something called Dane

Lager and hands me one.

'Pay for yours. I might get some crisps.'

When I get to the counter, the woman smiles, but merely says, 'ID.'

I haven't got any, just a bank card, which I show her.

'That's not enough.'

By this time, Addison has arrived next to me.

'What's the hold up?' she asks.

'ID,' the woman states again.

'We don't have ID because we've just got out of prison,' snarls Addison. She pulls up her right sleeve to reveal a large, smudged, horrible, prison tattoo. She flips her arm over which clearly shows what even I know are track marks from injecting drugs. They don't look six weeks old. Addison holds out a £10 note with her other hand.

'This beer's leaving your premises now, bitch. It's up to you if you want to get paid for it.'

Addison grabs her four-pack, throws the tenner on the counter, then walks past me. I'm not sure what to do. The assistant's eyes are wide and trained on me. Then I see her hand reach out and grab the tenner. She punches the numbers on the till, there's a ping, then she hands me back a £2 coin.

I'm tempted to say keep it, but we don't have that luxury. I take the money. She looks away from me.

Outside, Addison is halfway down the street. I have to run to catch up and give her the change.

'Come on,' she says. 'Let's get out of here before the cops arrive.'

The park she mentioned earlier is only around the corner. I drink the first two cans fast with my heart pumping. I could have got arrested and returned to prison before lunchtime. Surely, that would've been a record.

The fun has gone from the morning. Dane Lager tastes like something the Vikings clean their boats with. It's not even that cold. When I'm halfway through the third can, I gag and only just manage to stop myself throwing up. I lie back on the grass, feeling tired and drunk.

'Are you okay?' asks Addison.

I cock an eye open and watch her drinking a small bottle of wine. Her gullet opens and closes three times, and then it's gone. She lies next to me.

'Got a place to go?'

'Kind of. You?'

'A friend. Maybe.'

'What will you do otherwise?'

She looks into the distance. 'Get by.'

We lie on the grass together and watch the clouds float past. I feel mellow all of a sudden. I know I'm lucky. My mum wrote to me and said that our old neighbours, Mr and Mrs Thistle, would let me stay for a month after I got out. I'm not sure what I'm going to do after that. I guess what everyone else does. Find a job and pay rent.

I feel myself dozing off in the sunshine. It's nice to think there's nothing stopping me doing just that. The only sound is the hum of traffic from the nearby parkway. I drift away. After all, I haven't really slept for a year.

CHAPTER 18

I wake up with a start and a dry mouth. The sun has moved a long way in the sky, so I must have slept for a while. I look around to see Addison has gone. I drag myself to my feet and pick up my two plastic bags. One is much lighter than it was. I open it, but already know the score. My PlayStation has gone. I pat my jacket pocket where I put the envelope containing the release grant and find that's gone too. The sneaky cow even zipped my pocket back up.

I can only smile at my naivety. You'd think after a year in prison I'd know better. It's not the best news though, because every penny counts, although her need was probably greater than mine.

My mum encouraged me to save most of my restaurant wages, but I seemed to have a few issues with make-up and perfume. I couldn't stop buying either. There's nothing quite like being made up and smelling good. I get a waft of my breath. After running my tongue around my teeth to moisten them, I get my bearings. It's not far to my old house and The Puritans who lived next door. That's what my mum called them when I was there. Behind their backs, of course.

I pick up my bags and set off with a scowl. Dark clouds gather in the distance. I stride out to keep warm and beat the inevitable rain. Why the hell did I put my money in that pocket? I probably have five hundred quid in my current account, but that won't last long.

I take a slight diversion to walk past Jack Hunt School where I tried to do my A-levels. I press my face against the mesh fence and stare through into the playground. Two-thirds of the school's population were from ethnic minority backgrounds, the largest group being of Pakistani origin. Over half of the students had English as an additional language, and over sixty different languages were spoken at the school. I should have fitted in, but I didn't. Did this place reject me, or is the truth that I chose to be invisible?

The first school I went to was over in Stanground. It was a struggle there as well. Not that anyone was especially rude, but the students were predominantly white working class and had been in the same classes with each other since playschool. I was just making friends and settling in a bit when my mum found the place at Apsley Way, Longthorpe, which meant I would have to change schools. I couldn't complain because we'd overstayed our welcome at my father's friend's house while my parents tried to find their feet. I remember hearing the English phrase to work like a Trojan for the first time, and that's what my mum did to get the money together to move. Dad was too ill to work most of the time.

For someone like me at my age, Longthorpe was hell on earth. It's the kind of safe area that has neighbourhood watch signs on every third lamppost and no dog poo. Each house, or more likely bungalow, has wide, long front lawns. Rich people move there to die, but live for another thirty years.

It's a relief to get to Apsley Way and still be dry. A roll of thunder echoes overhead. It's almost a surprise not to see my mum in her seat by the window keeping tabs on the neighbours, but it's a much older lady in there. I walk next door to the Thistle house, wiping the cold sweat from my brow. I've become flabby, unfit and weak lying around in my cell.

There was a gym, but I was so little compared to everyone else that I never felt safe there. Angelica never wanted to go either. It was all too much aggravation. My thumbs are strong, though, from playing on that PlayStation.

Mrs Thistle opens the door before I reach it.

'Bella!' she says to me and pulls me into one of her spiderweb hugs. They are light on contact but tricky to escape from.

'Thank you for letting me stay, Señora Thistle.'

She always chuckles when I call her that. I see her teeth move as she grins at me

'Come in. Your room is waiting for you. We thought you'd be here earlier. We're going to have a *bellissima* time.'

I explained numerous times when we first moved in that Spanish is quite different from Italian, but she always just laughed. The Thistles were regularly in their front garden, so we spoke often. She and my mother quickly became good friends. Her dodgy Italian phrases and me calling her formally became our thing. It will be really good to be a part of it again.

I follow her into the hall where Mr Thistle is waiting. He shakes my hand, his eyes crinkling.

'I was getting worried they'd changed their mind.'

I follow him upstairs. They've put me in the spare room. It's a two-bed dormer bungalow like ours was, but most of the décor is decades old. I'm glad they didn't put me in their son's old room, which is downstairs. Mrs Thistle calls their only child, Ellis, a 'stuff-head'. That's her way of saying that he has so many things going around in his head that he never has the time to visit or ring. There's something more to it than that, but I can't imagine what it is. They're such lovely people.

I told them Ellis was selfish for not staying in touch once, but she wouldn't have it. Apparently, there was no drama, no scandal, he just moved to Liverpool for Uni, then settled in Cumbria and was terribly busy at work. Mr Thistle hinted at a sad event once, but I never pressed.

So, the Thistles have a lot of love to give but nowhere to direct it. I think that sad state is repeated all over the world. Judging by the box of chocolates on my dresser and the small teddy bear on my pillow, some of it's coming my way. My blood pumps a little faster at the thought.

God only knows what Black Magic tastes like, and there's a duck on the bedspread. Really? My culture loves old people for this very reason. They're all a bit crazy, and they don't give a shit about the stuff that isn't important. Life, or most likely death, has taught them not to worry about the small things.

I sit on the bed and look around at the dodgy, light-green wallpaper and tired, purple carpet. Funny how things work out, but I have to smile. Compared to Addison, I own the world. The room seems large after my cell's tight walls. Angelica always filled any space she was in. Those walls never seemed to close in when we were together.

Yet, I can't help thinking of my mother. My face falls. I wish she were here, but she said goodbye in the prison visits hall.

CHAPTER 19
Ten months ago

I strain my eyes peering around the prison visits room, but my mother isn't here. I glance across to the officer at the raised desk.

'Table forty-six,' he says while rolling his eyes at me.

The table next to me has a big twenty-one on the corner of it, so I walk down the line. I'm at table forty when I realise she's hidden from view by the back of a huge inmate. I beam when I can make out the top of my mother's head, causing the prisoner's eyes to widen as though I'm homing in.

'Mamá!'

My mum rises, face already covered with tears. She has lovely, plump soft-brown skin, never wears much make-up, and always looks beautiful. She covers every spare inch of my face with kisses until an officer wandering the aisles clears his throat with a smile.

'*Robertina. Porque?*'

'*Lo siento, Mamá. Fue solo un accidente.*'

My mother snorts, even though we've had this conversation before in here. She rattles through a speech she's clearly prepared in her head. It finishes with:

'I have given one month's notice on our home. You and your father were my reason to be in this strange country, but you have both left me, so I am going home.'

'In a month?' I reply when I manage to close my mouth again.

'Of course.'

I struggle to comprehend that she'll be on the other side

of the world while I'm stuck in here.

'Will you visit again before then?'

'No.'

'No?'

'Correct. I will still send things in for you, but it is time for you to live your life.'

'In prison?'

'Yes, in prison, and also when you are released. You have hidden away from the world, and I have let you.'

'But I'll have nowhere to go when I get out.'

'Perhaps you should have thought of that before your stupid acts.'

My situation was poor before today. Now it is terrible. I can't help tears streaming down my face, but I wipe them away. I don't have the right to feel sorry for myself and cause my mother anguish. She's always put our family first.

'No problem. I'll cope,' I finally say.

'Good.'

She grabs my hand and holds it against my heart.

'You are strong, Robbie. I know it. Believe in yourself. I will always be proud of you. You are in England, so enjoy. It is a dream, don't make it a nightmare. Visit their busy pubs and discos. Spend all your money on weird clothes. Make friends, make love, make a home. If you want to come back to Ecuador, I will be there, but take your time. There is opportunity here, if you want it.'

She's crying again now. We sit in silence, holding hands for a few minutes, her stroking my hair, touching my cheek. But it's hard for part of my mind not to focus on not having anywhere to live when I get out. Not only will I have no family in the country, I won't have any friends to ask either. It's times like this that I dearly wish that I had siblings. Angelica likes to call me her sister, so I should be grateful for that. I suppose she was an only child, too.

'*Mamá*. When I leave prison, I will be homeless, I might have to become a woman of loose morals.'

A little grin creeps onto her face.

'That's not so bad. Our people are used to handling bananas.'

I almost choke.

'Mamá!'

'And for a beautiful one like you, it will pay better than cleaning, and you can probably work from home. The Puritans might not like it, though.'

At my confused face, she explains that they have agreed to let me stay at their house after my sentence is over.

'I have told them that one month will be the maximum. They said you could stay as long as you liked, but no! You must challenge yourself. If they don't throw you out after a month, I will have my friends at the Holy Catholic Church burn their house down.'

I can't help laughing, mostly with relief. The Thistles attend a protestant church, hence my mother's nickname for them. Her face drops.

'Tell me, Robbie. What is the latest? What sentence are you looking at?'

I shake my head. I have no idea. They've charged me with manslaughter. If that sticks, the Thistles wouldn't be able to let me stay when I was free, because they'd be long dead.

CHAPTER 20

Present day

I spent yesterday afternoon sleeping in my new bedroom. The near silence of the suburbs was heavenly after the cries, snores and bangs of a night in jail. Mrs Thistle cooked us spaghetti Bolognese when I woke up. It was so good.

I went for a wander with Mr Thistle in the evening. His legs aren't great, but I wasn't in any rush. We walked mostly in non-judgemental silence. It's a unique skill, and one he's good at.

I woke with purpose this morning. There's so much to do. I need to reactivate my knackered mobile phone, apply for jobs, ring my probation worker, buy new clothes, find some confidence, pull a professional footballer, broaden my horizons, and win the lottery. It's time to be an adult.

I need a shower, but I can smell cooking downstairs and my stomach is rumbling like mad. I trot down the stairs and find the table set for three. There's an envelope at one of the chairs with my name on it.

'Morning, Robbie,' says Mrs Thistle. 'That card is from your mother to be opened on your first morning of freedom.'

'Wasn't that yesterday?'

'Well, you didn't get here until the afternoon, so I decided it could wait.'

I pick the envelope up and sit down just in time for Mr Thistle to slide a huge plate of fried food in front of me. I've read thinner books than the bacon. I place my mother's card back on the table. My stomach almost crawls out of my mouth to get to the food. I'm surprised I can't hear it yelping.

Ten minutes later, I've only managed half because despite all my stomach's bravado, it quickly raised the white flag. I smile, a bit sleepily after all the food, and thank them, then remember the card, so I open it up.

Two cheques slide out, both payable to me. They are for one thousand pounds each. Mrs Thistle hands me a new mobile phone and sim with a prepaid card for twenty pounds.

'Your mum said one cheque was for you to fly home with when you are ready, the other was for you to have fun. I'm not sure what she meant by that. Maybe she wants you to go skydiving or something,' says Mrs Thistle.

'Yes,' I reply. 'That's it. She said she'd pay for us three to do that the day after I got out.'

'Ooh, Stan,' says Mrs Thistle. 'Are you up for it?'

'I've already done a few dives this week, so I'll give it a miss. You ladies go. Edna, don't forget to take your teeth out.'

It's nice to be around such easy love. I watch Mrs Thistle squeeze Mr's shoulder as she collects the plates. He beams up at her. The Thistles are so lucky to have each other, but there will have been sacrifice, compromise and heartbreak on the way. I leave them to it and return upstairs to lay my full stomach on the bed. My eyelids feel very heavy.

What the Thistles have is what everyone wants. That feeling of knowing someone in and out, and understanding that they love you for who you are and what you are. Although, I'm still not sure if soul mates are people you meet, or if they are made by years of living together.

Strangely, the mobile phone package has been opened and resealed. I insert the sim card and turn the phone on. Full battery. I chuckle at the thought of my mother telling the Thistles to charge it for me. The call credit registers, and I commit my new phone number to memory. Right, let's get on it.

By midday, I've rung the mobile phone of my probation officer. I'm to go in next Tuesday morning at nine a.m. I already have a sign-on time and date for my benefits arranged when

I was inside, which is ten a.m. every other Tuesday, so that works out nice. I buy two lottery scratch cards online and lose on both, which is actually good because I don't want to rekindle that habit.

There was an online sale at Next which was a great find. It started two days ago, so pickings were slim, but I can fit in size small, which is often what they have left. I've bought almost an entire new wardrobe for two hundred pounds. That lot will be delivered within a few days. I silently thank my mother because I can throw most of my prison stuff away now.

I was on remand for nearly a year, so I could wear my own clothes for all that time. My mum sent them in at the start. A year in a dirty prison with industrial washing machines and fierce detergent means clothes don't last long. Thanks to Next, I will be smart for job interviews. Next had a small business suit for just £25. Maybe I can get a nice little job as a secretary, smiling flirtatiously at rich business people. I suspect my mother wants more from me.

My prison stuff goes in the bin, apart from the odd item that's still serviceable like my trainers. I studied English while I was inside, mostly in my cell from an advanced textbook out of the jail library. In prison, I never met a single person who could speak Spanish. Two Romanians who had worked in Spain spoke a little. It's only now that I've finally stopped translating in my head before talking. I like to think my English is perfect, although my Spanish accent will mark me as foreign forever.

I'm ploughing through my list, but there's no sign of a footballer or much chance of meeting a soul mate in this bedroom. Mr Thistle brings me up a ham and cheese toasted sandwich just like I used to have when I was growing up in Ecuador. It feels like I could go downstairs and find my mum swearing good-naturedly at the TV.

It's a different parent I need to visit though. Angelica's mum has passed, so it will be her dad, Trevor, who I need to speak to. He works in construction, so I'll see him this afternoon and get it out of the way. I can't say I'm looking

forward to it. We met once before.
    It was a Christmas Day to forget.

CHAPTER 21

Sixteen months ago
Christmas Day

Angelica agreed to meet me up the road before we headed around her house for Christmas lunch because I was nervous. She told me to dress up, so I have a little black number on that mum gave me last night as my main present. Ecuadorians tend to hand presents out on Christmas Eve. My mum insisted she drive me over to Werrington, even though Peterborough is so multi-cultural that taxis aren't outrageous at any time of the year.

My mum smiles when I tell her to drop me off at the corner.

'Call me if you need a lift home. You look beautiful, Robbie. I'm ecstatic that you have a job and friends now. It's time to begin your adult life. Your dad would be very proud, too.'

The dress goes well with my kitten heels. It also complements both my hair, which I have up in a messy bun, and my make-up, which I spent hours on. I still feel a bit like a hooker waiting for Angelica on the street corner near her house, especially when an old dude beeps his horn at me as his car crawls past. A middle-aged woman strolls past in a yellow onesie pausing regularly for an ancient, stiff-limbed terrier.

'Morning,' I say.

'Rain later,' she says.

'Yes, we're a long way from Spain.'

She seems to consider that fact for a moment, then nods and walks away.

I don't know why I ever arrive on time because Angelica is always at least five minutes late. Why don't I arrive ten minutes late? See how she likes it. Instead, I've got nothing to do but wait and worry about lunch. When Angelica invited me, I had the impression it would be a traditional family Christmas dinner, which I'm well used to. My dad reckoned if you hadn't thought about vomiting at least once by the time you went to bed, then you hadn't celebrated hard enough.

That's one of the things I liked about my father the most. He seemed to always know that life was for living. Wring out every moment. Celebrate every chance you get, love the company you keep, just enjoy, because we aren't here long. I wonder if, on some level, he knew that his time was short. That must have made the job he chose to do difficult. He would have known the danger.

Angelica, however, is the opposite of my dad. Whereas he taught me to accept, or even embrace, other people's opinions even if they were quite different to my own, Angelica would rather have a row. After I agreed to come today, she said lunch with her family had turned into a big argument for years. I thought she meant every Christmas Dinner, but I later realised it was more or less every time the Hemming family sat down together, they had what she called a ruck.

Obviously, I wanted to cry off, but my mum told me to support my friend. I think my mother wants some peace and quiet because she has a few days off this year for a change. Although, I bet she spends most of it on the phone to back home.

Angelica arrives in a taxi. She moved out a little while ago. She's fifteen minutes late. She has what appears to be a wedding dress on with some sturdy hiking boots. It's an interesting combination. At six feet tall, she is an imposing presence. We look like a pair of eccentric lesbians off to get married.

'You look wow!' she says with comedy wide eyes. 'But hurry, or we'll be late.'

In my footwear, I have to scamper like an old lady to keep up with Angelica's long stride as she hastens back towards her house. When we arrive, their next-door neighbour has gone overboard on the outside decorations. Seeing as it's a mild, dreary day with a sky full of heavy, grey clouds, it all looks a bit tragic. Especially the lethargic, mechanical, listing elf who should be welcoming you inside, but could be beckoning people to their doom, Ahab style. I take some deep breaths as I follow Angelica around the back of the house to the kitchen door.

There are pots and trellises all over the place. The garden is apparently June's thing. Often when I've come, whatever the weather, she's outside in it. There are even two sections. One for fruit trees, all perfectly groomed, which reminds me of a fairy garden when all the blossom is out, and the vegetable patch which is long and carefully maintained. I can see the borders aren't full of flowers now, but they have been prepared. The patch leads up to a large greenhouse. The panes are misty, so it's hard to see inside.

I've met her mother quite a few times. She's short like me, but blonde and she has a big bust for someone who is thin elsewhere. She reminds me a bit of Dolly Parton apart from her accent which is pure Lewisham as opposed to rural Tennessee. I smile at my thoughts. Pure Lewisham is one of Angelica's sayings. I wonder why they left London because hearing June speak about living there, they were happy.

There's something not right about June, though. She's polite and offers me drinks and snacks when I see her, but I always feel like she'd rather I politely declined and left. I can't put my finger on it, but in a way, she reminds me of myself before I got the burger job. It's as though she has slightly detached herself from living. She's bright and bouncy, but skittish like a deer, even within the house. Apparently, she doesn't go much further than the garden.

It seems to me that she's swimming in the ocean, and the current is gradually pulling her out. She's realised, and fully understands the consequences, but still doesn't shout for help.

As for Angelica's father, Trevor, I've only ever seen him coming and going. June keeps the house spotless, so when Trevor comes home covered in dust and mud, he never fits in. When Angelica introduced me to him once, she did it in a confrontational way, which threw me at the time.

'This is the ruler here,' said Angelica, and wandered away.

'Hello, sir,' I said.

'I ain't no sir,' was how he replied when he walked towards me.

We stared at each for a few moments. Angelica, bless her, had inherited virtually all of her genes from her father. He was a real presence standing in front of me that day. Like her, he filled the room. He didn't say anything else, but I had a feeling he wanted to. It was blindingly obvious that he wasn't easy company. It's probably that which is making me nervous.

As I step through the back door, I have the strange sensation of being about to enter a boxing arena. The smell is good though. There's a huge steaming turkey on the side which can't have been long from the oven. I can see her petite mother checking a bubbling pan on the hob.

'Girls,' she says, giving us a stressed glance.

When she comes over, I kiss her on each cheek, although she moves her head for the second one and I end up kissing her nose. She giggles slightly, and it looks like someone's started celebrating early.

'Champagne ladies?' she asks, before moving to the fridge.

'It's Prosecco really,' whispers Angelica.

'Yes, please,' I say loudly. Having rarely had any kind of sparkling wine, either is fine.

June manoeuvres us through into the dining room, which is set up beautifully, then races back to the kitchen. There's a small but pretty tree in the corner with flashing lights and lots of Christmas cards on the heavy sideboard. Streamers have been hung against the coving. Their house is much larger inside than it looks outside.

I've only sat in the kitchen before, but now I can see that there is a big extension at the rear of the house which you access through this dining room. At the bottom is a large sliding door, leading to what looks like a real Christmas tree at the bottom of the garden. It twinkles in the darkness with lights in the lower branches.

'I'll give mum a hand,' says Angelica, 'Or it'll be Boxing Day when we get those drinks.'

'Where's your dad?'

'He'll be working,' says Angelica with a roll of her eyes.

There's a strange-looking snowman sitting on a small table in the corner. It's made of some kind of cereal box with cotton wool glued to the outside and black buttons for eyes. It looks slightly sinister to me. I can hear chuckling coming from the kitchen, which is nice to hear, and my shoulders begin to relax.

I wander through the open door into the extension and flick on the light. It's a lounge with a circular stairwell rising out of it to a mezzanine level. All very high end, except on the sofa there is a tired-looking duvet. There's a polystyrene takeaway box and a single bottle of Bud on a little wooden table next to the sofa. Like the rest of the house, it doesn't feel right, and it also feels as though I'm intruding.

When I return to the dining room, gold crackers have appeared at the side of each plate and there are four big glasses of something light yellow which fizzes. The table could seat eight, but it looks like we'll all have a side each. I take a big sip of my drink, enjoying the bubbles dancing on my tongue.

There are loads of photographs on the far wall, many going back years. Again, it feels like I'm intruding, but seeing as I'm still alone, I tiptoe over and look at a few. It's like a history of June and Trevor's life, starting with them being young with their parents in old sepia pictures or in fuzzy black and white. There's a photo of the pair of them outside a hospital with Trevor holding a large-looking baby which must be Angelica. Trevor has the biggest grin, shoulders back. He has a meaty arm over a tired-looking June's shoulder, but he's staring at the baby which he holds easily in one arm.

It's a great shot. There's nothing like photos of new parents. There's always a raw honesty to them. As if to say, this is what's important. I agree that moments like those are what life is all about.

My eyes stray to the final picture on the wall. Trevor and June again. This time June is cradling the baby as though it's made of fine china. Trevor is holding hands with a child who looks about five-years-old. I crouch down to get a close look. That child is Angelica.

CHAPTER 22

Angelica clears her throat behind me, almost causing me to put my head through the framed picture and the wall behind it. I recover, edge to my seat, sit down and smile. Angelica's gaze strays back to the photo I was looking at, then it returns to me. She smiles, too, but it's not an expression I can read. Her eyes are thinking, not judging. She drinks her Prosecco in two big gulps.

June returns to the room with another bottle of fizz. She hands it to me to open.

'I've never opened one before,' I say.

'Time to learn,' says Angelica. 'You don't need to do a Formula One style effort, where you spray us all with the contents. Just squeeze the cork out, and you'll be able to keep it in your hand.'

She shows me how to pull the foil off, and I try to ease out the cork. It's really stiff. June and Angelica start to lean back out of the way and begin giggling.

'Maybe you'd better point it out of the window,' says June. 'I'll need both my eyes to dish up.'

She opens the window to the back garden, and I point the bottle out, but still struggle with the cork, eventually getting it moving by locking the bottle between my legs, but then it comes out fast. There's a pop, then it shoots past my chin and hits the ceiling above me, making a large dint in the plaster. White dust floats down.

'Snow!' shouts Angelica.

I join in with the chuckles, but then the door opens. Trevor walks in. Everyone quietens. I half expect him to bellow but he just nods.

'Five minutes, I'll get changed.'

'Okay, honey. I'll put the veggies back on,' says June.

Trevor returns shortly. He has jeans and a plain blue T-shirt on. He hasn't showered because there's a smear of mud on his cheek. He takes the seat on my right, Angelica on his right, and June is on my left. We could do with the carving knife I saw on the kitchen table earlier to help with the atmosphere.

June returns with the first plate, which she gives to Trevor. He waits for her to deliver all the plates, then he gets stuck in with relish. It's a lovely plate of food, apart from the weird burnt things. I catch Angelica's eye. I mouth to her.

'What are these?'

Trevor surprises me by laughing.

'They're mother's specialities. Pigs in fire blankets.'

'It's a tradition,' says Angelica. 'If mum doesn't burn the sausages, it wouldn't be the same.'

Gradually, I begin to relax again, but June doesn't eat much, and Angelica and Trevor seem to be in a mad rush to finish. They do a little bit of reminiscing while I tackle mine, but it doesn't seem natural. June leaves the table and a minute later, brings in a large chocolate cake.

'This is another family tradition. Chocolate cake, not nasty Christmas Cake,' says Trevor. 'That was lovely, darlin',' he says to his wife.

She smiles at him, and they have a moment. It's the same sort of look my parents sometimes gave each other, and I see the Thistles share regularly. Those looks seem to combine years of strife and pain as well as happiness and hope.

Angelica is always moaning at work about being big-framed, but it does mean she can pack away the food. The piece of sticky cake her mum drops onto her dish with a splat, would last me for a week. Angelica starts spooning it in her mouth, but a piece slips off her spoon and slowly slides down the front of her dress like the trail from a tired snail.

'Perfect,' says Angelica.

Trevor looks up from his dessert.

'That is a shame.'

And just like that, it's like an electrical storm has swept into the room causing everyone to malfunction. June's head drops onto her chest as though she's short-circuited. The other two are like deviant machines coming to life. Red eyes ablaze.

'Don't you like my dress, Daddy, dearest?'

'What the hell is wrong with you, Alex? Can't you dress normally?'

'I told you, it's Angelica now. Is that so hard?'

'Okay, Angelica. Dress normally.'

'I'm sorry. I didn't realise there was a dress code in my own fucking house.'

'Watch your language in front of your mother. Why be so difficult?'

Angelica rises from her seat. For a moment I think she's going to lob her cake at her dad, but she settles for a snarl.

'What is wrong with you, you mean? Why does it matter how I dress?'

'Stop being so weird. You know it's annoying. Wear some jeans.'

'Just so you feel comfortable?'

'Exactly.'

'Look, you stupid dinosaur, you- '

'Enough!!!' cries June.

We all look over at her, but her head is still down. When she looks up, her face is a mask.

'I think she looks lovely. They both do. Coffee, anyone?'

She leaves her seat and exits the room without making a sound. Her cake is uneaten. Angelica rises next to me, but Trevor is already out of his chair.

'I'll help her. You've done enough damage.'

'That's it. I've had enough,' roars Angelica. She rests her hand on mine, but keeps her focus on her dad. Her voice quietens. 'I'm never coming back here. You can rot in this hell.'

Trevor shakes his head.

'It won't be hell if the devil has left.'

CHAPTER 23

Present day

To say I'm nervous about meeting Trevor again is an understatement, but it's something I must do. I suspect he needs an explanation, or at the very least, he must have questions. I've no idea what the prison told him after Angelica died. I want to find out where he buried her, or if there's a plaque somewhere.

It was only around four months ago that June died. Angelica went to the funeral, and she was withdrawn when she returned. I remember how I was when my father passed in a similar fashion. All I wanted was quiet. The impact of a parent dying is something very hard to explain. You know it's likely to happen, but not in your twenties. Both Angelica and I had some warning, but that doesn't lessen the impact much.

It makes you understand that life is not a dress rehearsal. If you want something to happen, then get on with it, before the opportunity gets taken away. Be fearless. If you can't, be brave. Let me know when you find out how.

I've been luckier than Angelica in many ways. Being in prison has made me realise that I've been dealt a good hand. I'm pretty, and people like me. Angelica often said it was time I played my hand with balls! With that thought in mind, I ask the Thistles if they have a bike I can borrow.

He beckons me to the kitchen where there's a door to the garage. I follow a smiling Mr Thistle inside, expecting him to wheel out a rusting boneshaker. Instead, there is a seemingly brand-new racer. He reaches down and squeezes the tyres, but he knows they are okay.

It must be their son's bike. I can't help thinking of them buying it and wrapping it for him on the big day. It looks unused. Thoughtlessness can be so cruel.

'Wow, I love it. Is there a lock?'

'Of course, there's a lock, and a helmet.'

He passes both to me.

I hook the lock over the handlebars and place the helmet on my head. It fits okay. He presses the button to raise the garage door. I mount the bike and ride away, but almost end up sitting in the hydrangea because the seat is too high. Mrs Thistle has appeared. She laughs and finds a spanner to adjust it.

They stand together on the drive, arms around each other's backs, when I'm stable and about to head off. I feel like crying for some reason but instead wave madly and wobble off into the distance.

It takes the half hour ride there for me to get used to being on two wheels again. When I reach Trevor's house in Gildale, Werrington, the sun is high in the sky and seemingly focused on me. I'm really out of puff and already dreading the return journey.

It's a nice street, full of large semis and grand detached houses. I smile because the neighbours have taken away the doomful elf. The guy two doors up from our old house in Stanground left his Christmas lights up all year round. He said someone had stolen his ladder, but I think he was just idle.

Trevor's van is on the drive, but there seems to be little sign of life in the house. The windows are shut, and the curtains drawn. If the front lawn doesn't get a trim soon, it'll get out of hand. I prop the bike against the porch and ring the bell.

Looking around, the place reminds me of the Thistles' neighbourhood. There are no people in sight, just pristine lawns and clean cars, excluding Trevor's of course. His van looks like he's been rallying in it.

No one comes to answer the door, which is a shame

because my teeth feel carpeted. Another thirty-minute trip isn't appealing without a drink. I try the gate to the side of the house and find it's open. After wandering down the passage, I knock on the kitchen door. No one comes. I try the handle, but it's locked.

I hear a sound from the garden. With a deep exhale, I edge down the path and look around.

'Trevor,' I shout.

Still nothing. Spring has sprung in the Hemming garden, but it's not the same place I came to before. It isn't because we've just had winter either. This place has been unloved for much longer than that. Longer than since June died. I think of what happened to Angelica and me. That was just over a year ago.

I ignore the vegetable patch which, with all the blackened canes and dead runner beans, gives off a menacing feel. A blackbird startles me as it rushes from under a broken terracotta pot. I slide open the door to the greenhouse, but it's more of the same, like a place for government experiments that have long since been abandoned. I'm about to slide the door back into place when I notice a trainer shoe stuck against a leg of one of the potting tables. It's too small to be Trevor's.

I step inside and reach down to touch it, but at the last minute decide not to. It's weird. The other shoe isn't in sight and this one is brand new. Even though the windows are still murky, the air inside isn't as fetid as you'd expect. Someone's definitely been in here recently.

A shadow across the bottom of the door makes me freeze, but it disappears. When I get outside, the sleek tail of a large cat disappears into the overgrown shrubbery. The fruit trees are in rude health despite the lack of attention.

I grew up amongst the forests of my homeland. It really is a concrete jungle in this country in comparison. So, I loved looking at this garden when I came before. It felt like a mini oasis.

I haven't got anywhere else I need to be, so I wander up

and down admiring the emerging flowers and budding trees.

Right at the bottom of the garden is an unusual sight. There's the tree I saw from inside the house that Christmas Day. It's actually a Yew Tree, eight metres high at least, which doesn't fit with the rest of the plants. I have an itch between my shoulder blades, but force myself to walk towards it. The graveyard in our village back in Ecuador is famous for its yew trees. They call them the trees of death because nothing grows under them. This one is no different, but there is something next to the trunk.

There's a small statue resting on a brick-sized piece of sanded light-brown wood. On the wood, there is something engraved. I use my fingers to scrape away the dirt and dust. It's just a single name, Felix. The statue, which looked like an angel at first, is actually a sleeping cherub. It's a beautiful ornament. Felix must have been a boy who died.

Something red catches my eye to my left. It's a small plastic seat. In the ground around me are holes where the feet have dug into the needles. A chill descends over my body. I turn around and look back at the house. There's movement at a bedroom window.

Trevor is there, watching me.

CHAPTER 24

Our eyes meet. Even though I'm over fifty metres away, I can feel his boring into my brain. The house looks large from the rear with the extension. He's obviously done a lot of work on it. I'm guessing he's in the main bedroom where there is now a Juliet balcony and French doors.

The huge frame that Angelica despised suits Trevor. The sun lights up his bald head atop the crown of grey, almost white hair. I'm not sure how old he is, but he looks healthy and strong. It wouldn't be the biggest surprise if lasers came out of his eyes and toasted me on the spot. His long arms reach out wide as though welcoming me, then he grabs the curtains and pulls them shut. I take a deep breath, then stride towards the house.

I spend five minutes knocking on the front door to no avail, before I get on my bike. Well, I can't say I didn't try. I'm about to cycle away when I remember his van is here. Angelica said her dad worked all hours. He doesn't strike me as the type of guy who takes a Saturday off to watch TV, so I stand against the garage door out of view and wait for him to come out. After fifteen minutes, I'm so thirsty I'm tempted to get stuck into the concrete birdbath in the middle of their front lawn. I decide that's enough, time to quit. I'm halfway down his drive when I hear the front door open.

I stop, get off the bike and leave it leaning against the birdbath. Trevor doesn't look over. He locks the door, then walks to his grey Volkswagen van, gets in the driving seat and fires up the engine. I stamp over, hands on hips, right eyebrow raised, and stand right in front of his bonnet. Our eyes meet again.

After ten seconds of head shaking, he winds down his window and beckons me over. I'm not falling for that, so I motion for him to turn off the ignition. I detect a small smile on his face, but he complies. I wander around to his window.

'You're persistent,' he says.

'I've found that you have to be when dealing with weasels.'

This time his smile is obvious, but I'm not here to entertain him.

'Why are you hiding from a little girl?'

He chunters before replying. 'I'm busy.'

'Too busy to hear about your daughter?'

The grumble becomes a growl.

'I'm late. I've got concrete coming next week which I need to be ready for, and I've got to run it. Even I'll admit it's brutal running concrete on your own. My lad's let me down.'

'What the hell are you on about? Don't you care?' I ask, even though I can see colour blooming on his neck.

'You know fuck all about me.'

'You knew fuck all about your Angelica.'

He shakes his head and turns the ignition back on.

He leans out the window and scowls.

'You've got a minute. Tell me what you want to say, then do one.'

I'm about to tell him to do one himself, when I realise what he's been through. I don't know much about builders, but I'm guessing they don't see therapists to handle their grief and anger.

'I'm not shouting through your window while you rev the engine.'

'Forty-five seconds left.'

My patience vanishes in a puff of smoke. I spit on the floor next to the van, surprising myself and Trevor. I bellow through his window.

'I'll be back tomorrow at midday. If you want to hear

what I have to say, be here. If you don't answer the door on the first knock, then I'll leave and not return.'

I step back from the car. He gives me a filthy glance, puts the van in gear and disappears in a puff of diesel smoke. I get on my bike and cycle hard towards the city centre. I forget my thirst. It's time to look for a job. Yet my mind is on Trevor.

What kind of man is he?

CHAPTER 25

The alarm on my phone goes off at eight a.m. on Sunday morning, but I've been awake for hours. Job hunting sucked big time yesterday. A couple of the restaurants I went to thought I was a foreigner and weren't interested. Others thought I was a foreigner and were interested, but only in paying me shit wages on zero hours contracts. The rest said to look at their websites for vacancies. You'd think they would know.

I've never really thought about prejudice in the workplace, only having had one proper job in the burger restaurant. It must be tough knowing that however hard you work, however well you do, it might still not be enough. Instead, you are going to be judged on the colour of your skin or the class you were born into.

On my prison bunk I had dreams of doing something great, making a difference somehow, living well, eating healthily and being generous with others. Yet I'm struggling to secure jobs at noodle bars. I went into recruitment agencies, but they even want experience for a minimum wage admin job. They said I fit the profile for factory work.

I debate not going back to Trevor's place, but the ride will do me good. I want to look and feel fabulous. Sitting around eating pasta at the Thistles' isn't going to get me in shape. The clock is ticking too. I've got to leave here in less than a month. I leap out of bed, knowing more sleep would be impossible.

There's a note from the Thistles on the fridge saying they've gone to church and to help myself to breakfast. In the fridge, there's a four-pack of natural yoghurt and a punnet each of strawberries and raspberries. I think again of luck. The Thistles know who I am and what I've done. Yet, they've welcomed me into their house. I only mentioned wanting to be healthy yesterday morning and they've been out and got all this for me.

Sometimes it's easy to think the world is against you, but it's often just a minority of bad people. Why does it always seem like it's the rotten few who have the loudest voice?

I open one of the yoghurts and top it with fruit, then head into the dining room. There's a small package with my name on it. Inside is a skipping rope. A tear trickles down my cheek. I push the yoghurt away, pull my trainers on and step out onto the patio. Four minutes later, I'm wheezing like a pensioner and my pyjamas are attached to me like Cling Film. The cold yoghurt tastes fabulous afterwards.

At half-eleven, after an hour of fruitless online job searching, I get back on the bike and cycle to Trevor's. It's a glorious spring day. My legs ache but apart from that it's an enjoyable ride. I don't expect Trevor to be there, so I don't feel any pressure. My phone rings just before I reach his house. I slow, but answer it while I'm still cycling.

'Hello.'

'Is that Roberta Ayala?'

'Speaking.'

'Stepstone Recruitment here. You came in yesterday about work?'

'That's right.'

'We have a job starting Monday if you'd like it.'

'Wow, okay, what is it?'

'A factory sorting job.'

'Sorting what?'

'Onions.'

'And the hours?'

'Twelve-hour shifts, six til six, seven days on, five days off.'

The money?'

'Minimum wage.'

I cruise to a halt outside Trevor's house. I suppose it's a job, although I don't like raw onions. How depressing, but it's a start. Damn, I have to see probation Tuesday morning.

'Okay, I'll take it, but I have an appointment Tuesday morning. Can I start Wednesday?'

'No, if you want to take it, we need you there tomorrow, and you must work all of your shifts.'

'I'm not sure if I can make it.'

'Okay, never mind.'

To my disbelief, she cuts the call. Bitch!

It's maybe for the best, though. One of the reasons my mum was pleased to leave Ecuador was because she was worried I'd end up working in a plantation. She and my father pushed me all through school so I wouldn't have to do that. I don't think I dare tell her I'd taken a job grading onions, although I suppose a job is a job.

When my father was alive, I felt positive about our prospects. I thought he would be healed. I didn't know that we were living on quicksand. It was the worst day of my life when he asked to see me to say goodbye.

CHAPTER 26
Three years ago

The smell from the dining room where my father's hospital bed is set up has drifted into the kitchen. It's a pungent aroma. He's embarrassed by his state, even though we ignore it whenever we visit him. He tries to stay awake and lucid at those times, but he is weakening fast.

The doctors said three months a month ago, but it's obvious he won't make that. He has few pleasures now except talking to my mother and me, but he can only last a few minutes. My mum leaves his room with a large heavy-looking plastic bag that she deftly tries to hide behind her body.

'Your dad would like a chat. This one is important.'

I wander through into his room, trying unsuccessfully to stop my nostrils flaring. There's a chair next to the bed. I slip onto the seat and stare down at him. He looks peaceful and, for the moment, without pain. He can hear I've arrived, but his eyes are closed.

'I want to say goodbye now, Robbie. There isn't much time left.'

What do you say to that? I take his cold, dry hand, the hand of a man much older, and give it a gentle squeeze. He opens the eye nearest to me and grins a little. I always wondered whether I would know what to say at this point, and I don't.

'It's not fair, *Papacito*. Why did this happen?'

I expect him to say it's one of those things, but he strains to sit up. His shoulders shake as he leans towards me. Bloodshot eyes burn in his weary face.

'It isn't fair, and it isn't only me who's paid with his life for the greed of the big companies. Look after your mother. This country isn't for her, but it's not safe at home. If she insists on taking you back, then don't let them get away with it. Maybe it will be a cause you can fight together.'

I smile, but it slips from my face as he collapses back onto the bed. I can tell he's passed out because his tongue lolls from his mouth. His breathing is shallow, then it becomes deeper and rapid, then it stops. Just like that. Gone. I return his hand to the bed, not wanting to feel it cool further. I flex my fingers which are slightly crushed.

I know my parents' story. I've heard about where they met, how they came to live in my mother's village, but I didn't know of this anger. How can I have been so naïve about the early deaths in our villages and who was to blame?

I reach over and kiss my father on the forehead. It's so quiet in the room. I don't really feel anything. Not even sad. We grieved our loss some time ago, and said we loved each other many times over the last month. Right now, it's hard to imagine anything else but him being ill, so I'm even a little happy that his suffering is over.

My mum returns from pegging washing out on the line. She's about to joke about the dodgy clouds, like she always does, then she sees my face. I nod.

'Are you okay?' she asks.

I nod again. 'Come and say goodbye, Mamá.'

She walks in and sits on my seat. Her face is a picture of devastation that is so sad that I can't bear to be near it. I trudge upstairs to my room and wriggle the mouse on my computer to bring it to life. The information on pesticides causing cancer in Ecuador and many other poor countries is everywhere. Everyone knows, yet still it carries on.

I feel a righteous rage burning in my heart. Why hasn't anything been done? I grab a pad and make pages of notes. Hours pass and still I scribble, until I'm exhausted and fall asleep.

In the morning I wake with a heart full of pain, but I do what I'm best at, which is nothing.

CHAPTER 27

Present day

Trevor surprises me by opening the door before I reach it. I wouldn't be shocked if it was to tell me to clear off. As I wheel the bike towards the house, he walks inside leaving me to follow. I rest the bike against the birdbath again. Despite it being a bright, warm day again, it's immediately cooler, darker and oppressive when I step into the hall. It must be how the police feel when they enter a house after a neighbour has called them to say they haven't seen the owner for a month.

All the curtains are drawn and it's too dim to see what I'm treading on. I won't be taking my pumps off, that's for sure. Trevor waits for me in the kitchen. He puts the light on. I glance through to the dining room. It seems to be the same place. Obviously, June and Angelica are gone, but it feels like Trevor left some time ago as well.

Yet, the surfaces are clean, the sink is empty, the floor has been swept, and I don't think it's all been done just because I've come. The air is stale with a faint whiff of bleach. I can't put my finger on what else is different until I recognise the slight shadows on the wallpaper where picture frames used to hang. It's so clinical here, he could rent it out to the city hospital for minor surgeries.

'I like what you've done with the place,' I say.

'I don't want to be reminded of anything. I'm sure you can understand that.'

I consider my answer for a moment. Would I want constant reminders of everything I'd lost?

'How do closed curtains and constantly circulating farts

help?'

I'm not expecting the big booming laugh that Trevor lets out.

'Fair enough, darlin'. Alex told me you were funny.'

'Angelica.'

'Yeah, right. Alex was my dad's name, so I didn't like the change.'

I acknowledge that with a nod.

'How are you coping?'

'The neighbours brought stuff around, you know, after June. Then they did it again after Angelica died. I can't get any peace.'

'Is it so bad that the neighbours show you kindness?'

'It is, as it goes. There's a time for flounderin', but then you need to move on. I've hidden all my emotions away now. To a place where they can't hurt me.'

It's true, I think, as I stride past him to open the blinds and the windows, and the kitchen door. In prison it was random kindness from officers or other cons that would break me. I'd end up sobbing in bed. Although when I recovered, it was the memories of their actions that made me stronger.

I walk into the dining room and lounge, pull back the curtains and open the windows as wide as possible. There's a gentle breeze and the smell of cut grass. The distant buzz of a lawnmower enters the room.

'I don't mind the gloom, or the smell,' he says with a grin.

'I'm not airing your house. I'm stopping you from suffocating.'

'Okay, darlin'. Spit it out. Why are you here?'

I've thought long and hard about what I would say given the chance. There's actually too much. I could start anywhere, even near the end, and still not finish. It's easier if I ask what he wants to know. Does he want to understand? Perhaps he already knows as much as he wants to.

'I thought you might like to know about Angelica's frame of mind over the last few years. She said you were close when she was young, but you drifted apart.'

Trevor's eyes drop as he thinks back over the years. He rubs his chin, then looks up.

'That's true. I didn't understand her behaviour. It was like she was on self-destruct, which ironically is what she did in the end.'

I waggle my finger at him. It's a cold way to describe suicide.

'What would you like to know?'

Trevor shrugs. He turns around and pulls two mugs out of a cupboard.

'Coffee?'

I nod. He puts the kettle on, then turns back to me.

'I don't think I want to know anything.'

'Really? You're happy to let it all end, and move on.'

'Yeah, basically. What's the point? They're both fucking dead. Dragging it back up don't help.'

His anger fades rapidly.

'Do you mind if I ask you something a bit personal?'

'Yes.' He smiles though.

'Why didn't you try to get to know her?'

'Like I said. I didn't get it. We'd have the police around. She'd be stoned at the breakfast table. School would ring because they hadn't seen her for days. Every time we spoke about it, we had a right battle. Things almost got violent, so I eased off.'

Angelica never mentioned that to me, but she was a pretty hands-on person herself. She very much believed there was a time for talking, then there was a time for fighting. I supposed that explains how things ended up that terrible night.

Trevor pours boiling water into the two mugs.

'Milk, sugar?'

'Just milk. Continue, please.'

'That was more or less it. June carried on trying to get through to her, but nothing seemed to help. Angelica wouldn't see anyone. She spent her time looking at weird shit on the internet. It pushed June over the edge. I gave up and worked 'til my fingers bled. I couldn't be doing with the agro in me own drum.'

I raise an eyebrow as he hands me the drink.

'What's a drum?'

'Rhymin' slang, darlin'. Drum and bass, place.'

I nod, although I'm not really sure what he means. Angelica had loads of weird sayings and slang. I guess she must have learnt them off her Cockney dad.

We stand in silence while I sip my drink. Trevor must have a cast iron throat or have loads of milk because his is gone in less than a minute.

'I've gotta shoot in a few minutes. My lad let me down big style.'

'What's a lad?'

'It's a labourer. I'm what you call a jobbing builder. I do everything, but some stuff is a two-man job, so I have a youngster to help me out. Anyway, my one's gone and left me right up the creek. I'm in the ground tomorrow and it's no fun on your own.'

'Can't you just get a new one?'

Trevor laughs that loud laugh again.

'No, Miss Fix-it, I can't. They're like hen's teeth at the moment. It messes me up, though, because I've got a big job week after, and I'll be late starting.'

'What do they do, these lads?'

'Everything. Digging, carrying, prep, loading, fetching, you name it.'

'Is it crap money then?'

'It's a ton a day.'

I almost drop my drink.

'A ton? You mean a hundred quid. For one day?'

'That's right. Why, you gonna do it?'

'They paid me two quid a day in the prison for cleaning the wing.'

'Too right. Do the crime, do the time. When did you get out?'

'Few days ago.'

'You on the Adrian Mole?'

'What's that?'

'The dole.'

'What's that?'

'Fuck's sake. Benefits. Universal credit.'

'Yes.'

'How much is it?'

'About £250 a month.'

Trevor's eyes scan down my body and back up. He smirks, picks up the mugs and puts them in the sink.

'I'll do it,' I shout, surprising myself.

'Nah, you can't do it,' he replies without turning around.

'Why not?'

He comes and stands next to me, towering over my head.

'One word. Core strength.'

'Isn't that two words?'

'Come on, get out. I'm busy.'

I follow him to the door.

'I'm stronger than I look.'

'You'd need to be.'

'Jesus, Trevor. I'm reliable and hard working. Like my mum. I won't let you down. Just give me a chance.'

Trevor flinches at the last comment, almost as though I've hit him. I wonder if Angelica said the same thing to him at some point.

'Okay, it's your funeral. Where do you live?'

I give him the address.

'I'll pick you up at seven sharp. We're working out in the sticks. Eat as much breakfast as you can keep down. If you last more than two days, *I'll* eat my shorts.'

We step out into the sunshine. My bike's still on the lawn, which is a relief because I forgot to lock it.

'Will I get paid a hundred pounds?'

'No, you need to be on a ticket for that. Don't stop your benefits, cos you won't last. I'll pay you cash in hand.'

He walks away and gets in the van. The window winds down and he sticks an elbow out. I raise my chin.

'How much, then? What am I worth?'

He curls his lip, looking me up and down again.

'You're about half the size, so a bullseye.'

At my confused face, he grins.

'Fifty nicker, darlin'. Better than the Adrian Mole, and that's straight in your skyrocket.'

He winks at me, revs the engine, then he's gone.

I pick my bike up and wheel it down the road, feeling strangely exhausted. That's not a good sign for tomorrow, but I can't help smiling.

I think back to the first few times I met Angelica. She was in my face, too, but I decide that I quite like Trevor as well.

CHAPTER 28

The alarm on my phone wakes me up the next morning at six. The promises I made to Angelica swam around in my head for a while when I first went to bed, but then I slept like a baby after all the cycling. I feel refreshed, almost reborn, and definitely ready to go. And nervous.

Yesterday, I told the Thistles about my new job. They hugged me as though I'd just won a big promotion at a huge stockbroking firm. I can hear plates and cutlery being moved downstairs. It sounds like they're both up for some reason.

I race down to the kitchen.

'Morning, Robbie. What would you like for breakfast?' asks Mrs Thistle.

I remember Trevor's words, but my tummy is rolling.

'Weetabix, please.'

'No problem. I've done you a pack-up. It's next to the door, and don't worry. You'll be great.'

'Thanks. Can you look out for a delivery for some clothes I ordered? It might come today.'

I eat two Weetabix, then two more, followed by a yoghurt, an apple and a banana. By the time I get back upstairs, I look three months pregnant and feel all dopey. I realise I should have asked Trevor what to wear. It's cooler today, so I stick to a T-shirt and my old prison jeans and fleece. I pull my relatively new trainers on and look in the mirror. I don't look like a labourer, even if I sneer!

I scrape my hair back into a tight bun and pull a baseball cap on. It's the only one I have and pink, unfortunately. There's a toot outside. I glance out of the window and see Trevor's grey van. After three deep breaths, I trot down the stairs, grab the carrier bag at the bottom, shout *adiós* to the Thistles, and walk to the van with a swagger that's a long way from how I feel.

'Morning,' says Trevor with a blank face.

'Morning,' I reply with the same passion, getting in and pulling the seat belt on.

'We're in a place called Ramsey Forty Foot today. The job's a small extension at the back of a big house. We're only doing the footing as a favour to a mate. Brickies are in next week, roofers week after, plasterers week after that, painters, then flooring. Peachy.'

'Ah right. So that's why you're stressed. If you don't get it done in time, there's a domino effect.'

Trevor gives me a quick sideways glance. 'Spot on.'

My nerves haven't settled, so I try to probe what it's like.

'Are there many people like me on building sites?'

'Whadda ya mean? Like small, weak people. No.'

'I meant women.'

'It's just you and me this week. Sites have changed in my time. I'm sixty-four soon, so I've seen it all. I've got a job lined up on a proper site next week. If you're still around, you'll see every type of person you can imagine.'

'I can imagine quite a few.'

'There'll be a few birds like yourself. In fact, one of the plasterers is a tattooed lezza. Don't tell her I called her that, cos she'll rip me to shreds. There'll be a couple of poofs on the roof and the carpenter's a queer Chinky. There are loads of gypos about, although not too many coloured people. I don't think they like the cold. We all get on well, though, and have a bit of a laugh to be honest.'

Trevor gives me a big smile as he swings the van through a chicane at what seems a dangerous speed. I can't believe the offensive terms I'm hearing. It's as though I was sent to prison in 2021, but got released into 1965.

CHAPTER 29

I sit in silence and seethe for the next twenty minutes of the journey while Trevor whistles to himself. Angelica spent our entire relationship encouraging me to challenge outdated views. It's no wonder she was at loggerheads with her father. I'm tempted to stay quiet, though. It's what I've always done, but a small spark of fury has started to burn in my chest.

'Trevor, you recall the terms you used a few minutes ago to describe people on building sites?'

'Yep.'

'Quite a few of them are offensive.'

'Yeah, which ones?'

'Black people, which includes mixed-race people, prefer the term people of colour, not coloured people.'

'What's the difference?'

'Seeing as you're so old, you must remember the sixties.'

'I was about ten, so the summer of love passed me by.'

'Yes, but you've seen phrases like no coloureds on waiting rooms and buses.'

'Yep.'

'Well, that's probably the main reason. It's an offensive term from an offensive time.'

'Right. Splitting hairs, aren't ya?'

'I suppose to a certain degree, but seeing as one phrase is liable to upset someone, I think it's necessary to do so.'

'Okay, what else? Actually, I told one of the poofers last week I fancied a Chinky, and he told me that it was offensive to some people.'

'He was right. It is offensive, and what the hell is a

poofer?'

'It's the combination of a roofer and a poof. And I bet Chinky is mostly offensive to rich, white people's student children who have no money worries to occupy their time like the rest of us, so they spout shite instead. Okay, we're here. I'd put on some boots if I were you, or you'll fuck them trainers right up.'

CHAPTER 30

We get out of the van and walk towards a tall thin man in a thick sheepskin coat who's leaning against an ancient looking Land Rover. He shakes hands with Trevor.

'Morning, Ronald,' says Trevor.

'I didn't know you had a daughter, Derek,' he says.

'It's Trevor, and I don't.'

Trevor walks past the bloke so close that he leans out of his way. It reminds me so much of what Angelica used to do to people that I'm grinning like a cat by the time I follow.

Ronald looks at me like I might have the mange, then follows us through an outbuilding, talking in a posh voice.

'Hopefully, you'll remember me showing you what was needed. I'm afraid I won't be present to provide pots of tea and things, but here's a key for the toilet. We're off to the outlaws for the week. I'm also afraid this is the only access to the rear.'

'No worries. I've got eyes. It's all in the price. Two and a half grand, including the skip, payable Friday.'

We reach the rear, where I can't decide if it's a field or an untamed garden. There's a concrete slab about three metres by four next to the back of the long house. It's exposed, and there's a keen wind racing across ploughed farmland beyond a dilapidated fence. I've never heard of Ramsey Forty Foot, but it seems to be in the middle of nowhere.

'Righty-O. And you'll definitely be finished by then?' says Ronald while staring at me.

Trevor nods, but doesn't turn around. The man hovers for a bit waiting for a response which doesn't arrive.

'Lovely. I'll be back Friday afternoon at four. You have my

number if there's an issue.'

Trevor doesn't move or reply, just stares at the concrete slab which I assume is where the extension is going.

Posh boy slopes off. After a minute, Trevor turns around and stares at me.

'Ready?'

'Yes, but I only have these trainers.'

'Say goodbye to them then.'

We both hear the sound of a large vehicle arriving outside. When we circle to the front of the property, a skip lorry is reversing into position. Trevor directs him where to place the biggest skip I've ever seen. It all seems very industrial with the grinding gears, screeching metal and thudding of heavy weights.

Trevor places a large piece of plastic sheet on the block paving and guides the swinging skip in. It slams into place. Trevor has a quick chat with the driver while one of the chains from the lifting mechanism swings perilously close to his bald head. There are no goggles or helmets in sight. This is the place that health and safety forgot.

The driver spins the lorry around and roars up the road, leaving a deep gouge in the grass verge that makes me imagine the weight on my chest.

It spits with rain. I pull my thin fleece around me.

'You won't need to worry about being cold,' says Trevor, who is dragging a variety of lethal-looking tools out of his van. He passes me a holdall of some kind which I immediately drop. I notice there's a trainer in the back of the van. It's the matching pair to the one I saw in Trevor's greenhouse. I point at it.

'Bit small for you,' I comment.

Trevor stares at the shoe for a moment.

'It belonged to my wanker labourer. He said he couldn't find the other one. He used to come in a pair like that and change into his boots. You're going to need some boots, by the way.' Trevor drops a heavy bag of metal stuff on the floor.

'Bring that in.'

He pulls what looks like an enormous electric screwdriver from the back of the van, slams the door shut, then swiftly strides out of sight. I shiver, and wonder if it's just the breeze.

CHAPTER 31

I can barely lift the holdall and more or less drag it through the outhouse door. When I get inside, Trevor is unwinding a power cable and plugging it into a loose socket with exposed wires hanging off the bare brick wall. I follow him out to the rear where I'm pleased to see a blue crack in the grey cloud.

'Right, darlin'. We've got a simple day ahead of us. We need to break up this concrete base so I can dig the footings for the extension.'

It seems a shame to have to smash the concrete up.

'Why don't you just build on top of it?' I ask.

'Building regs. They'll want at least eight-hundred mil down. Overkill if you ask me, but them's the rules.'

'Fair enough. Do we use a digger or something?'

Trevor laughs.

'That's why I'm here and why he's paying me two and half grand. There's no access, so we can't get any machinery in. Instead, me and you are gonna do it by hand. There are five black buckets in the back of the van and a shovel. Fetch them, but to start with it's easier just to carry the bigger chunks out to the front.'

'So that's my job today. Carry the rocks and put them in the big tin outside.'

'You got it, baby. And it's a skip. Pace yourself, too. This will take all day. If you bust a gut early doors, you won't last.'

He walks over, reaches down and grabs one of my hands, lifting it up so it's between us. Again, I realise what a big unit he is. My hand looks like a child's within his paw. It's not helped by the bright red nail varnish with stars that I put on a few nights ago. Trevor reaches into his fleece pocket and pulls out a pair of work gloves. He hands them to me.

I pull them on, surprised they fit. They're brand new, too, so he must have picked them up this morning. I assume building merchants open early. After nipping back to the van to fetch the buckets and shovel, I return to find Trevor holding the big screwdriver vertically on the concrete. The silence is broken.

I was expecting loud, but the drilling fills the air to the exclusion of everything else. I'm not surprised to find that Trevor doesn't have a helmet, goggles, mask or ear defenders. He wears a black bobble hat and his normal glasses. I begin to wonder if he has some kind of death wish, but, surely, he must know what he's doing.

The first big chunk comes away from the concrete, I pull it away. Even though it's not that big a piece, it's heavy. I lug it to the front and lob it inside the skip where I get a satisfying bang and rattle. I suspect it's going to be a long tiring day.

The concrete floor resists Trevor's drill as though it's personal. Bits starts to chip away, but it doesn't give up easily, which is a state that probably won't apply to me.

By midday, I'm punch drunk. The sun has mostly kept away thankfully. When it did come out, I cooked in my fleece, but I didn't want to remove it because the rocks were already scratching my arms as I carried them.

'Lunchtime,' says Trevor, dropping what he said is called a Kango into the rubble.

If you take out the odd tea break, he's probably been at it for three hours. It's nothing short of hard-core, and it's difficult to believe he's doing something so physical when he should be thinking about retiring.

As for me, I got into a rhythm, and it's been strangely okay. There's too much noise for talking, so I plod along in silence. I can't quite get the measure of Trevor. When he's seen me struggling with some of the bigger pieces, he's walked over and broken them up or stopped drilling for a moment and carried them through. I was expecting some piss-taking but it's as though he's entered a zone, too.

Trevor brought a twenty-four pack of bottled water with him in the van. We neck a bottle each when we get back to it.

I jump in the passenger seat and grab the lunch that Mrs Thistle made for me. God, I'm so hungry. Angelica used to joke that she could eat a killer-whale on a lolly stick. I reckon I could do two. When I open the bag, I receive a nasty surprise. It contains a load of cleaning cloths, some wipes, and two cans of Flash kitchen spray. I let out a gasp which is half sob, half cry.

'I brought the wrong bag,' I say to Trevor, showing him the contents.

Trevor grins. 'It's going to be a tough afternoon with an empty belly. You won't forget to check tomorrow though, will ya?'

He grabs a small holdall and pulls out a large white roll. It's about the size of my face. I can see it's stuffed full of ham and tomato because the contents are falling out of the sides onto his lap. I'm so hungry, I'm tempted to do a seagull move. That's how Angelica described food theft in the prison. The meals were enough for me, but I was one of the smallest on the wing. Everyone else was always hungry, except for the oldies. If you weren't careful, people would swoop past and nick your chips straight off your plate. I even had my whole burger in a bun removed from my fingers once. The thief, a prostitute called Sam, opened the roll and ate the meat in one smooth move.

I sobbed then, too, more from shock, I think. It was the first sign that Angelica wasn't going to take any shit. She saw how prison worked right from the start. The next afternoon, the staff ran to the laundry where they found an inmate weeping with pain. Sam had been the victim of a ferocious assault. No one stole my food again. No one looked at Angelica in the same light again, either.

Trevor takes three huge bites of his roll. I've watched jackals show more finesse. He reaches back in his bag and pulls another plate-sized roll out and passes it to me.

'You lads never bring enough food first shift,' he says. 'You could eat all day long and never get fat doing this.'

After I devour the roll in a similar fashion to Trevor, it occurs to me to ask about his recent labourer.

'Why did the last lad quit?'

Trevor pauses while he roots around in his mouth with a muddy finger to dislodge a piece of food.

'This is a transient business. People just chip off. A lot of the pay is cash in hand. People don't want to pay any tax. If you move around, it's hard to trace you. My labourer was a dodgy fucker anyway, and we had a few rows. In the end, I'd had enough, but he'd vanished by then. Said he was going up north for work.'

'So, he just disappeared?'

'Cleared off is the term I use. There aren't enough labourers to go around. In fact, at the moment, there aren't enough of any tradesmen. So other firms offer more money, and your men don't say goodbye, they just go and take it. There's no fucking loyalty nowadays. I had a huge plastering job on my last contract. The team were all booked in, then never showed. I collared the guy a month later, and he gave me some pony about going on holiday. I already knew he took a job in London. I know everything that goes on, round here. Afterwards, I had a word in his shell like. He won't do it again. Not to me, anyway.'

I glance across at Trevor. His eyes have narrowed, and his molars grind together.

CHAPTER 32

Trevor carries on with the drilling after lunch, but he starts to flag around two p.m.

'Can I have a go?' I ask.

Trevor wipes sweat off his grimy, moist forehead and nods.

'Careful of your feet, you really should have steel caps. It's straight down, though, so you should be okay.'

I grab the Kango off him. It's heavy.

'Do that new patch over there,' he says, pointing to the last area of flat concrete. 'I need to make a few calls, then I'll climb in the skip and flatten the stuff you've thrown in. Take it easy, okay?'

I wait until he's out of sight, then I fire it up. After a few seconds, I release the trigger and the revving stops. It operates like an incredibly heavy hedge trimmer. There's a sticker on the side saying 30kg, which is over half my weight. I switch it on again. The Kango skitters around on the surface of the hard floor like it's doing a drunken waltz. I'm pleased Trevor's not there because I nearly let it go. My shoulders are already throbbing from this morning, and they struggle with a tool that seems possessed.

I manage ten minutes. Salty sweat stings my eyes. It races down my face and off my nose. The vibrations have turned my knees, elbows and wrists to jelly. It's most definitely not a job for someone with loose teeth. I've only broken off four bits of the base. I grab one and walk outside.

'Finished?' asks Trevor with a big smile.

"Yeah, no problem. I popped around the neighbour's

house after, and did his drive for him seeing as I had some time to spare.'

He laughs.

'That's not easy work. No one wants to do it. The youngsters don't mind sitting in a cab and operating the plant machinery, but ask them to get in a hole and they ain't interested.'

'It's so heavy.'

'You'll get there. The building game is not about big muscles, although they will grow. It's about core strength, and that takes time. Fair play for having a go, though.'

We continue in our original roles, but it's slow going for both of us. Trevor struggles as much as I do, but he makes it personal. He fights that concrete out of the ground like his life is at stake. We're both subdued on the way home.

'What time tomorrow?' I ask.

'Are you positive you don't want to quit?'

'Yes, I thought it was going to be hard, but it wasn't so bad.'

We giggle a little, but even my jaw feels like it's seizing up.

'Seven-thirty. Different job.'

'Shit,' I reply. 'I've got to sign on, then see my probation worker in the morning. Shall I get the bus to the site after?'

'Tell you what. Forget tomorrow. Trust me, you'll want to quit in the morning. That's assuming you actually wake up before dinner. I've got a few nasty jobs that need doing anyway. I'll pick you up Wednesday morning, although parts of you will hurt worse by then. I'll beep my horn. If you don't come out, I'll know. You don't need to explain.'

'Will you be all right?'

Trevor gives me a strange look that I can't discern.

'On my own? I've been on my own for years.'

We drive the rest of the way in silence.

The Thistles are pottering around in the front garden when we pull up.

'Who are they, then?' asks Trevor.

'Mr and Mrs Thistle. We lived next door, but my mum went back to Ecuador when I went to prison. They're letting me stay for a month.'

Trevor has a slight smile on his face, but I'm not sure why.

'You're on your own, too,' he says.

I'm about to just nod, but decide to explain.

'I am. I've kind of made a mess of everything. I've got a year of probation to do, then I'm going to go back to Ecuador. But first, I want to enjoy life, make friends, meet people, do something. Live a little.'

'And you think a building site is the place for that?'

'Who knows. If I survive, at least I'll have a good body. Do you get many nice handsome men working with you?'

'We'll see if you last. Remember I told you about the work on a proper site next week?'

'Yes, is it the same money?'

'Better. They've been let down as well, so they're paying good wages, but the bloke with the cash is a dickhead. There will be handsome men about, but I doubt any of them will be nice.'

'No husband material?'

'I'd get a dog if I were you, or better still, a hamster. See you Wednesday. By the way, why do you call them by their surname?' he says, gesturing to the now waving couple.

'Respect,' I say. 'I was young when I first met them, and I was taught to respect my elders. Now, they're helping me when they didn't have to, so I respect them even more.'

Trevor looks at them, then back at me. He gives me a wink.

I step from the van. The Thistles stride over to greet me. They're well into their seventies, but it's me who walks like a geriatric. I watch Trevor's van reverse off the drive, but then he gets out and walks towards me. He counts out five crisp ten-pound notes.

'A bullseye,' I say.

'That's right, darlin'. Five Ayrton Sennas, straight in your skyrocket.'

I wave him off, then attempt to limp past Mr Thistle, but he stares at me with concern.

Are you all right?'

'I'm fine, just very, very, very tired.'

'We thought you would be. I laboured when I was a young man, so did my boy, Ellis. Edna has gone in to run you a bath. How tasty were those dishcloths you took?'

'I very nearly ate them, but Trevor came up trumps. Whatever the pack up was that I left behind, I'll eat for tea.'

Mr Thistle looks up the road at Trevor's disappearing van.

'That was very good of Trevor.'

I can't reply. I've never been so exhausted. The bath makes me so drowsy I have to get out before I slip to the bottom. I stagger back to my bedroom where a cool bag sits on my bed. I remember seeing it at the bottom of the stairs as I left this morning. God knows why I took the carrier bag of cleaning products.

I lie on the bed and steadily munch through the contents. It's funny to think of Mr Thistle as a young man doing what I did today. It's even more strange to think of Trevor still doing it at his age.

I unlock my phone and get Google up. Skyrocket means pocket, cockney rhyming slang. Trevor uses this slang all day long. I try to recall what else he said. He told me mid-afternoon that he had to nip into the main house for an Eartha Kitt. Yuck! Nasty.

Ayrton Senna, tenner, or ten pounds. Deep sea diver or Lady Godiva, fiver, or five pounds. It's quite clever, really.

Angelica didn't think it was ladylike, so she didn't use them unless she forgot or was very angry. Or drunk. Actually, that was most of the time. I remember she called the police a bunch of fucking planks when they turned up that fateful night. I flick through the pages of the screen, but it's not there. Perhaps it isn't rhyming slang, merely insulting.

I ache in places I never knew existed. It's only seven p.m., yet I'm shattered. Even my eyeballs seem to have had a hard day. I feel good though. Most importantly, I feel safe at the Thistles'. I had to spend ten days on the wing once without Angelica after she got sent to the block for fighting. She was only defending herself, too.

Without her, I was lost. There were bullies on that wing, and worse. When Angelica was gone that first time, they came for me, and it all became too much.

CHAPTER 33

Four months ago

It's almost lock up time, and I'm waiting in my doorway as usual. Angelica rushes from her cell and races around the landing. She stops at the cell next to me and stealthily slips something into McNulty's hands, who is also watching the wing. McNulty backs out of sight.

Angelica steps over to me and pushes me into my cell. She pulls me into one of her crushing embraces. When she steps back, I see her face is free of make-up. The multitude of red marks and scratches all over her face are clear to see. Her right eye is already half-closed, and there's a splatter of blood up her T-shirt and down her jeans.

'I'll spend time in the hole for this, even though it wasn't my fault,' she gasps.

'What's happened?'

'I haven't got time to explain. Be strong, Robbie,' she says, glaring into my eyes. 'You're going to need to be strong. Please, hold it together until I get back. Talk to that officer who likes you, Mr Exton. They won't transfer me, so just take whatever they throw at you. I need you to be street tough. You can be tough, Robbie. I know you can.'

It's obvious when one of the officers has pressed their personal alarms. The noise instantly rises, and a lot of officers come running onto the wing. Angelica sits on my bed with her head in her hands. We hear dozens of heavy boots hitting the floor, gates clang back on their hinges, senior officers raise their voices as they order their underlings onto the wing.

'Behind your doors,' echoes around the landing from

multiple shouts. 'Bang up.'

I step out of my cell, lean against the railing, and peer across the wing to Angelica's cell. An officer is supporting one of the most unpleasant prisoners on the entire wing, Kelly, who is trying to stagger from the cell. There's blood everywhere. The officer's shirt is no longer white. Kelly has claret all over and slumps to the floor like a dead weight.

The senior officers wear red badges instead of blue. A red badge reaches the scene. The officer who appears to be attempting to stem the bleeding from the victim's neck listens for a moment, then points in my direction. Red badge roars out an order. At least five officers descend on us.

I turn to Angelica. The blood all over her registers.

'Are you hurt?'

She shakes her head.

'I am hurt, but only from words.'

A strong hand roughly grips around my bicep and drags me towards my cell. There's a primeval roar from Angelica.

'Get off my friend,' she screams and barrels towards him, scattering the other officers until a big one, who I recognise as Hardwick, places a meaty paw around the back of her head and slams her to the ground, where she is pinned by the other men.

Exton shoves me to the back of my cell, steps outside, slams the door, and the lock clunks into place. My ears strain to hear what's going on, but it's surprisingly quiet apart from the thudding of other cell doors as inmates kick them. I can make out heavy breathing from under the bottom of my door.

'Lift her up and get her down the block,' says Exton.

A few seconds later, they are gone.

I am alone.

CHAPTER 34

The next morning, instead of being unlocked and left to get my breakfast, I'm greeted by two officers and given a thorough rub down search. They take me to an empty cell without even a mattress in it and leave me there. I ask them what's up. One growls that my cell is being searched. I sit on the metal bed and wait.

Two hours later, I'm returned to my cell which looks like a tornado's been through it. The rules stating that they're supposed to put things back where they found them have been ignored this morning. They unlock the rest of the wing, but I ask the officer to lock me back in until lunchtime. I don't plan to go anywhere unless absolutely necessary until Angelica returns.

The wing is quiet over the next few days. By the third day it's obvious that Angelica and Kelly aren't returning soon. Kelly is still alive, though, because there are no posters. Whenever there's a death behind these walls, they stick posters up or put messages on the pods where we choose our food saying we should ask for help if the death has distressed us.

It's almost funny. Everyone's permanently distressed. A death is just another thing we have to bear. It's no wonder everyone collapses at some point because it's too much. Atlas would have put his globe down long ago in here. Then he'd have smashed it to pieces and savaged himself with one of the shards.

When I return from fetching my evening meal, I am again shoved into my cell, but it's not by officers. It's Penny and Braithwaite. They don't say anything. Penny grabs the sausages from my plate, eats one, then throws the other two into my toilet. They both root around in my belongings, taking my shampoo and deodorant. Penny leans into me, all sausage breath.

'Everything you own is ours, understand?'

They both clip me around the back of the head, hard, as they leave. I can feel my resolve vanishing. There's a gentle knock at my door. It's McNulty.

'Here's Angelica's blade, Little Mouse.'

McNulty hands over a small palm-sized circle of red plastic. A long thick nail has been melted into it. I knew Angelica had it, but have no idea where or how she got it. She showed me the shoving technique to use it. You hold the plastic disc with the back of the thick inch-long nail against the ball of your thumb. Then you puncture whatever's in front of you. Could I ever use such a brutal weapon?

McNulty hasn't left even though I'm miles away. Worried eyes search mine.

'Be careful, Little Mouse. The food is just the start.'

CHAPTER 35

There are worse dangers on the wing than Penny and Braithwaite. One of them is called The Gorgon. This foul excuse for a human being was involved with trafficking people until the gang was caught. I've never met such a hideous creature before. Heavy and pudgy, long greasy hair in ringlets, but strong and wide. By all accounts, a rapist of men, women and animals.

I've barely eaten for two days even though McNulty has been fetching my food. I've heard nothing about Angelica. Exton, who is my best chance, hasn't been on the wing since that day and everyone else I asked has feigned ignorance.

My underwear smells, and I need to use the kiosk to order next week's food, so I scamper along the edge of the wing when they unlock us. It's Hardwick on shift today. I'm relieved to see him because he doesn't take shit from any of the prisoners. He still might not tell me about Angelica, though. I smile at him.

Feeling safer with him on duty, I take my clothes to give to the laundry dude who is usually friendly, but the room is empty. When I step back onto the landing, I can sense a strange vibe. There are surprisingly few prisoners out of their cells. I could do with a shower, but there's no chance I'll risk that. The kiosk is free, so I order some quick canteen items seeing as those bastards stole my stuff. I choose next week's food menu, then hasten back to my cell. My door is wide open, when I know I had pulled it to.

I step into the room, but it's empty, then the door begins to close behind me to reveal The Gorgon waiting behind it. The

Gorgon strides towards me, pushing the door so it's completely shut at the same time. I'm overpowered, by the size, strength and malevolence that envelops me. Rough hands molest me all over. My nipples are crushed.

Then I'm turned around and pushed against the barred window. A damp, foul-smelling hand smothers my face. I should bite down, but I can't do it. I can hear the Gorgon lick something, then her hand is rammed down the back of my tracksuit bottoms and a thick, wet object penetrates my arse.

'You love it,' breathes The Gorgon over my shoulder. 'You are mine now. My plaything. You dirty little whore, you belong to me.'

We both hear someone clearing their throat. The digit is slowly removed from my bum. McNulty is in the doorway looking petrified.

'The screws are coming.'

McNulty vanishes without saying anything further. Hardwick appears in the doorway.

'What's going on here?'

'Just being friendly,' says The Gorgon, who walks out of the room under the disbelieving stare of Hardwick. I gasp in relief giving him confirmation of his suspicions.

'Are you okay?' he asks.

I attempt a smile. What do I say? Grassing makes little sense in here. I've seen the paramedics take away those who've broken that unwritten rule.

'I'm okay, I suppose. But can I ask you a favour?'

He's a tall man. His big eyes squint in his russet-brown face, and the hint of a smile drops.

'What is it?'

'Please keep looking out for me. I don't feel safe.'

'You've been here long enough to know the rules. If you want off the wing, you need to name names.'

'You know I can't.'

'Then I'll struggle to help.'

'Please, sir. I know you're fair. If there's anything you

want from me, then...'

I leave the implication hanging in the air.

Hardwick smiles, but it's a sad one.

'Actually, I do quite like you, Robbie. There's something so engaging about you. I read up about your case, and it does seem quite unfortunate. But there are rules, and I obey them. I need to be better than everyone that gets locked up here. It's the only way to keep people safe and to maintain control.'

It feels like another slap in the face, but I try to keep control of my emotions.

'Okay, I understand.'

But I don't understand. I wipe a tear away with the back of my hand.

'I'm on all day,' he says, then ducks his head under the door arch and leaves.

I stand there, staring out onto the landing as the wing comes to life. There are cheers and laughter from somewhere. The Gorgon walks past my cell and looks in with a leer that makes me want to vomit.

I stand on my chair and reach up to where the lights are. I close my eyes and take a deep breath. No sane thought comes. I remove the screws, then the panel, and take out Angelica's shiv. I rub my index finger over the tip of the nail and feel that it has been sharpened to a fine point.

After sitting back down, I place the plastic disc in the palm of my hand, push the cell door shut, and use the weapon on myself.

CHAPTER 36

Present day

I wake up in the same position on my bed as when I rested my eyes with the cool bag still on my stomach. It feels like I've been asleep for two or three seconds, but the curtains are still open, and I can tell from the light it's morning. I try to swing my legs out of the bed, but my stomach muscles scream in protest. What did Trevor say? Something to do with core strength.

I roll off the bed and onto my feet. Various muscles complain all over my body. I'm unsteady going down the stairs, but I can smell fried food.

'Morning,' says Mr Thistle. 'Edna's cooked you *empanadas de vimto*. We thought you'd need a good start this morning for another day at the coal face.'

'Empanadas de viento!' she laughs, playfully cuffing her husband. 'I found the recipe online. They look a bit greasy if I'm honest, so don't force them down if they are.'

'They look and smell amazing,' I reply, honestly. 'I think I could eat about ten, but I'm not with Trevor today. I need to sign on and speak to probation. Trevor said I'd be stiff, too, and he wasn't wrong.'

Mrs Thistle slides a plate in front of me. Thinking of Trevor and me eating that ham roll yesterday, I slow down so I actually taste them. They're good, but not quite the same as at home. I really appreciate the gesture, though.

'They're wonderful,' I say to Mrs Thistle.

She beams at me, but then her husband stands up next to her. He nods at her.

'Stan and I would like to say something,' she says. 'Well,

we've known you for quite a while now, and we understand it's not been easy for you, and we'd like to help out, if you'd like, and we want..., sorry, I'm rambling.'

'What my lovely wife is trying to say is you can stay for longer than a month if you want. We'll email your mother and ask her. We both imagined our retirement to be spent with grandchildren, but it hasn't happened. We're loving having you here. It's kind of giving us a reason for living.'

I choke on the fried pastry in my mouth. I try to wipe my mouth in a ladylike way.

'Thank you. That really means a lot, but don't email her. She wants me to step up, you know, take responsibility for my life. Of course, I'll stay in touch. I'll come for breakfast.' I gesture to the food.

They both look a little sad, which sets me off. I really need to stop crying so much.

'Don't cry, Robbie,' says Mr Thistle. 'And call us Edna and Stan now, please.'

I think of Trevor and smile.

'I'll call you that when I come back after I've found my own place.'

'Fair enough, do you need a lift into town?'

'No, I've got all day, so I'll walk, but thank you.'

I help Mr Thistle with the washing-up.

'How was Trevor? He's getting on a bit to be doing that kind of work.'

'Yeah, that's what I thought. Wait. Do you know him then?'

'I was a building inspector for the council for decades before I quit to train to be a planner. I haven't seen him for years, but I know most of the tradesmen in the area, good and bad.'

'And which of those was Trevor?'

'He was very good, but he could also be volatile, so keep on the right side of him.'

We're finished by then, so Mr Thistle smiles at me,

takes the tea towel out of my hand and disappears into the garage where the washing machine and dryer are. I'm still considering his comment when he returns.

'Should I be careful then?' I ask.

'No, he'll look after you. It was a terrible shame what happened to his daughter, Alex, and of course, his wife was also too young when she died.'

I ignore him getting her name wrong because the terrible day that Angelica found out about her mother still lingers in my mind.

Was that the moment she gave up?

CHAPTER 37
Three and a half months ago

It's been two weeks since they stitched me up after what they called my self-harm incident. I was lucky in that only the point of the nail was sharpened as opposed to the sides, so I stabbed my arms as opposed to slashing them. A lot of blood came out but at a much slower rate than if I'd managed to open up the veins, otherwise I would be dead. Hardwick found me fifteen minutes later having been concerned by my state of mind.

It's a strange thing to wake up after doing something like that. I can't believe I did it, but for a fleeting time beforehand, it was as if I didn't have any other options. My mind had ceased to function properly. For those few minutes, I lost all hope.

There was no pain, even though it hurt when they stitched me up. Incredibly, as blood oozed from my wounds, I felt some peace for the first time since we were locked away. Yet now, I feel ashamed. I can't stop thinking about my selfish actions. It's like having a dirty secret but it's written on my face because everybody here knows.

I'm so angry with myself. I can barely think what my suicide would have done to my mother.

A doctor spoke to me briefly in the hospital, and I told him the truth. I don't want to die. I want to live. When I got back to the jail, they put me under observation for ten days in healthcare and checked on me three times an hour to make sure I wasn't making another attempt. You hear such dreadful things about prison, but most of the staff are professionals.

One of the governors came to see me and asked if I

wanted to return to my old wing. The Gorgon, whose real name turns out to be Grace, had been shipped out to stricter conditions having already assaulted an officer on the wing and attacked a prisoner in the showers. I asked what stricter conditions meant, but they wouldn't tell me.

I said I would go back to the wing when Angelica returned there. A healthcare officer knew what had happened because it was all over the prison. He told me Angelica got two weeks in separation and care, which is where they segregate prisoners, for the injuries she inflicted on the wing, but there were no official charges. CCTV clearly showed Kelly walking towards Angelica's cell holding a pool cue. Kelly made no comment upon questioning and was moved to a wing on another houseblock after the hospital had patched her up.

A mixed-race officer with beautiful teeth and bad acne arrives at my cell.

'Are you ready?' she asks.

I nod and grab the few things I have that they fetched from my cell. I'm returning to my old room which they've kept locked for me. When we get outside healthcare, Angelica is waiting there with the tall, handsome Asian officer. Angelica and I have a good hug. The officers smile at each other, which makes me grin. Even down here in the gloom, amongst the pain and the madness, the flowers of romance can bloom.

The route has been cleared so the only people we pass on the way are a few prison officers. When we reach the wing and get let on, it's as though nothing has happened. Except to McNulty, who stares at me through two black eyes. That reveals who the inmate was whom The Gorgon assaulted. Nevertheless, I receive a smile as I pass by.

It's nearly lunchtime, so they leave Angelica and me out on the landing. She follows me to my cell, and we sit on the bed next to each other, staring forwards. The pictures of my mother and her family, and some of my home village, are stuck on the wall in front of us. I shake my head.

I'm not sure what to say. My cell looks the same. They've

mopped up the blood that I slipped on as they pulled me off the floor. But I can't help feeling I don't belong here.

'I'm stupid,' I finally say.

Angelica puts her arm around me.

'I was the stupid one. I owe you everything and you owe me nothing. Please tell me you'll never try that again.'

'I'm not sure why I did it. It's like I became someone else for just a few moments. What sort of person does something like that?'

'Robbie. Everyone thinks about that in here. You know how I like my stats. In places like this, on these wings, over eighty percent contemplate taking their own lives.'

'Yes, but I actually tried to do it.'

'You aren't the only one. Before I came in here, I read online that in America for every successful suicide there are twenty-five attempts. And over a quarter of those people deliberated for less than five minutes before acting.'

I nod in agreement, wondering why she would look that up.

'Sometimes a minute on your own is an eternity,' says Angelica, standing.

I still feel ashamed, so I don't reply.

'Did you know someone dies in a male prison by their own hand every three days?'

'What about women?'

'The article said they only had figures for men because there are so few women in British prisons.'

'Is this supposed to make me feel better?'

'Look, no one gives a shit about our predicament, or our mental health. We're locked away in here and forgotten about. Out of sight and out of mind. We have to do something about it. I've just done two weeks in the block. It's all I could think about.'

'Think about what?'

'We need to let the world know what goes on in these places. People are locked up, then blood flows off the wings, and all they do is mop it up. We need to get in people's faces. Be on the news.'

'Angelica, you know I'm not like that.'

'Rubbish. Remember what you said when we first arrived here? You said it was like walking into a dark pit. You compared it to a coal mine. One where we had to stay until people who don't give a damn about our fates decide to let us out. You have to sing to the world, Robbie.'

I can't help laughing.

'Why do I have to do it? I'm not a militant person.'

'You're beautiful, Robbie. People respond to you.'

'They respond to you, too.'

'No, they're scared of me, and that's different. You can't create change through fear.'

I look out the window. She's right. You can't force people to change their views. You can only shine a light on the truth. Let them understand. Let them see how things should be another way.

'They told me my mum died this morning.'

'God, Angelica. Why didn't you say?'

'Don't worry about it. You don't care about her.'

'I care about you.'

'I'm fine. I'm only bothered about people understanding what it's like here. Otherwise, nothing will change.'

A voice reverberates around the wing.

'Yankee One! Medication to the gate!'

We both stand to join the queue.

'I'm so sorry,' I say.

Angelica's face is earnest as opposed to full of sorrow.

'Think about it Robbie. They're going to sentence me to years and years. There's very little I can do in here. I wish I could spread the word.'

'You'll be able to do something when you get out. Or you can write to the newspapers. Maybe we'll get a break when they sentence us.'

'No, Robbie. It can only be you, my friend.' Angelica gives

my hand a squeeze. 'You are the one.'

CHAPTER 38

Present day

I have a sense of someone being near my bed as I stir on Wednesday morning. I crack an eye open and see Mrs Thistle hovering over my bed.

'It's seven o'clock, Robbie. Time to rise.'

I smile and grumble that I'll be up shortly. The bed is so cosy and soft. In prison you have a thin mattress on a metal bunk. For two days I didn't even have that after someone stole my mattress when I was getting my lunch. It's funny what you get used to.

I did a load of stretching exercises last night, but there's still a steady throb over most of my body. A day with Trevor filling a skip doesn't appeal.

I force myself out of bed and look out of the window. The branches wave at me from the tree in the centre of the garden. I pull on the work boots I bought yesterday, which feels like putting my feet into two concrete blocks, and stomp downstairs. After three bowls of cornflakes and an apple, I'm ready. There's a toot outside, so I lift the waterproof coat I found for a quid in a charity shop off the banister, grab the cool bag this time, and head outside.

'Morning, darlin',' says Trevor, out of the window.

I get in, but Trevor doesn't drive off straight away. He gestures with his head back to the house. The Thistles are in the doorway, waving.

'They're so lovely,' I say.

'No one's that nice,' barks Trevor. 'They're probably serial killers.'

'Don't you know Stan?'

Trevor growls, then pulls away. We hit the parkways and head towards Ramsey. Trevor is surprisingly talkative.

'How did you get on yesterday?' he asks.

'Do you mean at probation or the job centre?'

'Both.'

'Good. Are you allowed to joke about the Gestapo nowadays?'

'I do.'

'Well, the job centre was a bit like that about what I'd done to find a job. They said I needed to prove how hard I was looking, or they'd stop my benefits. Probation, on the other hand, were pretty supportive, telling me to take the time to find my feet.'

Trevor laughs.

'Right,' he says. 'Good for you. Now, I've been making enquiries about that big job on the site I told you about. The position I was after was taken by an unreliable Scottish maggot I know, so that's off for the moment.'

'Oh, won't you need me then?'

'Darlin', there's work all day long for those prepared to graft. The brickie who was doing the walls on our base next week has taken a contract in London for more money. Told posh boy he could stick his extension where the sun don't shine. I know a brickie, so I said I'd sort it for him. For pound notes, of course. But the guy I know is old and half retired, so we're going to do the donkey work for him.'

'We're going to labour for him?'

'Too right. It's relentless work. The bricks and cement are coming. We need to mix the muck, tee him up, locate a bit of scaffold, keep 'im going. Then I'll get them gay roofers on the job, stick in a Velux, order the UPVC, sort the insulation, beg for a plasterer, steal a sparkie, and Bob's your uncle. That's a month's worth of hard work for me and you for good money. Sweet as.'

I smile, not having understood much of what he said.

'Will I be paid officially? It'd be nice to do it above board and get the social off my back.'

'Going to hang around, are ya?'

'I think so. It felt good to do a manual job. Even now I feel a little stronger. I need to find my own place, too.'

'Fred and Rose West throwing you out, are they?'

'Something like that.'

Trevor keeps quiet until we arrive at the site, clearly deep in thought. As he parks up, a heavy squall buffets the van and rain lashes the windscreen. He chuckles.

'If you last the week, I'll take you on at a hundred a day on the books.'

'That's brilliant. I'm no quitter.'

'You will be. I doubt you'll last today.'

'Why is that? What are we doing today?'

Another blast of wind violently rocks us again.

'Muck and bullets, darlin'. Muck and bullets.'

CHAPTER 39

The next four weeks passed in a blur. Muck and bullets turned out to be Trevor excavating a metre deep ditch for the foundations by hand with the Kango and a spade. Not quite digging a World War One trench using a shovel with overhead cannon fire, but not far off. I've never seen or imagined anything like it.

It rained for four hours solid. He put waterproofs on, which he said was for the wind chill. He sweated so much inside them that he was soaking wet anyway. I still had a chill the following morning and struggled badly for the rest of the week, but I persevered.

The running of the concrete nearly finished me off on the Friday. On big jobs, or those with access, it gets piped or tipped in. Trevor didn't want to pay £400 for the pipe, so the man swung out the hopper and filled up our wheelbarrows. We then wheeled them along planks of wood in the doorways to reach the rear.

It was vicious on my back, and it felt like my arms were being pulled from their sockets. I kept shouting at the man to do me half loads after the first few. Obviously, he knew Trevor, and they both had a good chuckle as I wobbled around.

I tried my best not to have a barrow tip over, but finally one got the better of me. It lurched to the side and the acidic poison concrete slurry poured all over the drive. Trevor and the skip driver's faces fell, then they laughed their heads off. *Bastardos*. The driver was supposed to charge extra for us taking too long to unload the truck, but he liked Trevor and let us off.

Trevor was a machine. He gritted his teeth, ploughing on and on, with his wheelbarrow full to the brim of heavy slop as he ran it up the planks and tipped it into the footings for the building. I felt cheeky taking my bullseye when he dropped me off at the end of that vicious shift, until Trevor told me his day rate was two ton. It was definitely a fair split that day.

We got the extension done on time. The old bricklayer turned out to be a man nearly a decade younger than Trevor. He described Trevor as a legend and one of a kind. There was real companionship between them. In fact, the sparky, who turned out to be an electrician, the chippy, who turned out to be a carpenter, and the roofers and the plasterer all turned out to be nice people. They were welcoming, worked hard, never complained, and there was respect for Trevor. I'm not sure why I imagined they would be a bunch of shady dossers.

The female plasterer, who Trev introduced as batting for the other side, was hilarious. She could imitate Trevor almost perfectly. When Trevor started complaining about stuff that was mostly his fault, she would send him up and have me in stitches. Trevor laughed loudest of all.

As the foundations were built, it felt like it was me, rising from the ashes. My body has changed in ways I could only have dreamed of. I can just about make out my stomach muscles and I finally have some little guns. The weather was mostly mild but cool, which was ideal to work in, but my skin turns deep brown very quickly due to my mixed heritage. The building is finished now, and it looks strong. I feel the same way.

I'm off the dole, and probation are pleased with my progress. I speak to my mum regularly, and I've been too tired to spend much money.

We pack the tools away as it's the last day of the job, then hang around in the weak, late afternoon sun for Donald, the posh guy, to arrive and pay Trevor.

'You did well, Robbie. That's a good building.'

'Thanks. Now what?'

'We've got a job at that site I was telling you about before. They're putting up four executive houses. Million pounds each. That Scots maggot who took the job has left them in the lurch, so they're desperate. We're going to make some decent spondulicks. The first house has the walls and foundations built, and the roofers you met are doing their work on it, but we have the rest to do.'

'Great. More Kango action.'

'No, there's access this time. We'll have diggers, and we won't have to run the concrete. The rich guy in charge will pay for it to be hosed in.'

We hear a car pull up outside. Ronald walks in with another similarly dressed man. They are all grins when they see the quality of the work. He hands Trevor an envelope.

'First class effort.'

'Cheers,' replied Trevor. 'We'll be off.'

'I have another property needs extensive renovation. Would you like to quote for it?'

'Email me,' says Trevor, who then walks away.

I follow with a chuckle. We get in the van and leave. I'm tired, but not like I was in prison. It's a chilled, steady vibe that gives me peace.

'Fancy a Chinky?' asks Trevor.

'If you mean a Chinese takeaway, then yes, that would be very nice.'

'Good. I'll pick one up. And I'm ready.'

'Ready for what?'

'You asked if I wanted to hear the truth about what happened that evening when that police officer died. I paid no attention to the court case but I'm ready. Tell me now.'

Trevor pulls his sunglasses down. I moisten my lips, then begin.

CHAPTER 40
Thirteen months ago

I check my watch. It's nearly eight p.m. I'm all dressed up with nowhere to go. Angelica was supposed to have rung to tell me she was back at her flat so I could meet her there, but her phone is off. We planned this night a few weeks ago and have tickets for a local club who are doing a seventies night. Angelica knows the DJ, apparently.

My mum is stressing.

'I told you she's unreliable. Why don't you get some nice friends?'

'I thought you liked her.'

'She's gone off the boil. I know when someone's losing their mind.'

'I'm going to get a taxi around there.'

'Robbie. Be careful tonight.'

I can't be doing with my mum wringing her hands next to me while I wait, so I step outside after ordering it. She's not wrong about Angelica. We were doing great while the restaurant was open, even though I decided not to move in with her. I'm not sure if it was a second sense that it would be trouble or just more evidence of me choosing not to take risk.

I did have my first club experience in London with her, which whilst scary as hell at the start, blew my mind. We had such a good time. Then the bank foreclosed on Gordonsburger, and that was it. One minute I had three weeks of shifts lined up, the next it was a closing up party the following night.

Angelica has started hanging around with some shifty characters over the last few months. I met a few in the pub, and my radar told me to stay well clear. The place Angelica eventually rented after too many blazing rows with her dad is on the other side of town. I don't know how she's affording the rent. Neither of us are any good with money, but when the restaurant closed and we lost our jobs, my mum stopped charging me board.

My mum and I have had a good couple of months together. I took her to London, and we had a very different experience to the one Angelica and I had. My mum made all the other tourists laugh outside Buckingham Palace. She stood at the railings for ages with her mouth open, saying, '¡Qué magnifico!', loudly every few seconds. She thought the tube was some kind of novelty roller coaster for the tourists.

She hasn't said anything, but she's ready to go back to Ecuador. I'm not a kid anymore, and I'm realising that others have feelings and hopes as well. She wasn't too gutted when the burger joint closed because she thinks I can do so much better. From overheard phone conversations, there is a movement back home that's gathering pace around environmental issues. The locals have finally had enough of the big corporations stripping the forests and polluting the rivers and land. It's a noble cause to be involved in, but I feel like I'm just getting my own life sorted here.

I've had a few dates and kisses, but nothing more. Perhaps it's the Catholic in me.

The taxi driver beeps the horn, which makes me jump. I was so far away with my thoughts that I hadn't noticed it arrive. My lounge curtains twitch as we pull away. The driver guns it around the parkway and stays silent. Angelica's flat is on the middle floor of a block of six set alone near the central park.

We drive past the prostitutes on the corner. The taxi driver doesn't turn onto the forecourt; he must know it's covered in broken glass. Only two cars are parked up and calling them non-runners would be very kind.

'You sure this is where you want?' asks the bald-headed

guy driving.

I nod and pay him.

Despite it being spring, someone is letting off fireworks. There are loads of youngsters in the street, giving it a carnival atmosphere but without the joy. The masks on faces are real. I can hear the TV from the flat underneath Angelica's when I'm still fifty metres away.

The window of the entrance door is smashed as usual. Debris crunches under my feet. I'm glad I have hard-soled sandals on. The drunks leaning against the car park wall start singing YMCA to me. One of them shouts out, 'Fancy a snog, Geronimo.'

Angelica told me my outfit was guilty of cultural appropriation, but I don't think it is if you have Indian heritage.

I skip up the stairs quickly seeing as the light has been fixed. It still smells like my rabbit's cage from long ago. I can just make out the voice of Angelica's favourite, Beyonce, coming from her flat. With all the competition, I have to kick the door many times for her to hear and open it.

'Robbie, hey, was just ringing you. Dance right in. We're going to have some fun.'

I'm tempted to go home. She's so wired, you could run a city off her. Taking a deep breath, I walk in. It's a mess. There are so many clothes on the floor, sofa, chairs and hung on the curtain rails, that five people could live here. Angelica is limping.

'Hey, what happened?'

'Nothing, just partying.'

Angelica's voice copes with the lie, but she is betrayed by her eyes.

'Tell me! You have a scratch on your face.'

She shakes her head, sits on top of the clothes on the sofa, then picks a ten pound note off the table and rolls it up. She's only wearing underwear except for the crown part of her Freddie Mercury outfit that is perched on the back of her head.

She snorts up a line that could have come from a Peruvian mountaintop. It makes her eyes blink. Despite what she's just done, she leans back looking exhausted, then holds out the note to me.

I tried coke with her once when she first started on it. I swore never again. It supercharged me. I felt like the world was mine to conquer. My life had no problems at all, until the morning. My mental health is not strong enough to cope with downs like that. Looking at the whacked out skinny woman in front of me with the unfocused eyes, I'm not the only one.

'Not for me. Let's have a coffee.'

Angelica shakes her head and mumbles something.

'What did you say?'

She uses her stomach muscles to pull herself up. They ripple and bunch.

'I need to forget!' she roars at me, causing me to stagger back.

'Forget what?'

Angelica pretends to shoot me with her fingers. 'For that, you need to join me. Come on, I'll explain everything.'

'No, tell me anyway.'

Angelica shakes her head and starts building two lines. I walk to the kitchen and put the kettle on. While it boils, I have a moment of clarity. I need to escape Peterborough. Either I go home, or I go elsewhere. One of the girls I chatted to in London last time said Manchester was good, if you can cope with the weather. Otherwise, Brighton is the place to be if the capital is too much.

I take off my headdress and leave it on another pile of clothes on the table in the kitchen, then make two coffees. The work surfaces are clean even though the sink is full. On closer inspection, it's only brimming with cups and spoons. No knives or forks, no plates, pots or pans.

When I get back to the room, there's only one line left on the table and the laptop which was playing Beyonce has been silenced. Angelica has gone. The song from downstairs is so loud I didn't hear the door go. Then the music down there stops as well. It's replaced by shouting.

I walk outside the flat and look over the railings into the stairwell to see and hear Angelica bellowing into the face of the prick who lives underneath. I trot down the stairs. He points at me when I reach them.

'You as well, eh? Fucking piss off, or I'll ring the police.'

I drag Angelica away, unable to stop myself giggling. She went downstairs in just her underwear and crown. Her grin is manic as she passes me and stomps up the stairs. I notice bruises on her legs and back. I follow her up and shut her door gently.

I head into the lounge, pick up the rolled note, and snort about a centimetre of the long line of powder. It stings my nose, but it only takes a few seconds for my heart to strengthen.

'What's happened?' I demand.

Angelica looks close to tears which is unlike her. She takes the crown off and throws it in the corner. Then she paces the room, running her hands through her hair. It looks like there is a clump missing near her right ear. After a minute, she calms, then sits and markedly attempts to control her breathing. She puts another tune on her laptop but keeps it quiet.

She sings along for a bit, then turns the music up.

'They tricked me,' she shouts.

'Who did?'

Angelica pauses as we both hear sirens approaching despite the various rackets. I stand and signal for her to turn the music off, but the sirens have stopped. Through the dirty net curtains, there are flashing blue lights. Angelica stands, pushes the curtains to one side, and looks out of the window. I sit quietly with a bad feeling building.

After a couple of minutes of nothing, she turns around. We both smile at each other, until the door vibrates with two hard knocks. Then another two.

Angelica strides past me and yanks the door open.

'What?'

Two police officers are outside. There's a stern-looking, older woman and a shorter, younger man. They look up and down Angelica's body. They both narrow their eyes. The younger one steps forward.

'We have cause to believe an offence has been committed,' he says. 'Are you the occupier of this property?'

'None of your business you fucking planks,' snarls Angelica.

'It is our business. Are you Alex Hemming?'

'I'm Angelica Hemming. Alex Hemming is dead.'

'Cut the attitude,' the little cop says. 'A very serious allegation has been made against you.'

'And what is that?'

'The woman downstairs said you threatened to kill her if she didn't turn her music off.'

'That's right. She's turned it off now, so it's all good.'

'It's not as simple as that. She says you assaulted her.'

'Out!' bellows Angelica, shoving the policeman away so she can close the door.

Both officers push her back inside. All three of them barrel towards me. I step out of the way and watch in amazement as they roll around on the floor. The police eventually manage to get Angelica on her front with her arms behind her back. I watch the snarling female officer pull Angelica's right arm up to cuff it, which makes Angelica scream.

Something snaps inside of me. Even though I immediately know it's the cocaine that's causing me to act, I am powerless.

'Get off, you're hurting her,' I shout.

I grab the woman's lapel and, with a strength I never knew I possessed, haul her over Angelica's back and push her away. The woman is much heavier than I imagined, and she doesn't go far. She turns and punches me hard in the stomach.

The wind vanishes from within, and I drop to the floor.

She quickly cuffs me. I look up, gasping, and see that the smaller copper has lost control of a much larger Angelica. He draws his baton, but she snatches it from him. He grabs her hair, and they struggle in a silent dance with him bouncing against the door. Angelica has her eyes on me. They widen, then bulge.

With a terrible howl, she roars at the top of her voice, and twists them both through the doorway.

'I said get out!' she snarls.

She shoves the baton under his chin causing him to stagger backwards, but Angelica keeps advancing until they slam into the railings, they both go over the edge and vanish from sight.

CHAPTER 41
Present day

We've reached Trevor's house by the time I've finished telling him the story of that night, but he drives around the corner and parks outside a Chinese takeaway.

'What do you like?'

'Everything!' I reply.

I can still hear his throaty laugh after he's shut the door. They seem busy, but he's only gone ten minutes. We get back to his house, and I follow him in. Even though the curtains are open this time, it still feels like when you go in a caravan after it's been shut up for the winter. It's been a cooler day, and it's a bit chilly inside.

'Does the heating work?' I ask.

'No idea,' he replies. 'Do you want a jumper?'

I follow him into the kitchen, clean my hands with a bottle of squirty soap from the windowsill, then find some cutlery and plates in the cupboards and drawers. There's a single bowl and spoon in the sink which makes me feel a little sad. Trevor washes his hands, then opens up the trays on the kitchen table like we're having a picnic.

'What have we got?' I ask.

'Balls, ribs, spicy noodles and gooey stuff.'

'Like life itself.'

'Beer?' asks a chuckling Trevor.

'Sure.'

He opens the fridge and hands me a bottle of Corona.

'I hear your lot like that.'

'My lot? Do you mean people from Ecuador or Mexicans?'

I think he's serious for a moment until he replies.

'I meant bandits.'

I almost spit the contents of my mouth across the room.

'Yeah, well, you should have got yourself a bottle of Desperado.'

'Why's that?'

'Look at this place. It's depressing. You aren't living. You're existing. What's the point in you working all the time? What's it for? Are you saving for a luxury coffin?'

'I have a life. I've got mates.'

'Good, but you can still have a nice home. There are no photos, no pictures, most of the furniture is older than me, and none of it is as lovely.'

Trevor pauses his shovelling for a moment.

'You are lovely, you know. I find you very easy to talk to. Alex. Sorry, Angelica was tough to have a conversation with. We rowed like mad.'

'That's because you were the same, and she had some issues. Even she would admit that. It wasn't easy being Angelica, and she had some temper. It was scary seeing her in action. Prisons are full of trouble. People have given up and don't care about losing the little they have. They cause fights and don't back down. That is until they lie down.'

'She hit them?'

'Yeah. She had your long arms and shoulders. No one expects a punch like that from a lady.'

Trevor laughs, but it turns into a gurgle. I stand and slap his back. He pushes my hand away, and I see his eyes are moist. Without a word, I retake my seat.

'I fucked up. She was my blood, and I let her down.'

I'm about to say it wasn't his fault, but it kind of was, so I let him continue.

'I couldn't be doing with all the bullshit, especially the drugs, so I worked. Harder and longer. I was never here. Until she was gone, and it was too late. What I'd give to tell her that I loved her.'

'Oh, Trevor. She always knew.'

I reach over and put my hand on his. He looks at me, tears flowing out from under his glasses.

'I just let her go.' His voice breaks into a croak. 'I was sand, when I should have been concrete.'

He closes his eyes for a moment, then rises and leaves the room. I hear the toilet flush, then he comes back to the table and starts chowing down like he hasn't eaten all day. It's as though the recent conversation never happened.

'How's the house hunting going?' he asks.

'Badly. I'm supposed to move out tomorrow. When I went for one last look at a place that was okay, the landlord told me that if I was ever short of money, I could pay by helping him out.'

Trevor coughs a pork ball back onto his plate.

'Yeah,' I reply. 'At first, I thought he meant like do some painting for him, or mow the lawn.'

'I can go around and straighten the fucker out if you like.'

'No, it's okay. The other places were either dodgy as well or really expensive. I don't want to waste all my cash on rent, because before I go home to Ecuador, I plan to move to a bigger city to see if I like it.'

'Move in here.'

I slowly finish chewing my noodles, then put my fork down.

'You'd have me here?'

'Yeah, I told you. I like having you around.'

'Wouldn't it be a bit weird? For me, that is. You probably sleep in a dusty crypt in the basement.'

'Cheeky mare. There are three rooms to choose from. Angelica's old one has a lock on it. On the inside before you make a joke. You can't do better than rent free. I can keep an eye on you then.'

Rent free sounds good. His eye on me doesn't. He gets out of his seat and starts clearing up the trays even though I haven't finished yet.

'I reckon Angelica would like it, too,' he says.

I let out a deep breath and consider that. He's right. She would approve.

I rise from the table and hold out my hand.

CHAPTER 42

It was late by the time I left Trevor's and got back to the Thistles' last night. I didn't sleep that well. All that greasy food lay in my stomach like I'd swallowed a large squashy pillow. Perhaps it's an insight into being pregnant. I still feel full this morning. I'm also not looking forward to telling the couple who have become like my adoptive parents that I'm leaving, but it feels right. I swing my feet out of bed and go downstairs.

After a cup of coffee and a bite of an apple, which is all the space my stomach has, I tell them the news. I half-expect a guilt trip, but of course, I'm wrong. Instead, Mr Thistle offers to drive me to Werrington to drop my things off at Trevor's place. I tell them Trevor's picking me up at midday to show me the building site we're starting at tomorrow so I can get a feel for the place beforehand.

Packing doesn't take long. I've brought a huge rucksack that's almost as tall as me. It's perfect for today, and for the future. I'm going to go backpacking at some point, too. Something's changing inside me. I can feel it. I'm going to see the world. It really feels like I'm ready for the next stage of my life.

I'm off benefits and on Trevor's books, and probation think I'm doing great. My body feels slim but strong. I've got some money saved, and there are people who love me. My rucksack almost pulls me over when I yank it off the bed, but I've coped up ladders with heavy roof felt over my shoulder. I get my balance, like Trevor showed me, and it's no trouble.

At the doorway to my bedroom, I glance back around at the walls, the carpet and the ceiling. It could have been another cell, but instead it was my sanctuary. I've left a big canvas photo on the bed. It's from a picture that I got Trevor to take when they came to see me off one morning. In the shot, Stan, Edna and I are standing outside the house, arm in arm, grinning like cheesy cats, or whatever the hell that phrase is.

I recognise the beep of the horn from the street and step downstairs. The Thistles follow me outside. They stand against the door, like always. Trevor gets out of the van for once, takes my bag off me, and puts it in the back. It's hard to know what to say to the Thistles. They've been more than friends.

'Edna, Stan. You've been perfect. I don't have the words in your crazy language to do justice to what you've done for me.'

Edna is crying so hard she can't move, so I give her the biggest squeeze I can manage. Stan is more composed. He hands me a big, thick card.

'Thank you, Robbie. Come back whenever you feel like it, at whatever time, for whatever reason. Your room will be waiting.'

We have a long hug. For once, I don't cry. I run to the van. They both wave as we pull away. Strangely it's only now that I see how small they are. It's only at this point that their grey hair, lined faces, stooped backs and dated clothes register. I know, though, as I wave until we're out of sight, that's because until this moment, they weren't people. They were titans.

Trevor smiles at me from time to time as we drive through the streets to the housing estate on Oundle Road where we'll be working.

'You okay?' he asks.

'Great,' I reply and mean it.

'I bought you a moving in gift.'

He reaches over to the glovebox, which makes the van weave alarmingly, and pulls out a carrier bag which he's taped up.

'Did you know there's a funky thing nowadays called

wrapping paper?'

'I didn't have any.'

'Shops sell it.'

'Just open the present.'

The idiot's taped up the bag with builder's tape. I eventually reveal a small book. It's a beginner's guide to cockney rhyming slang. After a flick through of the first few pages, I give it a little kiss.

'Perfect,' I say.

'You'll need that, living in my gaff.'

'Excellent. Now is probably a good time to tell you that from now on I expect you to do all your apple tarts outside or in the toilet.'

Trevor laughs his guttural laugh.

'And you'd better have been joking about the heating not working.'

I open the card next from Edna and Stan. A load of notes fall out. I count two hundred pounds. They've written on both sides inside the card. I read the left-hand side first.

Spoil yourself, Robbie. If you can't do that, buy Trevor some manners.

Smiling, I read the right-hand side. There are only three words.

To our girl.

CHAPTER 43

We arrive at a long row of laurel and birch trees with a big iron gate in the middle. Trevor gets out and fiddles with a padlock. He climbs back in, and we trundle up a hundred-metre dirt track. I kind of imagined the building site to be something like the little plot we worked on in Ramsey but on a slightly larger scale. I've underestimated, considerably.

It's clear there are four huge plots. One has a concrete base, walls and some of a roof and looks half-built, one is just a base, and the other two are mud squares with a trench around one of them. There is equipment and machinery all over the place. I spot a big excavator which would have taken a few hours to dig the base that took Trevor and me a whole week. There's a squat compactor parked in the left corner, numerous skips, and there are huge piles of bricks, breezeblocks, tiles, plasterboards, insulation and hand tools all over the place. Some of it is under a marquee in the far-right corner, but the rest is exposed to the elements. The chunky cement mixer makes the one I'm used to resemble a kid's toy.

'This is it,' says Trevor. 'Our home for the next three months. Looks like chaos at the moment.'

I'm slightly overawed by it.

'How can it only take three months to finish all this?'

'I'm only responsible for the shells being put up, then keeping the site moving forward. They'll start painting inside while we're here, but we're done when the last fitter leaves.'

'It still seems a big task.'

'There'll be a lot of people here. Two teams of brickies, chippies, sparkies, blokes on the roofs, those gay guys you keep protecting will do all the lead work.'

I give Trevor the finger. The poofers, as he calls them, helped on the last job. They spent nearly all their time on the roof or drinking coffee in their little van. Stevie and Chris seemed a lovely pair of gents in their mid-fifties. They were unfailingly polite and respectful to everyone, me included. Stevie has a Jesus style haircut and carries a few pounds, whereas Chris is thin and has a shock of grey hair. I liked them at once too, but didn't get chance to chat much.

Trevor drives me back to his house after we wander around the site. I spend the rest of the weekend with him, my new roomie. We watch a movie, go for a walk around a nice park nearby and feed the ducks, and generally have a bit of a laugh. He has to nip out early evening to fix a neighbour's leaking tap, so I clean the house. I pop into his room without thinking and hoover, but when I see all the photos of him, June, Felix and Angelica on his walls which used to be downstairs, I leave.

At ten p.m. on Sunday night, Trevor yawns and tells me he's hitting the sack. I hope that doesn't have anything to do with masturbating. He dawdles in the doorway for a moment.

'Don't worry about tomorrow,' he says. 'It'll be different, but it'll be fine. I'll look after ya.'

I grin at him. I'm sure he will.

'I'm just worried that I'll stick out like a sore thumb.'

'You will, but so what. They won't have seen an air gunner like you before.'

He leaves and I hear him trudge up the stairs. I pick up his guide and look for air gunner, which makes me smile.

It stands for stunner.

CHAPTER 44

We drive to the site at seven the next morning. Trevor wants to get there early. Despite him telling me it's all going to be cushty, he's a bit nervous too. When I tell him that, he nods.

'Places like these can be jungles. It's a man's world, and there are always knobheads. Over the next three months, there are going to be fights, thefts, and accidents. People are going to get hurt. The owner of the site is so far up his own arse that he eats his food twice.'

'What happened to all this *"it's a modern world now"* you were telling me about?'

'It's the nature of the game. Stay away from the idiots. If anyone steps too far out of line, I'll get rid of them. They'll be aware I'm taking over today. I'll know most of them already, and the ones who don't know me will have heard of me.'

'Now you tell me.'

'It's a building site, not a soft play centre. These are real men's jobs. Admittedly some women do them, but it can be a harsh environment. There's pressure to get the job done, and you're always battling the weather.'

We've arrived by this point. I step out of the van into beautiful morning sunshine. The birds are singing. It smells like summer.

'Wipe that grin off your face. This is England. It'll probably be bloody snowing this afternoon.'

He wanders around the site. We start reorganising the equipment. Trevor tells me if we're already grafting when the others turn up, it'll set a good example. Before I know it, there are twelve people working on the site.

There's a team of Albanian bricklayers who speak poor English but are very keen. Trevor passes most of the morning shouting at them. They seem to think he's joking and spend the morning laughing at him.

The Chinese carpenter, queer according to Trevor, arrives to have a look around. Trevor introduces him as Johnny Chan. His work won't start until they've made a bit more progress on the first plot, but he wanted to check the first house out now the roof is nearly on. He's the only one who really stares at me. I can feel his eyes boring into my back. He looks familiar too for some reason, but his jeans and checked shirt are immaculate and he has a full face of make-up and beautifully coiffured hair. I'd definitely remember someone like him.

The second team of bricklayers are English. There's a couple of quiet, strong guys who sound like travellers. They both nod their greetings, smile and say something, but they have thick accents. They work like trojans. The other two are my age. Samson and Scott. Samson has long hair, which means I'm guessing Samson is a nickname. He talks to me non-stop. I often find him looking at me. Instead of glancing away, he does a thumbs up. I can't decide if he's good company or irritating.

Scott looks Italian. He's really attractive. He knows it, but wears it casually, if that makes any sense. We share a little moment for some reason when we stare at each other and smile at one of Trevor's comments as though we're already friends. I find I have a skip in my step after we're properly introduced.

Just after lunch, the foremen turn up. Trevor tenses as they get out of their car. He explains to me that the foremen's job is to organise the labour, machinery and materials. Trevor runs the site, but it's on them to get the entire job in on time and within budget.

'Be careful of this pair. Especially the younger one, Jacko. He's tougher than a brick wall and about as bright. Even my younger self was a pussycat compared to this fella.'

They look a little like military men as they walk over. Almost marching together. They are clearly fit. They even have a similar uniform: blue jeans and white T-shirts. Jacko has a broken nose and visible scars on his face. His head is completely shaven and well-tanned. I can almost hear the seams of his white T-shirt creaking as they struggle to contain his biceps.

Eduardo is leaner, older, and has a crewcut. His T-shirt is fitted and looks expensive. He has ridiculously white teeth that seem to flash when the sun catches them, which takes the edge off what would otherwise be a classically handsome face. The main difference in their attire is that Jacko has work boots on, while Eduardo has brown loafers.

The complex smell of expensive aftershave wafts over me. They don't offer their hands to Trevor. Eduardo grins at me. It's hot by now, but I shiver in response. They both make me feel uneasy but for different reasons, so I wander off and pretend to be busy.

I spend the next ten minutes moving bricks over for the brickies, but we can all hear the visitors arguing with Trevor. It gets so heated at one point, I suspect I'm about to see one of the fights Trevor told me would happen, but it's not what I expect.

When they finish arguing with Trevor, they start on each other. It's not banter. They square up, bellowing in each other's faces. Trevor steps back. The bigger twin eventually shoves the older brother so hard he ends up on his arse. Trevor shakes his head and walks away. The disagreement lasts another minute, but the older one, Eduardo, backs down and they eventually leave.

The site settles into a rhythm, and I do, too. By late afternoon, it feels as though I've worked here for years. Trevor answers his phone just after four, then shouts to everyone that the owner is on the way. We're all tired by then, but we give the plots a once over. Trevor's obsessed with maintaining a tidy site, so it doesn't take much.

When we hear the crunch and revving of a powerful

vehicle drive up the dirt track, we all stop and wait. It's about knocking off time anyway, but it feels like we're waiting for someone incredibly important. The vehicle is so big when it comes into view past the trees, that it could be the royal barge arriving.

The man who opens the door of the enormous Range Rover is hard to age due to a Fedora pulled low over his ears and Aviator shades obscuring his eyes. He is understatedly well-groomed in a cream polo neck. He moves his leg from the footwell, but looks down where he's about to step before he gets out. His trousers ride up to show off a pair of shiny brown crocodile brogues. I take a dislike to him immediately. I'm surprised he doesn't ask one of us to lie down for him to walk over so he doesn't get his shoes dirty. He removes his hat.

I'll admit that he is George-Clooney-handsome with salt and pepper hair and a strong jaw. His grey beard and moustache are neatly trimmed. When he takes his Aviator sunglasses off, his piercing, seemingly black eyes drill into mine and my stomach lurches. I've met this piece of shit before.

I can't believe it's him. It was only once we met, but the whole experience was so unnatural for me, that I'd never forget it. Angelica said she was seeing someone which was unusual. I knew she had the odd lover every now and again, but she usually glossed over the specifics. People found her attractive, despite what she thought of herself.

She wanted me to meet him, so we took a taxi to the Marsden Hotel. It was the type of place I'd never been in before, but I wasn't unnerved by that.

For the first time in my life, I felt the presence of pure evil.

CHAPTER 45

Fourteen months ago

The taxi pulls up outside the hotel in the pouring rain, but they have a doorman who hustles out with an umbrella.

'Evening, ladies,' he says.

We get out and teeter in our high heels through the front door into a posh atrium, which is all reds and golds. The ceiling is high above us with large chandeliers casting reflections off the walls. The thick carpet tugs at our footwear. A woman in a three-piece suit approaches us.

'Good evening. Are you dining with us tonight or staying?'

'We're meeting Mr Landsman.'

She pauses, a second too long.

'Very good. He said to expect two young ladies. Follow me, please.'

We walk through quiet corridors, then she knocks on a varnished wooden door that sounds a foot thick. She opens it and ushers us through. The door closes and clicks behind us like it's a trap.

'Ladies, join me.' says Landsman. 'I've taken the liberty of putting a variety of drinks on ice for you. Help yourselves.'

Angelica grins at me as though she's fallen out of an air balloon and landed feet first on a superyacht. For some reason, I conclude that he believes he's too above our station to fetch us our drinks. He sits at the head of a glossy table that could seat about sixteen. There's a place set out either side of him. We pour ourselves glasses of something fizzy, then sit down. He only looks at me.

'I'm always keen to meet Angelica's friends, especially one so beautiful. She told me how you met. How do you like our country?'

I smile at him, not wanting to seem rude, but he seems so slippery, and more than a little creepy. I don't like being stuck out of sight in this room at all.

'Nice. You have some strange foods, and the weather is pretty odd, but mostly the people are nice.'

Landsman nods as though he is the nicest of them all, but he is far from convincing.

We chat about inconsequential things. Angelica and I finish our drinks quickly. He has a thick glass tumbler containing a little splash of brown liquid, but he doesn't touch it. He practically orders me to top up our glasses. While I'm away from the table, I hear his low voice and Angelica's titter, but I can't make out the words.

By the time I return, Angelica has risen from her seat.

'I'm just off to the ladies,' she says. She disappears through a different door to the one we came in, leaving me alone with him. I feel myself begin to perspire.

'I hear it's just you and your mother in the UK?' he asks.

'Yes.'

'Do you have plans for the future?'

'Not really. The restaurant we work at is struggling, so I'm not sure of the future. I'd like to do something more serious if you know what I mean.'

'Of course, of course. I have many businesses and many contacts, so let me know which direction you fancy heading towards. Maybe I can open a few doors for you.'

'That's very kind.'

He raises his glass and takes the tiniest sip.

'I like helping young people. It's a tough and expensive world.'

'It is.'

'Well, Robbie. I have a party coming up at my place. Lots of fun, just a few select guests. Youngsters like yourself, too.

Angelica will be there. You should come. Let your hair down.'

'I'll see if I'm free.'

'Excellent. I'll give the details to Angelica and have a car pick you up. You won't need to spend a penny. Everything is free.'

My mum has a saying for such things. She would rather scratch the underbelly of an exhausted elephant. It applies now. I almost gasp in relief when Angelica returns. We have one more drink. Angelica is very loud and talkative when she returns. We are ushered out as though our time is up after the third drink. He stands and kisses both our hands when we leave, but his cold lips linger on my fingers for longer.

It seems I've passed an interview for a position that I never applied for and didn't even know existed.

CHAPTER 46

Present day

Mr Landsman only hangs around at the site for about ten minutes. He makes Trevor line us up like he's a general inspecting the troops. He doesn't offer his hand to anyone. When Landsman walks away, he puts his arm around Trevor's shoulder almost in a fatherly manner, but I can tell he's being too aggressive by the way Trevor is unbalanced.

I get distracted by my phone ringing. It's my probation worker. We talk for about five minutes, but there doesn't seem to be any purpose to the call. I can't shake a paranoid feeling afterwards that she's lurking in the woods behind the site. I tell Trevor later, and he says she's probably ringing up on the off chance that I'm drunk.

The first week of the job flies by. Everyone works hard. Jacko and Eduardo's method of motivation is bullying. It works on everyone except Trevor, but I can tell they are secretly pleased with the progress of the work. Sometimes, when I look around, it reminds me of those scenes from the American West where they're laying down the railroad. It's the sound and sights of hard and honest labour.

I was stupid to worry about people being off with me or thinking I wasn't up to the task. I'm holding my own. I mix a lot of muck for the brickies, but there are things I can't do. I can't carry two twenty-five kg sacks of cement at the same time like Trevor and Scott can, but then neither can a few of the others. Trevor's arms are long. He calls it his wingspan. He flips doors and sheets of plasterboard around like they're dominos.

By the time Friday comes around, I'm ready for a few

beers. Trevor brings a crate of chilled Stella Artois from a cool box in his van, and we all sit in the sunshine drinking them. I find myself next to Scott, which seems to have been a regular occurrence over the last few days.

He's a quiet guy really, but we don't seem to need to talk. I can make him laugh with a raised eyebrow or a Spanish curse said with gusto. Every now and again, I turn around quickly and suspect he was staring at me. He changed his shirt this morning, and I got a glimpse of a tanned back. I had to take my own fleece off even though it was spitting with rain at that moment. It's supposed to be baking next week, which I'm looking forward to.

He grabs another bottle of beer and chinks his with mine.

'You did well this week,' he says.

'For a girl.'

'For an anyone. If you can keep up with our team, you're doing well.'

'*Muchas gracias, señor*. Too kind.'

He always smiles when I speak Spanish. I find I'm doing it more.

'I heard about what happened to Trevor's kid.'

My mouthful of lager goes up my nose. I thought things were going too well. Does he know I was involved? It's hard to think what to say, so I nod and put my sunglasses back on.

'I used to go to school with Alex,' he says.

'Angelica.'

'Yes, sorry. It must have been hard for her in prison.'

'It was tough for all of us.'

His face falls like a curtain coming down. Even though the sky is a vast sea of turquoise behind him, it feels like the sun has gone behind a cloud.

'No way. Were you there too?'

'Yes, it was a nightmare. The police were heavy handed when they arrested Angelica, so I pushed one of them.'

'Surely you don't go to prison for pushing a policeman.'

'It was a policewoman actually, but yes, apparently you can get six months. Unfortunately, because I pushed her, that allowed Angelica to get up and attack the other officer, which led to him dying. We both tested positive for cocaine as well, which they said was an aggravating factor. They also found nearly eight grams of it in a drawer.'

He raises an eyebrow at that.

'Yes, we're lucky not to have been prosecuted for drug dealing as well, but they knew they had Angelica for at least manslaughter, so they left it.'

'It still seems harsh.'

'To be honest, I was relieved they didn't charge me with manslaughter, too, which is what they were planning to do from the beginning. Eventually my solicitor got the CPS to drop that charge and instead I was prosecuted for assaulting a police officer and a charge of threatening to kill.'

Scott chuckles, which is a relief.

'That sounds like something Angelica might do, but not you.'

'That's because she was guilty as charged! The so-called witness said it was both of us, but I didn't have much choice. Our credibility was shot to pieces because a copper was dead. My solicitor recommended I just plead guilty to the lesser offences. We'd been on remand for nearly a year anyway, so she reckoned they'd give me two years, serve half, which was about the time I'd done. I just wanted to get out by that point. She was right on everything.'

'At least you're free now.'

'Yes, but even though I didn't kill that officer, I often find myself carrying some of the responsibility around with me. A man died. He had family and friends whose lives will never be the same again. It's like having a small stone in my shoe all the time, reminding me I don't deserve to be happy.'

'A mate of mine got sent down for a similar thing to what Angelica did,' he says. 'He got into a fight with an aggressive junkie who fell over and banged his head on a lamppost. The junkie got brain damage, and my pal got five years.'

'I met quite a few inside with similar stories. I'm fortunate that it's over and I'm able to get on with my life. Poor Angelica didn't have that luck.'

'Yes, it's very sad.'

'By the way, you should really say person with drug dependence rather than call someone a junkie.'

'Eh? Why?'

'I lost a friend to drugs, and people always referred to her as that fucking junkie. Everyone thought she was injecting drugs, but she wasn't. Calling her a junkie reduced her to solely that. She was a beautiful person inside and out who struggled to cope. That's all.'

'Erm, okay. That sounds reasonable. Does that apply to smackheads too?'

I give him a playful shove. A loud shout interrupts us.

'Hey, Boyband,' shouts Trevor. 'Why's this cement not covered?'

Scott takes his nickname in his stride. I suppose it could be worse.

'It's not supposed to rain for a week,' replies Scott.

'What are you, a fucking weather forecaster now? Cover it up. I don't want so much as a squirt of squirrel piss on it.'

Stevie and Chris are sitting next to us and start laughing.

'Trev does make me chuckle,' says Chris.

'How do you know him?' I ask.

'We met decades ago when we were all young. Back in the day, we worked for a company called Beavis Homes. The management accused us of nicking a load of gear. Went to the police and everything. We were looking at jail until they found it in some ponce's garage. Anyway, they didn't give us our jobs back, and the building game is a small world. Ask Trevor. He knows everything and everyone. Nobody wanted to go anywhere near us afterwards.'

'Even though you were innocent?'

'Yeah. Mud sticks. We could only get the odd domestic job. Both of us got miles behind on our mortgages. Then Trev rang us up. He had some work. When the gaffer on that job found out who we were, he told Trev to get rid.'

Stevie takes up the story.

'Trev said to him that if we go, he goes, so the boss had to suck it up. We're good at our jobs, and lead work is a dying trade, so after a while it was all forgotten, and we got our lives back on track.'

'Yeah, if it wasn't for Trev,' said Chris, 'We'd have lost our homes.'

'And our marriages,' laughs Stevie. 'So, he owes us for that.'

When my face drops, the pair of them roll around in their seats laughing.

'What's so funny?' I ask.

'Your face,' says Stevie. 'I take it Trevor told you we were gay.'

'Yes, he did.'

'We've both been married for donkey's years, to women. Chris has two kids, three for me. You remind me of my youngest. She's small but packs a punch.'

I smile back at them, while cursing Trevor. Although, I'm pleased to hear that others on the site see me as tough. It's true, I'm brimming with confidence. Who'd have thought I'd find my soul on a building site?

'I used to have long hair,' says Chris. 'And Stevie's was longer than it is now. We used to fancy ourselves as rockers. Trev used to accuse us of being shirt lifters, even though he'd been to my wedding.'

'Didn't you mind?'

'Not at all. Life can be hard, especially in this game. When you get to our age, you'll have lost friends and relatives for no real reasons at all. Good people. So having a craic at work helps. I know you shouldn't say those sorts of things nowadays, but I miss the old banter.'

I shake my head.

'How can you miss the banter? Trevor's still saying it.'

I have a good giggle about some of their stories, in particular about Trevor falling through someone's kitchen ceiling and landing on the table while the family were having breakfast. Apparently, he got up, buttered himself a slice of toast, and told the father he might have a hole in the main bedroom floor.

When it's time to go, Scott is the last to leave apart from me and Trev, which is what most people call him. It suits him. Scott slows his truck as he drives past and gives me a wink out of the open window.

The weekend hasn't begun yet, but I already can't wait for it to be over.

CHAPTER 47

To my surprise, Monday comes around quickly enough. I forgot about tall Scott and his brown eyes because Trev and I had such fun. We got some beers in and paid for the boxing on Sky Sports Box Office on Saturday night. Trevor was funny. He got right into it for a local lad in one of the earlier fights and was stood shadow boxing with him. I nearly wet myself when his fighter got knocked out in the sixth.

Beer is Trev's Achilles' heel, and mine I suppose. We both fell asleep and missed the main fight. That's manual labour for you. We rewound it, but the fight was over after two rounds. Dazed, we both went to bed. Before I turned out my light, I could hear Trev talking in his room. I'm pretty sure it was to his wife, June.

Trev went food shopping Sunday morning while I was in bed, then he had a list of jobs all afternoon for various neighbours, so I tagged along. They were for little things like fixing toilet seats and loose cupboards. He even changed three light bulbs for a lady in a wheelchair and unblocked a drain for a guy he called Old Bill, who was closer to my age than Trev's. I didn't ask how much he charged them, but I never saw any money change hands. We had pizza Sunday night.

We're first on site this morning. The forecast is for thirty degrees. A scaffolder's van is next to arrive. The brick walls for the second house have reached the height where scaffold is needed. I watch the three men get out, who weirdly all have big beards. They greet Trevor like a returning war hero.

It becomes clear to me at that moment that I've been wrong about Trevor's life. I thought he'd given up and was just treading water until he died after he lost his family. It's clear to me that this is his family now: the men and women who work these dangerous jobs in any weather. They support each other and watch out for those who are struggling. It's a cutthroat game where people let others down at the drop of a hat for the sniff of a pound, but Trevor has created a community within this turmoil.

The owner of the scaffold is a guy called Thin Jim. He accidentally knocks over a row of the Albanians' tools. They turn as one to give him some grief, then look at each other and break out laughing. Jim's not particularly thin, but he is seven feet tall. I'm getting fond of the Albanians. They're like a team of mischievous but happy puppies.

'So, you're young Robbie,' says Thin Jim. 'The Whirlwind told me you were tasty. I usually eat babies, but you'll do.'

'You've probably got a couple in that stinky beard,' I reply.

His chuckle is like the rumble of distant thunder.

'Why do you call Trevor the Whirlwind?' I ask.

Thin Jim looks over at Trevor who's throwing heavy planks over a wall as though they're toothpicks.

'Need I say more?'

'I suppose not.'

I grin. That name suits Trevor, too. I love all their nicknames, politically incorrect or not.

'Efficient but dangerous,' says Thin Jim. 'He's the last man I'd want to fight.'

I stare at the giant next to me in surprise. He looks like he could crush most people in his shovel hands. I'm distracted, though, by Scott's Jeep arriving. He gets out and swaggers over, but the beaming smile on his face betrays his cool. He has red shorts on and a blue T-shirt.

'Morning, Robbie, Jim. Lovely day.'

'How you doing, Boyband?' asks Thin Jim.

'Good, you?'

'Yeah, you can't beat England when the weather's like

this. Fancy dress later?' asks Thin Jim.

Scott looks puzzled.

'I don't get it. What do you mean?'

'I was guessing that's why you're dressed as Pamela Anderson.'

Scott shrugs. I smile.

'Very funny,' says Scott. 'Let me know if you want your shoelaces doing up later.'

I laugh out loud. It's going to be a good day. Scott puts a hard hat on, and I put mine on too. I've braided my hair into tight pig tails today, so the hat fits better. The youngsters tend to wear all the safety equipment, whereas Trevor, Jim and the roofers don't bother.

By mid-morning, the sun beats down as though it's trying to scorch the earth. By midday, most of the men are topless, whatever condition they're in. Even the roofers let it hang out. I have a sports bra underneath, so I look around, then slip off my T-shirt. I've got a pretty flat chest, so it's not like a strippergram has arrived. I feel a bit self-conscious, but I'm only on the mixer, and it's boiling hot. Sweat has been pouring down my back and face, stinging my eyes and dampening my clothes.

Trevor returns from the builder's merchants. He walks over to the second house and chats to the bricklayers. He strides over to me, raises an eyebrow but doesn't comment.

'The Albos need more bricks up top.'

'What are Albos?'

'Albanians.'

I shake my head at him. They're up the scaffolding, so I grab the hod, load it up with eight bricks and climb the ladder. They're fast workers when they stop arguing and joking with each other, so I get into a rhythm. An hour passes, and I barely notice. I never would have guessed just how good it feels to be really fit and healthy.

I pause for a drink from a bottle of water, then take my helmet off to wipe the grimy sweat from my forehead. I can't resist pouring the cold water over my forehead, letting it run down my face and chest. When I look up, all the bricklayers on the second plot are leaning against the scaffolding in a line, staring in my direction. I look behind me.

'What?'

They all get back to work. Scott is the last to go. Even from a distance, I get the same smile I received when he turned up this morning. I feel a rush of heat in my groin, which burns hotter than the simmering sun overhead.

Just before we down tools for the day, one of the Albanians badly twists his ankle jumping down from the scaffold. It's one of those things that seems to happen on sites, but it swells up fast, and he's in a lot of pain. Trevor carries him to his van like he's a toddler who fell off a swing, then drives him to the hospital, leaving me to lock up and secure the site. Trev says to ring him when I'm ready to be picked up.

When I get outside the front gates, Scott's jeep is parked up on the kerb. He gets out and wanders over.

'Hey, can I ask you an important question?'

'Sure.'

'Fancy a beer?'

I can't help grinning. 'I could kill a beer.'

We wander over to the Gordon Arms and order two pints of Fosters. The bartender is very friendly. Scott scowls at him when his back is turned, making me smile again. We find a table in the beer garden. It's right next to a busy slip road, so it's not very romantic. I gulp most of my pint down in a few minutes. Scott has a little designer moustache of froth that makes me think of Orlando Bloom. I point at it.

'You have one, too,' he says.

'Oh, sorry. It's Trevor. He's turning me into a cavewoman.'

'It's not a bad look.'

For the first time in my life, I really flirt. It's brilliant. All the other people there, even the fumes from thousands of passing engines, disappear. We both have a soft drink next as he's driving, and I don't want to end up drooling. Our knees keep touching under the bench, unnecessarily so.

'Would you like to go to a party on Friday night?' he blurts out as we stand to leave.

'It's not that fancy dress thing Jim was going on about, is it?'

'Funny. No, it's a house party. A mate of mine has rich parents. He passed his degree with a first so they're throwing him a bash with waiters and a DJ. It won't be anything too crazy, fifty people maybe. Barnaby's pretty quiet.'

I don't hesitate.

'I'd love to.'

'I'll pick you up at seven-thirty. What's your address?'

'I'm staying at Trev's.'

Scott doesn't look surprised.

'What's the dress code?' I ask.

'God knows. Smart. You know, they love posing and then posting it on social media. His girlfriend has a fashion blog. I don't really get it. Seems to me they're busy taking pictures which look like they're having a good time, instead of actually having a good time.'

We walk back to his car. We briefly hold hands as we cross the road.

'Hey, how did you know I was at Trevor's?'

'I overheard him telling Jim. It's good. It can't have been easy losing his wife and Alex so close together.'

'Angelica.'

'God, sorry. It's just I knew her so well as Alex from junior school. Did she change her name officially?'

'No. She was going to before she got out. Alex Hemming will be forever the cop killer.'

'Was it an accident?'

'Kind of, but Angelica pushed him over the banister using his baton as leverage. They both banged their heads on the stairs, but he went home and must have had some kind of bleed. I suspect he cushioned her fall. He went to bed and never woke up. If you strip the incident down to the basics, she caused it. That makes it manslaughter at the very least.'

We reach Scott's car where we stand a little bit in each other's space. He looks like he's going to move in for a kiss.

'Didn't you read about the case at the time?' I ask.

'No, I was working as a holiday rep last year. I want to start my own building business at some point, so I thought I'd have a wild year first. Loads of my mates went to university, but I'm dyslexic. I know that people are more aware nowadays, but it does make it harder, and I've always loved doing stuff with my hands.'

'I'm sorry.'

'No, it's cool. The school were good about it, but I was never going to work in an office. I left school at sixteen and learned plumbing, but I didn't want to work with my head in someone's U-bend, so I retrained as a brickie. Angelica and I weren't close by the time we left education, so I never heard what happened. I only found out when I returned to the UK. Someone told me on the last site I worked on that Trevor's kid had died.'

I decide it's time I blurted something out.

'Robbie's not my first name, although that's what it says on my passport and bank statements.'

Scott grins. 'Interesting. What is your first name?'

'I was christened Alfredo Roberto Ayala.'

CHAPTER 48

I thought his face fell when he heard I'd been to prison with Angelica, but, right now, he looks as if he's just been given a terminal cancer diagnosis.

'Your name is Alfred Robert Ayala.'

'If you like, yes.'

'You're a man.'

I try to stay positive.

'I was assigned male at birth, but I felt like a woman from the moment I had any kind of conscious thought.'

For a moment, I don't think he's going to do what everyone normally does when they hear for the first time, but then he follows the crowd. Angelica called it the sausage scan. His eyes track down my body to my shorts as though he expects to find a marrow sized bulge there, or some kind of trunk dangling against my leg.

'Wow, you should have said.'

'Really?'

'Yeah, of course.'

'Why?'

'I wouldn't have…'

He trails off. By my bunched jaw, he's aware that he skates on thin ice.

'You wouldn't have talked to me? You wouldn't have asked me for a drink?'

'Erm.'

'Or you wouldn't have fancied me?'

'Well, it's not norm…'

'I'm dishonest AND abnormal now.'

He squints as he tries to wrap his head around it all.

'No, it's not that. I'm surprised, that's all. You're so attractive, and hot, I guess, that I never expected you to say that in a million years.'

'Can't trans people be attractive? Should I wear a T-shirt in future? Maybe one with "Packing Meat" on the front and a picture of a big salami underneath.'

'No, look, I'm sorry. It was a shock. I didn't mean to hurt your feelings.'

I exhale deeply and rein myself in. Maybe I'm morphing into the militant that Angelica wanted me to be.

'Look, it's okay. I know this sort of thing doesn't happen every day. It's who I am. I'm a woman. There's a part of me that men have, but we're all created with the same cells, it's just how they divide.'

I stop. There's no point trying to persuade him that I'm his kind of normal if he thinks I'm anything but.

'Don't worry about it, Scott. It's okay for you to be surprised. It's why I told you now. Nobody got hurt here.'

Even as I'm saying it, I know it's not true. It felt like we had an incredible connection that has snapped like cheap string.

'Right, thank you,' he says, avoiding eye contact.

'We can still be friends. I think that's allowed.'

'Yeah. Look, I better go. I've got stuff on.'

'Okay. It's not a big deal, you know.'

'It is quite a big deal.'

I try to give him a confident smile, but I can't. He gets in his vehicle.

'Only if you make it one,' I whisper.

CHAPTER 49

I've seen slower starts in Formula One. Scott even accelerates away in the wrong direction from where he lives. I have to wait for twenty minutes because Trevor's still at A&E. The energy leaches from me so fast, that it's an effort to pick myself up off the grass when Trevor arrives. Trevor moans about the state of the NHS on the way to his, so he doesn't notice my watery eyes. When we get home, Trevor races inside, shouting that he needs a Jimmy Riddle. I stay in the van and give myself a juicy half hour of self-misery. It's not fair. Other people don't have to deal with crap like this.

Then I pull myself together. I know others have it worse. I'm healthy, and hot; Scott said so. It just wasn't meant to be. There will be someone nice out there who can imagine a different world to a binary one. Although, sadly, Scott won't be the only one to react like that. It's best he and I don't start anything, or I'll be in too deep and get hurt. Although, the way my heart aches, that's already too late.

It's why I've lived like a hermit, stuck in my shell. If you don't venture out, you can't get crushed. I clench my fists. If you don't take part, you can't win. I know that now. Admittedly, the first time I've raised my head above the parapet, it's been blown off.

I straighten my shoulders and hustle into the house.

'Trevor! Get the fucking vodka out.'

Trevor comes out of the kitchen in a black apron. On it, in big letters, are the words, "My wife says I only have two problems. I don't listen and something else".

'Oh dear. That doesn't sound good,' he says, looking

concerned.

'No. I told Scott about my special power.'

'Ah, I see. The rest of us on the site have been chuckling about love's young dream. I take it he didn't respond kindly.'

'No, you probably heard his tyres screech from the hospital.'

'If you've had a shock, you need brandy, not vodka.'

'Line them up, then Trevlar.'

'Trevlar?'

'Yeah, not sure where that came from. Maybe Gavin and Stacey. I watched a lot of Gavin and Stacey DVDs inside.'

'You had a DVD player in your cell?'

'No, but you can play them on a PlayStation.'

Trevor shakes his head as he pours us both an inch of brandy.

'Christ. It's supposed to be a prison, not a holiday camp.'

'Ahh, how sweet. Have you been reading the Daily Mail again?'

'You're there to be punished.'

'No, the punishment is to be sent there. We're supposed to be rehabilitated behind those high walls. Holiday camp? It wouldn't get much repeat business, would it? Yeah, I won't be returning next year. I was locked in my room for most of the day, where I couldn't sleep because of the howls from the insane. The wing was filthy and stank of B.O, piss and weed. The showers regularly had blood on the walls or shit on the floor, and I had to eat my disgusting meals with known child abusers, murderers and arsonists.'

Trevor knocks his drink back in one, and I do the same.

'I get your point.'

'Good man. Rack 'em up.'

'I've got to get up early.'

'It wasn't a question. We're getting drunk. It's times like these that a woman has to get shit-faced with one of her closest friends. We reveal our inner most secrets and become stronger together because of it. For a reason I definitely don't want to contemplate right now, I don't have any female friends, so you'll have to do. Although, in that poncey apron, you're halfway there.'

Trevor flops his wrist, which I think is his attempt to look camp.

'Ooh, was that a homophobic slur?' he says.

I scowl at him because he's right. He is listening after all.

It's also not only a woman I need right now. It's simply a friend. We neck the next brandy.

'Why have you got that apron on?'

'When I did the shopping on Sunday, I remembered you saying I was existing, not living, and you're right. I used to like cooking, but I stopped when June died. We used to do it together. If I think about it, when I wasn't at work, we used to do everything together.'

'It's good to start again.'

'Yeah, so I thought I'd surprise you, but it's made me think about things. It's made me acknowledge that I'll never see Alex and June again. I was crying before I got the onions out. When I think about my family, it makes me wanna give up.'

I don't correct him. He picks up the bottle and his glass, sits down at the table next to me, and slumps. I pat his hand and briefly wonder if that's the first time we've touched since he held my hand out to see if I needed gloves. Trevor really has become an island, but it's what I was. I'm trying now, and so is he.

'We need to move on with our lives, Trev. Let's do it together. Aim for the skies. Do you think Brad Pitt is into trans people?'

'All celebrities swing both ways.'

I titter, then chuckle, then we're both belly laughing. Trevor pours us another shot, spilling brandy all over the table in the process, which sets us off again. I'm not sure I need much more.

'What are you cooking?'

'Chicken curry. It's easy, and I've just finished all the prep.'

It's hard to picture Trevor pushing a trolley around a supermarket and selecting ingredients. I can't help thinking of it being a bit like dodgems at the fairground for everyone else.

'Very nouvelle cuisine.'

Trevor again puts on what a sixty-four-year-old man thinks is a gay voice.

'I'm not sure I like this new bitchy Robbie.'

'I'm allowed today.'

Trevor smiles at me. 'You are, darlin'.'

'Thanks, Trev. I feel better already. Now, tell me one of your secrets.'

Trevor takes a deep breath before he answers.

'I planned to kill my wife.'

CHAPTER 50

I peer at him through slightly double vision.

'What?!'

'Yeah.'

'I thought she was your soul mate.'

'She was.'

'Didn't she have a stroke?'

'She did, but it didn't finish the job, so I grabbed a pillow.'

'Holy fuck.'

Trevor pours another drink, just for himself, and downs it.

'Yep. Sleep doesn't come easy after planning something like that.'

My brain scrambles to keep up, but brandy's way ahead on points.

'I think you'd better explain, before I ring the police, or a taxi at the very least.'

'Me and June, we knew everything about each other. We met at school, ran away at sixteen, but we were too young. We ended up homeless and skint. June had no choice but to go home. June's parents hated me for obvious reasons, and I weren't welcome. Us splitting, well it drove me off my trolley. I ended up in prison for six months for ABH. When I was inside, a bloke on my wing was always spouting on about money in the building game. The day I got out, I walked past a site. A bloke was leaving, and I just asked him if he had any work.'

Trevor smiles at the memories.

'They paid me twenty quid a day, half money, for the first week. Same deal you got. I was built for it, though. I was only nineteen, but I was the strongest man there. I knocked out a bull of an Irish renderer in a packed city pub and never looked back. He became a decent *china*, as it happens. I spent the next two decades with him, drinking, working, shagging and fighting my way around London, but nobody ever stacked up to June. One day, not long past my fortieth, I was driving down a rainy East Ham high street, packed with Christmas shoppers, and I see her.'

Trevor's still sitting opposite me, but in his head, he's back in London many years ago. His eyes are moist.

'I nearly crashed the car. I just stopped in the middle of the road, horns were blaring, rain was hammering down, I only had a shirt on. She saw me running towards her, and her face crumpled, and I knew. I just knew. That was it.' He smiles a soft smile. 'She dropped her bags and ran towards me.'

Trevor clumsily wipes his eyes.

'Cheesy, ain't it'?'

I shake my head. 'Not at all.'

'And that *was* it for me. We got married three months later, moved up here to get a fresh beginning. She helped me start my building business, and she grafted as hard as I did. We had our ups and downs, but our boy was everything I dreamed of, until it all went wrong.'

'You mean when the trans thing came up?'

'No, before that. We had another little boy, Felix. He was sickly from the start. June was old when she had him, and it weren't an easy pregnancy. We kept having to take him to hospital after he was born. The last time we took him there, we didn't bring him home. Little man's heart wasn't strong enough.'

'I'm so sorry, Trevor.'

'Yeah, well. That was a long time ago, but it rocked us both. Then there was all the drama around Angelica. So don't give up on your bloke. I couldn't get my head around all this trans stuff. Born a man, you are a man. So I thought. The last conversation I had with Angelica went the usual route. We had a big argument. I asked her why she couldn't be normal. Can you believe it? I'll never forgive myself. Do you know what the last thing was she said to me?'

I shake my head.

'She told me there was this new thing where you can get all the information about what it was like to be her.'

'Yeah, what was it?'

'The fucking internet.'

I can't help laughing. 'And did you?'

'Not at first. She killed that copper, and I washed my hands of her. Just worked and worked, but June never got over it. She rotted from within. I couldn't get her to eat or laugh. Thank fuck she was brown bread before Angelica died, or that would have killed her.'

We laugh again, but it dwindles.

'June collapsed in a Tesco Express. They took her to hospital and did a load of scans. We waited a month, but there was little progress. She gave up. Her eyes were open, but there was no one home. She was going to be a vegetable. We'd lived in each other's skyrockets until Felix died. It was the best time of our lives, and we knew each other inside out. I knew she'd have done the same for me. So, I put a pillow over her face while telling her I loved her.'

It's uncompromising, but I can understand. Trevor stands with a wobble.

'But I was sand. I couldn't do it. Instead of pushing down, I took it away and sat beside her. It was weakness on my part.'

'Oh, Trevor.'

'Right, enough of this maudlin shit. I better cook this ruby. If we don't have any tucker after necking all this brandy, we'll wish we'd croaked it in the morning.'

Trevor busies himself at the oven and soon lovely smells have filled the room. I grab my phrase book. Ruby, means Ruby Murray - curry. Tucker, means Tommy Tucker - supper. China, means china plate - mate. Jimmy Riddle means piddle. And I know what skyrocket means. It's funny. Angelica's slang always came out when she was pissed.

Twenty minutes later, Trevor slides a dustbin-lid-sized plate in front of me, heaped with enough food for a family of six.

'Do you know what?' he says. 'It felt like June was staring at me when I was bringing the pillow towards her face. I reckon she was trying to say thank you.'

'Right. Let's hope she wasn't trying to say stop.'

CHAPTER 51

Saturday was a write-off, and Sunday wasn't much better. Despite Trevor's Ruby Murray being like eating hot coals, I woke up at the table. Trevor had put a pillow under my head. I'm glad I wasn't half-awake like June and could see him coming towards me with it.

Apparently, June died of natural causes a few days later, so he made the right decision. It's strange that he sees it as weakness.

It was a relief to sweat the toxins out at work on Monday. Trevor said he didn't half have what he called "the trots", and I did too.

The weather holds all week, and the time flies by. Scott and I circle each other like wary animals, but the tension begins to break, and we return to being a bit chatty. I try to convince myself I'm not bothered, but when he takes his shirt off, my tongue virtually rolls out of my mouth, cartoon style.

Trevor shouts over to me just before lunch on Friday.

'Triple C's coming early this afternoon. Can you look after him? We're running dry on cement, and there's none anywhere, so I've gotta chase some up.'

'Who's Triple C?'

'The camp Chinese chippy.'

'Trevor!'

He runs away laughing. He can be such a little kid at times.

I realise I'm looking forward to seeing Johnny. He's one of those people who make life seem fun just by being with him. I expected him to have something like a pink Audi TT, but he turns up in a dark-blue Ford Focus estate. It's quite the disappointment.

When he gets out, he's still immaculately dressed in 501 jeans and a short-cut leather jacket with seemingly nothing underneath it except a very blingy necklace, but he has no make-up on, and his hair is just brushed into a side-parting. He still gives me the biggest grin and a kiss on each cheek.

'Robbie! It's great to see you. You look a million dollars.'

I've got blue cut-off jeans on which are a touch on the small and short side. My checked shirt is buttoned quite low too. I lied to myself this morning by pretending I was decking myself out like this merely to feel good. The Albanians all pretend to fan themselves whenever I walk past them.

'Johnny Chan. You look like your outfit cost a billion dollars. You're more subdued today, but still very smiley.'

'I always try to bring sunshine, sweetie.'

'Come on. I assume you're here to measure up for the staircases and windows.'

'Yes, nothing but the best for these homes. Everything is oak and bespoke.'

We smile at each other. He's such easy company. He wanders around with a spirit level and a tape measure. I steal a few looks at him. His face does ring a bell, though. It's his teeth. They remind me of Freddie Mercury. He has the same attractive suaveness to him. Not to mention that due to my father playing his music all the time, Freddie is one of my heroes.

'How did you get into carpentry?' I ask him.

'Very boring. It's my dad's business. I helped out from a young age.'

'Trevor says you're better than your old man.'

'Yes, I'm good with wood.' He gives me a saucy smile. 'It's a shame I don't like it.'

'Wood?'

'Touché. Carpentry. Well, that's not completely true. It's okay, but I studied textiles and design at college. I want to work in fashion.'

'Why don't you then?'

'I'd just finished my course when my dad had a health scare, so I went home and picked up the slack for him. He's in remission now, so fingers crossed. I said I'd give him six more months, max, then I'm off. My future is not on a building site, darling.'

'Good for you.'

'What's your story?' he says. 'This doesn't look like the kind of place for you, either. It's like finding a rose in a sandpit.'

'Thanks, I think.'

We laugh easily again. I ponder giving him an airbrushed version of my prison escapades, but tell him the truth. He gives me a hug when I've finished.

'What doesn't kill you makes you stronger.'

'That's what I'm hoping.'

'You know, you'd look good as a model. Great arms and legs. The fitness look is very en vogue at the mo. You being trans would be quite the killer twist.'

'Did Scott tell you?'

'No, I guessed. I'm perceptive like that.'

Johnny looks over at Scott, who's topless and reaching up to lay his bricks.

'I see you've met Boyband,' he says. 'He's looking particularly fine today. Those abs could turn Trevor's eye. I'll wrestle you for him.'

'Scott's still living in the last century.'

Johnny doesn't reply, but his little smile tells me he understands.

'Did you know Trevor calls you Triple C?'

'Of course.'

'Do you mind? It's not very PC.'

'Mind? I love it. I've got a T-shirt with it on. I wouldn't be one of the dudes if I didn't have a moniker.'

'Oh right. I'm still only Robbie.'

The little smile is back.

'You'll never be just Robbie. It suits you anyway. Like Queen or Sting.'

'Or Batman.'

'More Robin, I would say.'

'I could dress as Catwoman.'

'I'm sure you could. You know, I like Trevor, but he's a bundle of contradictions.'

'That's my favourite English phrase.'

'It's one of mine, too. Yes, it suits him because he's such a mixture. He may be rude and uncouth at times, and outright racist and homophobic at others, but his heart is pure gold. He is changing though, which isn't easy when you're his age. He saved my life once.'

'Really?'

'Well, maybe from a kicking. I was doing a job for him a little while back, and some lads came past, drunk, and looking for trouble. Gay bashers. I was on my own at the front of the house. There were three of them. They started called me Wong Foo and threw stones at me, then they shoved me.'

'Was it racism?'

'It was everything. You know when you get that feeling where the atmosphere changes, and you just know something really horrible is going to happen.'

'I do. If nothing else, the prison taught me that.'

'Next thing, Trevor appears. He shouts out, what the fuck are you cockwombles up to? They were big lads, too, but Trevor had brought his nail gun.'

My eyes widen.

'He shot them with it?'

'Kind of. He hit one of them in the face with the handle of it, then chased them down the street firing it at them, while calling them cunts. They didn't come back.'

Worryingly, I can imagine the scene.

'He could have killed them.'

'Obviously Trevor hasn't trained you in the fine art of a nail gun. The little ones are useless at any distance more than two inches. You might as well throw the nails. Frightened the life out of those boys, though.'

After Johnny finishes up, I walk him back to his car.

'Can I ask you something?'

He sits in the driver's seat.

'Of course.'

'Why no make-up today?'

Johnny looks through the windscreen and into the distance for a moment. He slowly exhales.

'Sometimes, when I wake up, I can't be doing with the aggravation. So I conform. It shouldn't be like that, but that's the way it is for people like us. I suspect you sometimes feel the same way.'

'Yeah. I used to hide away, so I wouldn't get hurt.'

'Do you know? I used to do that. A friend once asked me what I was waiting for? He was right. We'll all be old, saggy and smelly soon, and we'll have missed our most brilliant moment.'

I beam at him. He touches my arm.

'Show them who you are, girl. You're beautiful and proud and trans. Shout it from the rooftops.'

CHAPTER 52

By the end of the day, I'm again ready to let off some steam. It's the builder's way of life. As we're all packing away for the weekend, a small red two-seater sports car slowly edges up the long mud drive to the first plot. It has a private plate, EST1R, and it looks brand new.

The woman who gets out of the car has poise and style despite being dressed in a pair of cut off denim dungarees. She flips up her oversized sunglasses and waves at Trevor, who looks like Christmas has arrived early.

'Esther,' he shouts. 'Great to see ya, darlin'.'

'You, too, Trev. It's been years.'

'Decades, probably.'

She looks around the four plots. I follow her eyes as she glances around, and I kind of see it for the first time as well. These houses will look beautiful when they're done. It reminds me of those Center Parcs holiday places, where all the lodges are surrounded by trees, giving it a secluded feel. This will be like that on a much grander scale.

Her gaze extends to include everyone here. She waves at Thin Jim and nods at the rest of us. Her eyes narrow slightly when she reaches me, but then she gives me a little smile. Up close, she is much older than I thought. She has delicate features and great skin, but I suspect she could be as old as sixty.

'Where are those imbeciles?' she asks.

'I assume you mean Jacko and Eduardo,' laughs Trevor.

'Yes, I've no idea why he keeps those buffoons on the payroll. I said I'd be here at this time, and I'm seeing my sister later, so...' She tails off looking annoyed, but then reaches over and gently squeezes Trevor's shoulder.

'I'm so sorry to hear about your family.'

'Yeah. Tough days. I'll miss them until the day I die, but I'm beginning to function normally again.'

Her eyes wander to me, and she gives me a smile.

'And who's this?'

'This is Robbie. Crazy cow wanted to try the building game. She was Angelica's best friend.'

Esther purposefully steps over to me, dodging the bricks and cement bags on the way.

'Lovely to meet you,' her eyes crinkle, and I get the impression she is a lovely, honest person. 'Careful out here. It can be dangerous for young women like you.'

A few goosebumps come up on my body at that comment, but she seems very genuine.

'Thank you.'

'What do you want from those two pecker heads, Esther?' asks Trevor.

'I'm trying to balance the accounts, but there are a few invoices missing. It looks like we've got half a tonne of cement free from somewhere and two tonnes of sand.'

'Ah, sorry. That's on me. I had to ring around for it because those imbeciles, as you so accurately called them, hadn't ordered enough. The merchants were out and they couldn't get any for a week. I rang around and called in a favour, so we didn't have to down tools. I had to find more today as well.'

'Bloody hell, Trevor. It's been doing my nut in.'

I can't help chuckling as I put the rest of the tools away. She sounded fairly posh at first, but she obviously came from the same streets as Trevor. I wander over to Trevor's van to wait for him to finish catching up. Esther and he are clearly old friends. Scott is hanging around at the back of Trevor's van looking shifty.

'Watch it, Boyband,' I say to him. 'Step away from the

vehicle. If you're hoping to nick one of Trevor's legendary ham rolls, we've already eaten them.'

'It was you I was after. I was wondering if you'll still be ready at seven-thirty tonight.'

To say I'm surprised is an understatement, but I manage to stay cool.

'You're lucky, Boyband. I've just had another date cancel.'

He looks cute, blushing, but he recovers well, too.

'I'd rather you called me Scott when we're at the party.'

'Scott it is. I'll see you later.'

He winks at me, rubs a hand through his lush hair, and saunters away. Overconfident git.

I watch Trevor get a sloppy kiss on the cheek from Esther, then there's the roar of a powerful engine, and a Ford Ranger pick-up truck hurtles up the drive. Whoever's at the wheel is driving too fast. The truck abruptly halts, skidding slightly. I'm not surprised to see Jacko step from the vehicle in another tiny white T-shirt. His face is pinched.

He stomps over to Trevor and Esther and starts gesticulating. Jacko hasn't completely lost control, but I can see Trevor has widened his stance and stepped back a pace. Esther does the opposite. She wags her finger in Jacko's face. She shouts at first, but then gradually softens her tone. Jacko reminds me of an excitable dog where the owner, Esther in this case, calms him down.

Trevor joins in with the conversation, but it's relatively relaxed now. Jacko nods, gets back in his truck and leaves at a more sensible pace. Trevor receives another kiss from Esther, then we all get in our vehicles and leave.

'What was all that about?'

'You remember the ruckus Jacko and Eduardo had the other day?'

'Yep.'

'It's been simmering for a while, and they had another big barney. Eduardo was supposed to meet Jacko this afternoon at Triple C's dad's showroom to make a final decision on all the woodwork and thrash out a final price, but he never showed. Jacko went to Eduardo's house, but he can't find him, and he's not answering his phone.'

'Why does Landsman put up with them?'

'He uses Jacko as muscle, even though Landsman used to be a professional boxer himself, and he's been pally with Eduardo for years, but both the brothers are notoriously flaky. I told you. It's a transient game. People come and go. Jacko is bad news when he's this riled up. I wouldn't want to be anywhere near him. Jacko and Eduardo have a warped relationship. I suppose a lot of brothers do. Eduardo's probably disappeared before their fight shifts up a notch and he gets a proper backhander. Eduardo once went missing right in the middle of another job I was working on. It was for an Arab, and he wanted it done pronto, so the dough was amazing. There were loads of us on that site. Anyway, Eduardo vanished one morning, and the police turned up that afternoon.'

'What happened?'

'Do you know what? I never found out. Eduardo wasn't heard of again for a few years, then he returned. He's always been a bit of a weirdo. I heard through the grapevine that he legged it back to Eastern Europe having been caught up in some kind of porn ring, but the case collapsed, so he felt it was safe to show his boat race again.'

Trevor's about to take the turn to his area of town when I remember Scott.

'Straight on, Trevor. I need to go to River Island.'

'What for?'

'I need a dress for a date.'

Trevor laughs. 'Boyband changed his tune.'

'Yep. Now tell me how you know the delightful Esther.'

'God, we've known each other for years. She was at my school in London, but three years below me. She was a cracker, then. She was always flirting with me, but three years was a bit too much. I felt a bit like a paedo whenever she linked arms with me in the playground. Then I met June, and obviously I left school.'

'She sounds posh. What's she doing up here?'

'She didn't sound like that at school. I ain't seen her for donkey's, but she was always gonna be a success, that girl. She was bright, too. The first time I did a job for Landsman, she came to the site. She was married to him by then.'

'You're kidding me.'

'No, he wasn't so twisted back then, and he's rich as Croesus.'

'Is his money dodgy?'

'Not at all. He borrowed big on housing and took a lot of risks, but property's been a one way bet in England, so he's laughing. I see her around every now and again. I think her and Landsman are going through the motions now, but you never know what's really going on in someone else's marriage. She runs his entire financial side, and he does the deals, but there have been rumours about him and prostitutes for yonks.'

'Poor woman.'

'Yeah, but she's a tough old bird. She wouldn't still be there if she wasn't getting something from it.'

'Why doesn't she leave him?'

'Who knows? There are people left who take their vows seriously. They've also got a girl in her late twenties who's in and out of posh rehab. More in than out. Esther's done her best, but the kid is a real fuck up. Esther probably hasn't got the time or energy for a divorce.'

I ponder what he's said for a moment. It's true. Some people endure their vows when times are tough. Others discard them easily. Makes you wonder what they were all thinking when they were saying them at the altar.

'She still fancies you.'

'Jog on, Robbie. I'm tired and not in the mood for your games.'

'You fancy her too.'

'I ain't interested in another man's wife.'

'No, but you can look elsewhere.'

'It'd feel like I was cheating on my June.'

'Come on, Trevor. June wouldn't want you to stay celibate for the rest of your life. You're so gnarled and grizzly, you'll probably make a hundred.'

'I fucking hope not.'

'Get back in the saddle.'

I can see he's thinking about it. He casts a cheeky look in my direction.

'Shag some old sort?'

'You're not going to get any with that kind of language.'

Trevor pulls into a parking space outside River Island at the Retail Park. I expect him to laugh it off, but he's serious.

'You're spot on. Look, I'm not good with words, but thank you. Before you turned up, I was only going through the motions. Stuck, with no chance of change. I was thinking of topping myself after Angelica did what she did, and June died. I couldn't see a future, but I can now. It helps you said Angelica didn't blame me.'

'Excellent. Half my work is done.'

'What do you mean?'

'Just before I got out of jail, and she did what she did, Angelica begged me for two favours. The first was to save a life.'

CHAPTER 53

I leap out of the van with Trevor gawping like a fool. That's another great phrase. Gotta love the English language. It's strange to think I spent nearly an entire year on remand with nothing to do but talk and watch TV. I picked up some brilliant phrases. I met a prisoner from somewhere called Acton Town and everything in his life was banging. Did you watch that film last night, it was banging?

'I don't get it,' says Trevor. 'Saved whose life?'

'Sorry, I'll be back in ten minutes. I'll tell you then.'

I slam the door shut and race into the shop towards the dress section. I receive a few funny looks while I check out what they've got. They probably think I'm the maintenance person. Then I see it on a mannequin. A black number. It's actually quite conservative in length and style, but the sheer material touches the mannequin in a way that's really sexy. I have some black heels at home which would match. They have the dress in a size eight, so I pull one off the rail and run to the counter.

'Hi, madam. That's a great choice. Ninety pounds, please.'

I cough and hand my card over.

She holds the dress up before putting it in a bag.

'This is so beautiful. Lots of people try it on, but this silky material is unforgiving. It will hang so well on your slim frame. You'll be prettier than Salma Hayek.'

Her kind comments take the sting out of the price. I remind myself it's about a day's wages, not forty-five days of cleaning in the prison. Trevor is still in the van. I'm not sure he's moved. Even his face has the same expression.

'Spit it out,' he says, as we pull away.

'Okay. Angelica knew that you didn't find having a trans daughter easy, but she told me that even when you were disagreeing, she always loved you.'

'Disagreeing is putting it mildly. She played merry hell.'

'Yes, but she knew that. It was hard for her, and you understand that. It took a long time for her to realise what was wrong. She had to wait for puberty to fully realise she was born in the wrong body. That causes problems for people like us. She said the hormones wrecked her head too.'

'I reckon it was more likely the recreational drugs that did that.'

'Yes, I'd agree, but she struggled so much. People were horrible to her because she looked different, and it sapped her confidence. Drugs are often simply a way to forget all the nastiness. She reckoned she was you in a dress, even though I told her all the time she was fabulous. She had your energy, but she also had your temper. It sounds like you've calmed down as you've got older, but Angelica was in the eye of her storm.'

'Okay, I get it, but what's this saving me bollocks?'

'She loved you, Trevor, and you were so similar, she knew how you'd react when June died. Angelica said you and her mum had the strongest love she'd ever seen. It was the standard Angelica judged all relationships by. It was what she wanted for herself, but she never got close. She thought she never would.'

Trevor desperately wipes the tears from his eyes, but it's a pointless task.

'She knew you'd give up and stop living, maybe even take your own life. She didn't want that because she felt it was her fault. Angelica asked me to come and speak to you to encourage you to start again. She told me a lot of people rely on you, and they do. I must admit we never expected me to end up living and working with you, but that's what occurs when you make honest promises. Good things happen. You're moving on now. It's not a betrayal to enjoy the rest of your life. Both of us have hidden away for too long.'

Trevor pulls up outside his house. He's weary, and, for the first time since I met him, he looks his age. He turns to me.

'You said there were two promises. What was the second one?'

I've tried not to think too much about the second one. There are obviously two types of promises. Some have the potential to change lives. Others to damage them.

'I've got a shower to run, hair to style, and slap to apply. Let's get a pizza tomorrow night and some wine, and I'll tell you about it. I'm warning you now, though. It's going to be tough to hear.'

'Okay, I get it, but why did she have to go and kill herself?'

I check my watch. It wouldn't be fair to leave him hanging.

CHAPTER 54
Three months ago

I look up to find Angelica standing in my cell doorway.

'Do you know what we're going to be?' she asks.

'Rich, I hope.'

'You will be darling, but only in love.'

'I'll take that. Can I be semi-wealthy as well?' I show her the Sunday supplement magazine from a four-month-old newspaper. 'I'd like some of these Hermès handbags. This one is only three thousand pounds.'

'Ooh, nice. No, sorry. Tesco carrier bag for you.'

I grin at her. We've been inside over ten months now. I never would have made it this far without her.

'We, Robbie, are canaries.'

'Okay. Isn't Drabwell in cell two a canary.'

'No, Drabwell is a Norwich City fan, that's a different type of canary.'

'So what kind are we?'

'We are young and beautiful. We light up and decorate this dingy hellhole. Remember what you said about this dark place when we first arrived.'

'That it was a pit.'

'Yes, and what is another word for a pit?'

'A dump?'

'No, we British also call them coal mines. So that's what we are.'

'You've lost me.'

'We're canaries in the coal mine.'

She looks really pleased with herself. I've heard of the

phrase, but I still don't get it. She huffs out a big breath and sits next to me, putting an arm around my shoulders.

'Think about it. Why do they send canaries down coal mines?'

'To check for bad gas. Ah, I get it. There is a lot of bad gas in here. You're responsible for quite a bit of it.'

'Cute, Robbie. Very cute. No, the concept, not specifics. I asked McNulty. It's called an idiom. The phrase is used to describe an early sign of danger.'

'I know that.'

'So, look at us. Look what they've done with us, where they've sent us. We shouldn't be on this wing, having our medication messed about with. We get abuse from the other prisoners and some officers. We need to be somewhere safer, at the very least. I know they let us shower separately and they give us access to make-up, but I want my hair to look fabulous, instead I'm starting to go bald like my dad. I want fabulous wigs and beautiful jewellery, so I can feel like a woman.'

It took two days to get my hormone pills and three for Angelica. It felt like we were going insane. The sense of panic was indescribable. It felt like I was changing into something completely alien to me. We couldn't function. I got put on report for refusing to clean. I felt like a werewolf. My dreams were filled with screams as I changed. It wasn't a long time, but that's how important it is for people like us. The only thing I can compare it to is like a cancer patient waiting to start treatment knowing damage is occurring. Your whole life comes to a halt.

Although, I suspect nobody in any kind of prison gets given nice jewellery or decent wigs. There has to be a punitive element to being a criminal.

'What's all this got to do with canaries?' I ask.

'We need to sing about our lives in here. Everyone must know what happens in these places. I want there to be newspapers and Panorama documentaries revealing our plight. You need to be proud of who you are, Robbie. Show the world that to be trans is to be normal. Let them know our story. Be a beacon for people like us who don't choose to be trans, it's simply who we are.'

'Why do I have to do it?'

'What can I do? They'll give me years. I'd love to make a statement, but what can I do to make them listen when I'm in here? You, on the other hand, are out soon. Besides, people like me scare them. Beauty opens doors. Then the rest of us can safely follow. Perhaps, finally, we can have people from our community of all shapes and sizes on gameshows and in magazines, instead of just the most cis passing members.'

She's right. There are some visible trans people but they tend to be cis passing, which means they resemble the gender they identify as. Whereas in reality, many of us overlap in the way we dress or present like men wearing make-up or having long hair.

'Okay.'

'Call the Guardian newspaper. They'll lap it up because at least they understand. We need to get the ball rolling.'

'So, we're canaries as in we go in first and make it safe for those who follow. I can understand that. If we kick up a stink and let everyone know how we've been treated, then they'll change their procedures. That way, it's safer for everyone who has to tread our path.'

'Precisely. Putting ourselves out there is a risk, but if we do nothing, then nothing changes. Yes, you might get abused, but in ten years' time, or whatever, trans rights will be as strong as everyone else's rights. It will be the way it should be. Our lives will have had purpose. Wasn't that what you always wanted? A cause to follow. Something noble to work towards.'

She's spot on. That is what I've dreamed of. What better thing is there than to make the world a safer place for those who don't fit in. Those without a voice need someone to speak for them. Angelica grins at me and turns to leave. Another thought appears in my mind. I grab her hand.

'Wait, Angelica. Don't the canaries often die?'

CHAPTER 55
Present day

Trevor looks at me with a confused expression.

'Where are you going with this?'

'I'm sorry. I've run out of time. I'll explain properly tomorrow.'

I rush upstairs to get ready. After a speed shower, I get dressed and put my make-up on. For some reason, I'm really clumsy, which isn't helping.

When I'm ready, I sit on my bed and try to remain calm. It feels like I'm waiting for my date on prom night. Not that our school had a prom. There was an end of school party, but I didn't go.

I keep sitting down for a wee, but nothing comes out. Finally, there's a knock at the door. I hear Trevor calling him Boyband and inviting him in. After two deep breaths, I walk down the stairs.

The look on their faces tells me I made good choices. The dress was tighter on me than on the mannequin. It must be the muscle tone I've developed while labouring. I've put my hair up into a bun on my head, leaving wisps hanging down. I have my mother's skin. It looks and feels smooth and is blemish free, so I need little make-up. I've mostly gone for a swipe of smoky grey over my eyelids, and layers of mascara to make my already long lashes thick and luscious. Light gold jewellery finishes the look down to a slim ankle chain, which makes me feel super sexy.

'Shut your traps, gents, I can see your tonsils.'

I stride outside to Trevor's deep laughter. Scott comes

scuttling out after me. We drive in silence, but I catch him grinning. We arrive at what I can only describe as a mansion. There are about ten cars parked outside, and a taxi drives away having left two elegantly dressed women at the entrance.

Scott parks up, takes my hand, and we walk in. I half expect there to be security guards at the door, but there's nobody in the hall. We walk through the kitchen where three people are chatting. There's food out. It looks like it's mostly canapes. I daren't eat anything or my dress might split.

Scott and I receive plenty of looks as we walk outside. We make a striking couple. He's got a pair of dark-grey trousers on and a lovely olive Superdry tailored shirt, above a pair of tan shoes. Scott gets me a drink, and I try again to be cool.

After about an hour, I wonder what all my worries were about. The host's mum is there, which I wasn't expecting. She looks uber glamorous in a short Azur dress. Her legs look fabulous above a pair of heels, which I would guess cost a hundred times what mine did. I enjoy a few seconds of envy. She chats to us and is really friendly. The guy whose party it is, Barnaby, comes over and spends ten minutes with Scott, laughing and joking, but he includes me.

Later, I meet his girlfriend, Chanelle, who comes over very confidently on her own. She admires my dress and figure, which makes me feel wonderful because she is so pretty. Scott nips to the toilet, leaving me a little exposed, but there are others here on their own. I spot a larger guy at the edge of the decking, so I wander over and introduce myself.

Daniel has a stutter, which he's conscious of and mentions repeatedly. He must also be nervous. I tell him I'm from Ecuador, so I'm used to people rolling their Rs. This makes us both laugh. He's really funny. He thought there would be a pool because Barnaby is so rich, so he almost came in his speedos.

Champagne always goes straight through me, so when Scott returns, I nip to the toilet. When I come out, there are two young lads in casual suits outside. I smile at them.

'Hey, fella,' says the black-haired one. 'You sure you're in the right toilet.'

The blond brays out a laugh which shows just how drunk he is. I give them another tight smile and walk past. I quicken my pace and rush outside to find Scott, who's still talking to Daniel.

'Are you okay?' asks Scott. 'You look flustered.'

'Fine.'

Scott glances over my shoulder and gestures for me to look. I turn around dreading what I'll see, but it's the mother walking over to a sound system, which is on a table next to the huge patio. She puts a Beyonce song on. *If I Were a Boy.* Scott and I share a look. Could it be more ironic?

We're so close to the speakers that I can feel the beat in my teeth. It reminds me of Trevor's Kango.

There's good-natured groaning from the youngsters, but people start dancing amongst all the tasteful garden lights. The way they've set it up with pillars and flowers makes it seem like there aren't that many people about. Scott looks very handsome in the flickering light. I think how Angelica would have loved it here.

Scott takes my hand and escorts me to the middle of the patio. We kind of half smooch, half dance. He's beaming.

'Did you ask her to put this on?'

'Yes. You said that it was Angelica's favourite.'

I rest my head on his chest. It feels like we're on our own, until Barnaby's mum comes over and steals him from me. Scott looks very flustered. I just laugh and return to Daniel.

'Do you want to dance?' I ask him.

'No, I'm heavy, and I have flat feet. Your feet would soon be the same if I danced with you.'

We chat for a bit, then someone taps me on the shoulder. It's the two jerks from earlier. The blond leans in, but speaks loudly.

'We're looking for women to dance with. Have you seen any?'

I ignore him and turn back to Daniel, who's wishing the ground would swallow him up.

'I'm sorry, Robbie,' he says. 'Let's go inside for a bit.'

I feel that flame light up inside me again. Why should we be the ones to leave? Why should we put ourselves out, when it's them who are out of order? I get another tap on the other shoulder.

'Do you know if it's legal to put a ring on someone like you?' says black hair.

I turn around fully this time. There are more people behind me than I imagined. They're all looking at me. The song changes to Don't Stop Believing by Journey. I feel like flinging the contents of my glass in his face, but manage to stop myself. I take a step towards him.

'Leave me alone,' I say as calmly as I can.

'Hey, relax. We like tranny porn.'

I can't help thinking, what would Angelica have done? Actually, I know. They'd both be bleeding by now, but I'm not Angelica. Scott returns slightly out of breath from his dance and immediately picks up on the mood change, despite the loud music.

'What's wrong?' he asks.

'We're leaving.'

'Why?'

I stare from blond to black hair and stride between them, making them step out of the way. I'm tempted to launch my champagne into the speaker tower, but I keep my arm tensed at my side. Then, I bring myself to a halt. It feels like a pivotal moment in my life. I walk back to the sound system, lift my drink up, pull my arm back, then stop again.

I place my glass on the table next to the speakers, then press the power button on the sound system. Nobody's talking because they're already mesmerised by the unexpected entertainment.

I glance at the people on my left, straight in their faces, and then to the right. Many look away. It's so quiet. I stride up to the two men and speak loud enough so everyone can hear.

'Yes, I'm trans. Yes, that makes me different, but I'm still a person. I was scared to come here tonight. I've spent my whole life not coming to events like this because I have nightmares about exactly this happening. So, thank you both, very much. You've made my dreams come true.'

Blond looks down, but black hair holds his angry stare. I direct my next comment at him.

'I don't know why you think you can speak to someone the way you have to me. I don't know why you would go out of your way to ruin my night. All I want is to be happy and make friends. Please, don't do this again. I hate to think you will make someone else feel the way I feel now.'

I turn around and recall how Esther walked from her car with such confidence in her walk. Blinking rapidly, I attempt to copy her style. Scott stands stunned with the rest of them as I try to glide past him. My heels click through the atrium, and I almost collapse with relief when I reach the car. Scott has caught up with me by then, but he doesn't know what to say. He probably thought like that himself a few weeks ago. He presses the button on the fob to open his car. I'm climbing in when Barnaby's girlfriend races out of the house.

'Robbie, Robbie! Wait!'

I sit in the seat, but leave the door open. Chanelle comes to my side of the car, crouches, and holds my arm at the elbow.

'I'm so sorry.'

'It's okay.'

'No, it's not okay. I'll have Barnaby throw them out. Come back.'

'No, I wouldn't feel comfortable now.'

'Please don't believe everyone thinks like them, Robbie. We don't.'

'I know, but their comments are hard to forget.'

I put my hand on the door handle. She steps back. Instead of slamming the car door shut, I look up at her.

'Thank you, Chanelle.'

She frowns. 'What for?'

'For coming out here. For saying that. For being kind. Now it's you who I'll remember.'

CHAPTER 56

Scott also apologises on the way home. It seems the only people who haven't, are the ones responsible. I'm not sad or tearful, though. I'm too angry. That's because situations like this aren't uncommon for trans people. I've been incredibly lucky in comparison. My school was very accommodating. They let me change in a unisex toilet for sport. They didn't enforce the uniform code, or otherwise I would have had to wear long trousers.

I remember Angelica begging that I become a canary, so I make a mental note to email the school and recommend that they alter their uniform code so it's more inclusive, instead of fudging it when necessary. They were getting there, though. The head of my year was lovely and regularly checked on me. The prison is going to get a strongly worded email as well, but I suppose the home secretary is the man in charge.

I can't help thinking about how those two bastards at the party knew I was trans.

'Do I look like a man?'

'No, of course not.'

'I must do, or how did they know?'

Scott's jaw bunches.

'I suspect Barnaby told them. He knew.'

I put my head in my hands, but I suppose Scott needed someone to talk to as much as I did.

Scott takes the wrong junction off the parkway instead of returning to my house. Then he indicates right and pulls into the Marriot hotel car park.

'What's going on?'

'I asked you out for a date, and I don't think that counts as one. Let's have a cocktail here and talk.'

We park and walk in. He holds my hand properly. It's quiet inside, and we almost have the place to ourselves. We choose a spot in the corner. He heads to the bar and soon returns with the drinks. I have a Sambuca, which I knock back in one. It makes me gasp. He sticks to sparkling water, saying he's already had his one drink.

'I think I have an idea what you and Alex put up with now.'

'Angelica.'

'Shit, sorry.'

'That's only the twentieth time. I know it's easy to do, but it's incredibly hurtful to the transgender person.'

'Why's it so bad?'

'Most trans people call it their dead name. Every time they hear it, even if it's someone shouting it out to someone else who's called the same name, it's a real shock. It jolts the person back to when their gender dysphoria was really bad. When they knew something wasn't right, but they didn't know what. They feel isolated and alone all over again.'

"Why do you say their dysphoria, and not yours?'

'Angelica was right. I was luckier than her. I knew I was female from the first moment I was aware there was a difference. There was never any doubt in my mind. I liked pink clothes, dolls, other girls' company, walked like a girl and talked like a girl. I haven't let anyone cut my hair since I was five. I refused to wear boys' clothes around that age, too. My mum thought it was a phase, so she let me go to school in a dress.'

'That can't have been easy.'

'I don't remember. My mum says some of the other kids laughed on my first day, but I didn't care. The most important thing was that I got my way. I loved dressing up as a girl. Back then, nothing fazed me. I wanted the world to see me in pretty clothes. I don't know where that girl went. I think I left her behind when I came to England.'

'Did you get any grief at senior school in Ecuador?'

'Of course, but not too much. It wasn't vicious like it can be here, but I lived in a village. The school was in a small town nearby, so everyone knew of me anyway. Most people are like you, they're a little shocked to begin with, but then they're okay with it. You usually only have to spend an hour with me to see I'm as girlie as can be.'

He smiles. 'Less than an hour.'

'Even though you've seen me covered in cement powder with sweat stained clothes?'

'Yes, you have a care to your work and other people that is very feminine. Think of how Trevor throws things around, whereas you place them. You take the time to smile at people and listen when you ask them how they are. I've heard you ask people about their families, remembering their names and concerns.'

I give him a small smile.

'Thank you. Poor Angelica had a much tougher time at school. She was bullied mercilessly by some, although most of them got silenced by her fists. She couldn't beat a whole school up though.'

'Is that why it was harder for her?'

'No, the reason she had it worse was because she realised why she was different a little too late. It was obvious for me, so my parents bought the hormone treatment that stopped me going through puberty. They supported my decisions, which was very important to me. Your parents are your world. If it was hard for mine, they tried not to show it.'

'You were lucky to have parents like that.'

'Yes. Angelica's parents were older. It's very much an age thing. The older you are, the more likely it's not as easy to understand. Men tend to take longer to accept what's literally staring them in the face. This isn't a game for us. It really is life or death.

'Was your dad quite a short person?'

'Yes, and my mum is tiny, and I didn't go through all the male changes, where your shoulders broaden, and your voice deepens. Angelica was already turning into a young Trevor when she realised she was in the wrong body, and you can't just click your fingers and get help in this country.'

'Ah, I see. There's a bit of a conundrum then. If you leave it too late to see if someone changes their mind, it's harder to reverse the changes that puberty brings.'

'Yes. There are obviously some risks in giving hormones like that to children, so it's natural the authorities are cautious. Angelica was more or less a man by the time she knew, and many of the changes she'd been through were permanent.'

'Was it an abrupt decision for her then?'

'No, she sometimes felt like she should have been born a woman, but it wasn't consistent. Puberty, or any kind of awakening or understanding, is not a light switch moment. By the time Angelica knew she was a female through and through, her outer being didn't reflect this.'

'I guess many people weren't kind.'

'No, they were not, but that kind of thing is improving. People like Angelica are putting themselves out there, even though it can be so tough. Because of that, society's idea of what is and isn't attractive or feminine is changing. As far as I was concerned, her power was her beauty.'

'What's the answer then?'

'To the hormone thing? It's obvious to me that each case has to be taken on its own merit. Of course, more research needs doing. It's true that some children change their mind, others don't know what they are. Sometimes they flip flop between the two. But I knew early, and I've never wavered. Apparently, my dad called me Alfie for a bit from Alfredo, but I hated it. One day I said call me Robbie, and that was it.'

'It's lucky that Angelica was so strong.'

'I'm not sure about that. She wanted to be a woman. She didn't want to spend her time fighting people for being horrible to her. The thing is, imagine if you weren't tough like she was. The bullying and name-calling can be relentless, and there'd be nothing you could do. It grinds people down.'

'You're strong, Robbie. It must have taken real guts to walk onto that building site the first day.'

I nod, but I had Trevor.

'Did you watch the boxing recently?' I ask.

'Yes.'

'It's like that. The boxers are big and strong, and they take blow after blow, time and time again, but each attack takes its toll. Every strike weakens them further. Soon, each hit is agony and eventually, they fall to the floor, beaten. Some never get up. Four out of five trans people have had suicidal thoughts. It's one in eight for CIS people.'

'CIS?'

'It's short for cisgender. It means a person is the same gender as their sex assigned at birth. Did you know that when it comes to those who take their own lives, a quarter take less than five minutes to decide to go ahead? In jail, you have a lot of five minutes for that to happen when you're all alone.'

He squeezes my hand. I'm turning into Angelica with my statistics.

'It must have been hard in jail,' says Scott. 'Were the women mean to you both?'

'Oh, Scott. They sent us to a male prison.'

CHAPTER 57
Fifteen months ago

Angelica and I were still stunned as they moved us into another interview room in the prison. We knew it was likely we would have to stay behind bars until the trial, but it was a terrible shock to actually arrive at HMP Peterborough and get searched. Now we've been put in another room with a big plastic window. The woman in the suit dismisses the male officer, but he only waits outside the window and stares in. She gestures for us to take a seat, and she takes one too.

'Hi, my name is Ms Parkin. I'm the deputy of the prison. We were made aware that you were coming here, so I thought it pertinent that I talk to you about where you'll be located while you're here.'

'Do we get to choose?' I ask.

'Not as such. We get to agree, if you like. There are a variety of places where you can be housed, but all of them have positives and negatives attached to them.'

'We'd like to be on the female side of the prison,' says Angelica.

Parkin nods.

'That is possible. Prison rules state that for us to house transgender people in a prison that corresponds to their gender identity, rather than their assigned-at-birth sex, then I need to see a Gender Recognition Certificate. Do either of you have one?'

Angelica and I shake our heads. Angelica slaps her hand on the table.

'That's out of order,' she says. 'We haven't had time

212

to apply for one. It's a bullshit rule when you can't get appointments with anyone to get the process started. I had to buy my hormones off the internet to start with.'

'We understand that there are issues for trans people in accessing medical help, so there are other ways. Do you have evidence of pursuing a permanent actual life in the gender with which you identify?'

'What the hell does that mean?' asks Angelica.

'I can see you're dressed as women and present as women, but do you have documentation going back at least two years to prove that you have been living as women?'

'Like what?'

'Is your passport in the name of Angelica Hemming? Or your driving licence, or benefits, maybe bank statements, credit cards, or even a rental agreement would help.'

I sense Angelica tensing next to me. I've seen her driving licence, and it's in the name of Alex Nathan Hemming. I don't think she has a passport.

Angelica rises from her seat. Her voice increases in power and depth.

'I've been living as Angelica for three years, but everything is in my dead name, or you can't get credit or claim benefits. It's all too complicated and costly.'

'Take your seat again, please, Angelica. I'm trying to help.' She slowly swivels her chair to me. Keen eyes and a slight tilt of her head show me who is in control.

'How about you, Robbie?'

Everything I have is in the name of Robbie Ayala. The passport that brought me over here is in the name of Robbie Ayala, but I had no ID on me the night we got arrested, not even a debit card. We both only take cash out as we're liable to get pissed and lose it, or get plastered and spend too much.

I can't leave Angelica though. It wouldn't be fair on her. She didn't mean for this to happen. That's not purely to help her either. I am terrified of going into either prison. Being with Angelica is the most important thing. I know she'll look after me. Together, we are both stronger. We'll be able to lean on each other.

'No, I don't have those things.'

'You can both apply for a certificate to validate your gender while you're here, but the panel will still need evidence.'

I reply quickly to stop Angelica blowing up.

'That doesn't seem fair. What do you do with people who are not 'out' yet, or haven't completely got to grips with their identity?'

'They are allocated to the prison which relates to their assigned sex at birth.'

My eyebrows hit the roof.

'But we're women,' I say. Are you seriously going to put us on a male wing?'

'As I said, there are options. I do have some understanding of the topic, and I've been head of diversity here for five years.'

I used to have a good radar, but I try to ignore it nowadays, because you shouldn't guess at people's sexuality. That's their thing. Even with pronouns, it's polite to ask. Maybe she was a lesbian who struggled with coming out. It's such a tough thing for so many people.

I had an uncle back home who we all thought was gay. He never got married, but often disappeared for weekends away on his own. We were close, and he was an important adult in my life because he was so affirming of my situation. It was him I went to after I checked things out on the internet when I was about eleven. I could relate to so many other people's stories, but it was confusing. He had a word with my parents for me because I was scared. I was so lucky that I didn't need to be.

I like to think he was going to meet a boyfriend for secret liaisons on his trips because the alternative is almost too sad to contemplate. Nobody should have no one.

For people like Angelica, though, it feels like they are

'coming out' every day. In this world, if you don't look like the gender to which you're presenting, then you are going to get judging looks as a minimum. That's why female to male trans endure heavy strapping to squash down their breasts and us male to female worry about our bulges. Often when we get dressed, our first thought is do we look like our gender. It's a privilege that CIS people don't even know they have.

'Let me sum it up,' snarls Angelica, 'Even though we haven't been found guilty of anything yet, you are going to deprive us of our freedom, and our identity.'

Parkin purses her lips.

'Angelica, I'm sure you're well aware how the world struggles with this kind of thing. The prison system is no different. Practically every woman on the female wings has been abused by a man at some point in their lives.'

Angelica shoots out of her seat again. She bellows her reply.

'Just by saying that, you are implying that if we are given the chance to be on a wing with people of our own identity, then we are going to attack them.'

The door bursts open, and the large male officer from before strides in.

'It's okay, Allan,' says Parkin. 'We're just thrashing things out.'

I turn to Angelica, grab her wrist and pull her back into her seat.

'Angelica. The rules suck, but they are the rules, so let's make the most of our options.'

Angelica stares down, her face curls into an unpleasant grimace.

'Why won't you fight for us?' she snarls at me, but she takes her seat again. Allan gets shooed outside by Parkin, but he leaves the door open.

"Thank you, Robbie,' says Parkin. 'I don't think trans people are predatory, but there have been incidents. Therefore, you'll be placed on the male side, but we will give you access to everything you need.'

'What about our drugs?' asks Angelica.

'Of course. We'll contact your GPs and get confirmation of your prescription. You'll be able to shower on your own once a day. You'll have access to razors, hair dryers and makeup. It's basic stuff, so if you want more or a better quality, you need to order it from the canteen via the kiosk system, which takes a week to arrive. I'll do an emergency paper order for you tomorrow.'

'How do we pay for that?' I ask.

'I'll put a twenty pounds credit on your accounts so that you can request some things straight away, but you'll either need to work or get money sent in after that. We don't do that for every prisoner, I can assure you.'

'Okay, thanks,' I say. 'So where can we live then?'

'One option is Male Separation and Care, but that involves being locked up on your own for most of the day. There's no association down there, but you won't come into contact with any other prisoners. It's safe. Option two is our healthcare department. There, you'll have your own cell, and you will be allowed out to associate on the landing. They also have a small social room. That wing only holds about fifteen prisoners depending on who's on the ward, so it has a higher staff to prisoner ratio and is generally a more secure environment.'

'Generally?' asks Angelica.

'By definition, it holds the inmates with the most serious health issues. That includes physical and mental concerns. There will be some troubled souls on there, who are liable to display extreme behaviour.'

'Jesus,' says Angelica. 'Both of those choices suck.'

'Yes, I agree. Historically we've housed others in your position on the VP wing.'

'VP or VIP?' I ask, but the tense mood doesn't lift.

'It's a wing for vulnerable prisoners, which would include you, hence the name. The population is mostly sex offenders. That includes those who've offended against children, both online and in person. It also includes those who've sexually attacked others of any gender. The old and infirm are on there, as well as those on various spectrums and people with special learning requirements. Anyone who can't cope with the testosterone driven physical environment in the rest of the male estate will also be housed on that wing.'

'Let me get this straight,' says Angelica, quietly and slowly. 'You want to put two pre-operative transgender women onto a wing which contains male rapists.'

'It's your choice, but you'll find that there are only one or two of those types of inmates, and nearly all of them committed their crimes whilst high on drink and drugs, which they don't have access to here. They are invariably repentant and quiet. There are also no gang affiliations on that wing, so it is quiet. Most people on there are average people who find children attractive. You should be safe.'

I decide to let the statement on access to drugs ride despite no prison in the world being completely drug free.

'Will we be on there together?' I ask.

'Yes, you can go in the same cell if you wish. I can't say there won't be comments and people won't try to bully you.'

'Nobody will be bullying us,' says Angelica in a tone which makes Parkin raise an eyebrow.

'It's possible that there could be the odd predator or chaser on there. The staff will probably make the occasional mistake with your pronouns, but it won't be deliberate. We have our most mature and sensible staff on that wing. They are well trained. If you have any problems, anything at all, any concerns, speak to them. If you aren't happy, ask to see me. I'll be on the wing every day for the first week of your stay.'

Angelica and I glance at each other.

'It'll do for the moment,' says Angelica.

'Okay, Officer Allan will escort you there now. Are you ready?'

I silently pray to God for strength as we stand up.

Angelica reaches over and holds my hand. She waits for me to reply. A nod is all I can manage.

How could anyone be ready for something like this?

CHAPTER 58

Present day

Scott asks me a few more questions, then I ask him about his upbringing. Ours are vastly different, but he didn't have it easy either due to his dyslexia. We leave just before the hotel bar closes. As he drives home, we make companionable chit-chat, as though neither wants silence. It's been an unusual night. The earlier unpleasantness hasn't had its usual shocking effect, but that's probably because I saw the guilt on the blond guy's face and because Chanelle came out after us.

It's midnight when we get back. Surprisingly, Trevor's still up if the lounge light is anything to go by. I'm tired, so I get out of the car. I crouch down to say goodbye.

'I won't ask you in for a coffee because Trevor will have a field day.'

'Wait a minute.'

Scott gets out as well and comes around to my side.

'I haven't properly apologised for acting the way I did when you first told me. I'm really sorry. It was just a bit of a surprise.'

'Which means?'

'I want to be with you.'

'It's not a deal breaker?'

'No.'

'Okay, Boyband, you may take me to the cinema in the week.'

'Hey, I thought you agreed to call me Scott.'

I laugh at him, then lean closer.

'I only said I'd call you Scott at the party.'

He grins, then quickly kisses me on the lips. I don't have a chance to move. He holds it for two seconds, rushes back to his car, gets in, waves, then accelerates off into the night.

I stand on the driveway like a statue, feeling as if at any moment I'm going to blast off into the sky.

CHAPTER 59

When I got inside last night, Trevor had gone upstairs, which was lovely of him, and a little unexpected. He's not as uncivilised as he likes to make out. This morning, he's serving us a fry-up swimming in grease for breakfast. I can't believe I eat this kind of thing nowadays. I was virtually a vegetarian before, but I'm so hungry all the time, I can't get enough of it.

'Pizza tonight?' asks Trevor.

'Can we have a vegetarian one?'

'No.'

'Okay. Actually, how about we go bowling? Stevie was telling me his wife and him go all the time. I've only been once before, and I didn't really concentrate on it.'

'I thought you were going to tell me about Angelica's second promise.'

'I don't think there's a no talking rule at the alley, so we should be okay.'

'I preferred it when you were less cheeky.'

His eyes crinkle as he says it.

'I'm busy this morning. There are a few things to do at the site.'

'Do you want a hand?'

'Nah, it's not much. You have the day off. Clean up your mess in the kitchen.'

Trevor's out all day. I clean and tidy again. Obviously, most of the mess was his. It's funny how I naturally want to have the place clean and fresh. But it's also funny how clean he kept it before I got here, but now he does bugger all. Men! I should charge him for living here.

I put rock music on my phone and dance around. My mum messages me, and we have text tennis, pulling each other's legs.

Scott took my number in the hotel bar, so I get one from him. We have some banter. He's one of those who always finishes the text with a question, so it's hard to escape the conversation.

I book a lane at the alley online for seven p.m., but by six, Trevor's not back. He doesn't answer his phone. At six-thirty, he strides in.

'Sorry, darlin'. I had the chance to get a bit of concrete cheap for plot three, so I've ordered it.'

'I didn't think they were quite finished.'

'No, but it was close, so I dug the last bit out this morning.'

'You could have called. We're going to be late now.'

'Chill. It only takes twenty minutes to wash my hair.'

I throw a tea towel at him, and he rushes upstairs. He's back in ten minutes, looking surprisingly smart. Nice black trousers, Ralph Lauren polo shirt.

'I did say bowling, didn't I? Not golf.'

'Enough of your sauce. Do you know what? I haven't bowled for yonks.'

I'm about to say we should have a bet, but I look at Trevor's orangutan arms and think better of it.

Trevor drives us to Hollywood Bowl in Bretton, and we're only a few minutes late. I like the atmosphere. It's all chintzy and American. It smells nice. Trevor says it's a combination of varnish for the lanes and sweaty socks. I paid online, so we're soon at the lane. I find a ball I'm comfortable with, which is half the weight of Trevor's.

After a few bowls, I love it. There's a party atmosphere. We order some beer and hot dogs and get in the swing. There's a family of four on one side of us, who are all as bad as me. The lane on the other side of us has two dishy black guys in it. One of them winks at me, but they're a bit wary of Trevor, who has an industrial style to his bowling action.

'Go on then, darlin'. Let's hear it. What was the second promise that Angelica bullied you into making?'

'She didn't make me, but I agreed. I wasn't entirely sure what she meant by both promises, but the first one seemed reasonable.' I stride down the lane and get a spare, then stand next to Trevor. 'I'm not sure I can follow through with the second one. Even if I wanted to, I wouldn't know how.'

'Spit it out,' he says, picking his ball up and striding to the line.

'The second favour was to take a life.'

Trevor was just bowling as I said the words. He slams his ball straight into the gutter. I'll have to try that more often. He turns around with a frown.

'She said what?'

'She wanted me to take a life.'

'And whose life was that?'

'Fabian Landsman's.'

CHAPTER 60

Three months ago

Angelica returns from the med hatch after receiving her morning medication. I'm next in the queue at the gate. As per usual, I can hear abuse coming my way from Z wing next to us. The other prisoners like to lean through the bars and proposition us both. Strong officers quickly move them back down the wing, but sometimes the baying goes on for as long as they can see us queuing. At least, today's is fairly good-natured. Sometimes it isn't.

'Robbie, can you come to my cell when you're done?' asks Angelica as she reaches the wing gates. She turns and gives the dickheads the finger. They cheer.

'Of course.'

I watch her shoulders sag as she walks away. When the officer lets me off the wing, a small prisoner with a ridiculous quiff at Z's gate pulls his trousers down.

'Howay, pet. Get your gums 'roond this,' he bellows.

'I can't see it,' I shout back, to raucous whoops from the others next to him.

Ah well, if you can't beat them.

Inside the med hatch, out of their sight, McNulty is getting his meds. He's a vile creature, really. Others on my landing told me of the repulsive crimes he's committed against children, but he's been exceedingly kind to me. It's hard to get your head around a character with such different sides. What kind of man is so incredibly pleasant, but so utterly perverted?

I return to the wing and climb the stairs. Angelica has her door open, but she gets up from her seat when I enter and closes it behind me.

'Do you remember when I said I wanted you to save a life?' she says.

'Yes.'

'I also want you to take one.'

'Come on, Angelica. That's crazy talk.'

'Listen to this, and then tell me I'm mad.'

I perch on the small side table that's attached to the wall.

'Go on then.'

'You know I was hanging around with Fabian Landsman.'

'You said he was your boyfriend once.'

Angelica hangs her head.

'God, I was so stupid. He's one of those men some trans refer to as a chaser.'

'I remember Parkin using that term, but I didn't know what it was then either. I forgot all about it in the horror of walking towards this wing that night.'

'There are a few different descriptions of what a chaser is, but in most cases, it's a heterosexual man who's extremely sexually interested in trans women. They really get off on the fact we look like women but haven't had bottom surgery.'

'Right. Is that so bad? Don't we want them to be interested in our bodies?'

'No, that's the thing. That's all they're interested in. They aren't bothered about us as individuals at all, just that we are trans. Landsman even called me his ladyboy a couple of times.'

'No way.'

'Yes. Anyway, he always booked us into top hotels. At the beginning, I got some nice presents. He was reasonably decent to me.'

'But not decent enough to tell you he was married.'

Angelica gives me a dirty look.

'Apart from the fact he only wanted sex. He never asked me about my life, what my hopes and dreams were. Nothing. He didn't care what I wanted to do. What I enjoyed during sex was not even on his radar. It was all about my penis.'

'Did he hurt you?'

'Not at first. He was a little rough, but nothing I'm not used to. You know I was struggling financially when we had our shifts cut, then lost our jobs at Gordonsburger.'

I nod, with a rising feeling of dread.

'He began giving me money to help. At the start he wanted nothing in return. I had too much free time with no work, and he kept calling round. He always had cocaine which he was generous with, but he rarely took any himself. Before I knew it, I was taking it all day long. One day, I ran out of it. I had to ask him for some more. That was the day he began to change. The day he really changed was after we met him that night at the Marsden Hotel. He started to ignore my phone calls, and I got desperate.'

'I bet he knew you'd get addicted, so he could control you. It's like he groomed you.'

Angelica turns her head to look out the window as she talks.

'I think he liked me at the start but got bored. He told me about his wife, then, because he obviously didn't give a shit anymore. He invited me to his house when his wife was away and said I could have some coke if I had sex with him and Eduardo. So I did. Then he brought another young lad into it. I don't know who he was, and I don't know what they gave me, but it wasn't just cocaine. I hardly even know what they did to me. It was a blur, but I think it went on for a long time. They weren't gentle. The next morning, I vaguely recalled Landsman recording us on a handheld camera.'

'Oh my God, that's awful.'

'I was so ill for the next few days, and I was covered in bruises. When I felt stronger, I went around his house. I was so mad, I was going to kill him, but he had a big muscley guy with him. Then his wife showed up and he panicked. Landsman offered me ten grams of coke to leave and forget everything.'

'You didn't take it?'

Angelica finally stares at me. Her eyes are bloodshot.

'Yeah, I did. Oh, Robbie. I was so disgusted with myself. Rock bottom is heaven compared to where I hit. I went home and hammered into it. Cocaine's a stupid thing to take if you want oblivion. I felt like I had lost my mind. We were supposed to go out to that fancy dress party at the club, but I didn't want you seeing me like that.'

'Angelica, we're friends. You should have just told me you were struggling.'

Finally, the tears arrive. Her shoulders shudder. I sit next to her on the bed and pull her into my arms.

'I'm not surprised that man rang the police,' she sobs. 'They weren't threats, I was going to strangle him to death. I was going to do to him what I should have done to Landsman.'

'Shh, it's okay.'

'No, it's not okay. Look what I've done to you. It's all my fault. I fucking belong here, with all these filthy perverts and killers because I am one. But I dragged you down with me.'

'Don't think like that. It was an accident, and you were exploited. Most of this is Fabian Landsman's fault, not yours.'

Angelica pulls herself from my grip and stands against the prison window. An orange sun rises behind her. She stares down at me. A God instructing a mortal.

'That's the truth of what happened. He must be stopped.'

'How the hell am I supposed to do that?'

'You'll find a way. There's always a way. There has to be.'

My mind races, looking for a solution I don't possess.

'Shall I tell your dad?'

'I'd rather you didn't. You're clever, Robbie. Expose Landsman somehow. I want his life to be over, one way or another. He's nearly sixty years old. I bet he's been doing this for decades. Will you do it?'

I look away.

'Robbie, please. I wasn't the first, and I won't be the last. Finish him. Please, swear you'll do it.'

I stare at the floor. She's my best friend, and she's right. It

has to end. I look up and hold her fierce gaze.
'Yes, Angelica. I promise.'

CHAPTER 61

While I'm talking, Trevor glares down the lane with a ball in his hands, completely still. He finally looks over his shoulder at me.

'Why the hell did you say that?'

'That I'd do it?'

'Yes.'

'What could I do? She was begging me.'

'You're going to murder him, are you? Take care of business.'

I shake my head. 'I know. It seems stupid now, but when I thought about it, she didn't actually say to kill him.'

'Sounds pretty clear to me.'

'Angelica asked me to take a life. That could mean taking the life he's living right now away from him. We could expose him somehow.'

'We?'

'Yes, she said not to tell you, but I can't do anything alone. He's a rich, white man in his home country. I'm just a little foreign girl.'

'I'd just leave it if I were you.'

Trevor turns away and bowls his ball down the lane. He's so tense, it bounces halfway down and only knocks a corner one over. I can't believe that he said to leave it.

'Don't you want him to suffer? It's not fair that he ruins people's lives, never mind that he's breaking the law.'

Trevor glares at me while he waits for his ball to return.

'Haven't you heard the phrase?'

'What phrase?'

'If you look for revenge, you dig two graves.'

I glare back at him.

'I don't get it.'

He pokes me in the chest. 'One of them is for you.'

Trevor's ball returns with a jarring thud into the hopper, which makes me jump. He picks it out and stands ready to bowl.

'Leave well alone. Your life is beginning. You said yourself that you're only just discovering who you are and what you want. Don't throw it away. Do you want to spend the rest of your life in the slammer?'

'No, of course not.'

'Then forget any thoughts of revenge. It's not going to bring Angelica back. She's gone.'

Trevor returns his gaze back to the lane and bowls the ball. The people in the surrounding lanes stop what they're doing and look over.

Trevor seems to have forgotten that the idea of the game is to knock the pins over, not shatter them.

CHAPTER 62

I sleep on Trevor's words, and he's probably right. Angelica wouldn't have wanted me to ruin my life. I went around the Thistles' house for lunch on Sunday and briefly discussed the issue with them. Not killing Landsman, of course, just exposing him. They strongly agreed with Trevor.

It was fabulous to return to their house. They were so pleased to see me. I think they thought I'd move on with my life and forget about them, like their son did. I might be a mouse, but I'm loyal like an elephant.

Work is fabulous for the next month. Scott and I try not to make our flirting obvious, but judging by the good-natured jokes from everyone, we fail miserably. We sneak the odd kiss in various parts of the half-finished buildings when we think nobody's looking. We've been taking it easy. I think we both needed that. Lots of kissing and nice dinners out. I love getting dressed up, but it's been obvious for at least a week the next stage is now.

He still lives with his parents, but they're going away, so Saturday night is *the* night. My mouth goes dry when I think about it. Trevor bellows over at me to be more careful when I nearly get hit by the digger.

Triple C has arrived at the site with his father to get started on the woodwork. His dad is smiley and enthusiastic, but he looks a little frail. They're both so funny. His dad is hilarious. Whenever I bump into him around the site, he pulls a stern-faced Kung Fu pose. Apparently, he did it all the time to Johnny when he was growing up. It cracks me up every time. I wonder what the politically correct lot would have to say about that.

I don't call Johnny his nickname of Triple C. Johnny suits him too much. I shout it out when I bump into him around the site, in the same way Baby does to Patrick Swayze in the scene near the bungalows in Dirty Dancing. It cracks him up. I've even got his dad doing it to him. I wonder if I can get Trevor saying it.

Trevor's been quiet. I think the word is pensive. He works hard, as always. I never knew how many different skills are needed to build a house, but Trevor does a bit of everything. It's amazing to see the first house now with the toilet and kitchen having gone in. He's currently handing huge sheets of plywood up to Thin Jim, who's leaning out of a first-floor window to grab them like they're sheets of paper.

My probation worker said she's coming to the site today. She arrives in a new Mondeo. She's a nice lady, about fifty. She reminds me of Barbara Streisand, but less groomed and with a smaller nose. I groan as she swings her high heels out of the car. She has a maroon business suit on with quite a short skirt, which I've never seen her wear before. She waves with a big grin. Then I laugh as she reaches across to the passenger seat and puts on a pair of trainers.

'Hi, Robbie,' she smiles.

'Come to check up on me, Mrs Richards?'

'Of course. Actually, it's a chance to sneak out of the office on a sunny Friday afternoon.'

She stares around the site with wide eyes, glancing up at the busy scaffolds.

'I didn't expect it to be so large a site when you said it was four houses,' she says.

One of the Albanians whistles. She blushes, but pushes her sunglasses back to see where the sound came from.

'You're doing really well, Robbie. I have no concerns, so you only need to come into the office once a month now. We can keep in touch by phone.'

'That's great.'

'No, you've earned it. I wish all my clients were as law abiding.'

Trevor wanders over at that point.

'Who's the cupcake?' he says.

I'm about to apologise for the dinosaur who seems to have wandered in from the Jurassic era, when she blushes again.

'I'm Mrs Richards, but if you show me around, you can call me Stephanie.'

Can you get lightning with no clouds in the sky? I watch them walk away. Trevor takes her arm and links it through his. I can just about hear him.

'It's dangerous here, darlin', but don't worry. I'll look after ya.'

I can't help smiling. Who knows what her story is? There are so many sad people in the world. Maybe she's a divorcee who paints a picture of happiness on her face at work all week, then returns to her cat in an otherwise empty house and spends the weekend alone.

Nah, she's probably a dominatrix, and Trev's about to get the shock of his life.

CHAPTER 63

I'm unusually self-assured as Trevor drops me off at Scott's house, but that confidence drains from my legs the moment he drives away. I take a moment, then ring the doorbell. Scott opens the door in black jeans and a checked short-sleeved Tommy Hilfiger shirt. He gives me a brief kiss and we walk in.

His parents' house must be one of the biggest on the Hampton Hargate housing estate, which is saying something. He reckons he isn't posh, but he went to the King's School in town, and his parents both drive Jaguar hybrids. Sounds pretty fucking posh to me. I realise I swear more now than I ever did before. Trevor's turned me into a potty mouth. I need to try harder in curtailing that because my mum will whack me if one slips out when I'm with her.

'Beer or wine,' he asks.

'Both, please.'

He grins at me and hands me a Budweiser from the fridge. We chink bottles. He puts Netflix on, and we watch a show that I absorb nothing of. After three beers, we both turn to say something, then begin kissing again. It's frantic stuff. I have a loose red and white gingham dress on which reaches to just above my knees. Scott's hand is much higher than that.

His other hand traces a line down my face.

'Robbie. I'm not sure what to do.'

'Make love to me, idiot.'

'That's what I mean. What does it entail?'

I push his hand away and sit up.

'What is love at its simplest?'

'Shagging?'

'Oh, that's funny. I thought Trevor had gone home. No, you muppet. I don't mean what men think sex is, which is five minutes of missionary and a kiss on the forehead afterwards. I mean, what is the point of making love?'

'To give each other pleasure.'

'Hurray! Give the dog a boner. Correct, let's go upstairs and explore each other's bodies. Make each other feel nice. I don't think it's any more complex than that.'

He takes my hand, pulls me off the sofa, and leads me towards the stairs. He stops outside the first door and slowly pushes it open.

'This is my room,' he says.

I take a deep breath and follow him in.

CHAPTER 64

I wake to the distant sound of a barking dog. It takes me a moment to realise where I am and what happened last night. I can sense some pressure behind me in the bed, which I assume is Scott, but my head is banging. He nipped downstairs after we had sex the first time and got a bottle of wine. He did it again after we made love for a second time. I can't remember much after that.

I try to moisten my dry teeth with my sandpaper tongue. Last night's events wash over me, making me feel hot all over. It was the first time I'd done some of the things we did. What the hell was I worried about? It was amazing.

I roll over to give him a cuddle, but the weight against my back is a pillow. His side of the bed is empty.

CHAPTER 65

I stretch out and pull the duvet over me. It was a surprisingly cold night, not that I felt it until now. Hopefully, he'll be up shortly with a cup of tea, and maybe some toast.

After twenty minutes, I get an uneasy feeling and check the time on my phone. It's only eight, so where can he be? Unless he's nipped to the florist!

I slip out of bed and pull my dress back on. My bra is on the back of a chair, but my pants are nowhere to be seen. I nip into his en suite and eat a bit of toothpaste in the hope of disguising my rancid wine breath in case he wants to kiss me. I don't think we're at the toothbrush sharing stage yet.

I find myself edging down the stairs as though there's a burglar in the house. I look through some empty rooms and finally find him with a mug in his hand sitting in the conservatory.

'Hey,' I say, giving him a smile for when he turns around, but he doesn't move. I have to stand next to him.

'Oh, hi,' he says, looking up at me with an odd expression on his face. 'Sorry, I thought I'd let you sleep in.'

'Thanks, but I'm so used to getting up early now, that eight a.m. feels like a lie in.'

He nods instead of laughs. The seconds tick by.

'What's the plan today?' I ask. 'There's a good film started this week. We might be able to get tickets to the morning show if we get a move on.'

'Sorry, I've got a few things to do.'

I'm confused by his cool front, when he was anything but last night.

'Oh, right. I thought you wanted to spend the day together.'

'Sorry, I forgot I had something to do.'

'Okay.'

All of a sudden, I feel unwelcome.

'I'll get going then.'

'Sure.'

I hover next to him for a moment, then return upstairs and fetch my handbag. I find my knickers entangled with his boxer shorts at the bottom of the bed. The crumpled sheets smell of sex.

I go downstairs and put my pumps on. He still hasn't come in from the conservatory. As my footsteps echo through the hall and kitchen, it feels like a different house to the one I was in last night.

'I'm going to get going, Scott. Call me later.'

He finally gets up and follows me to the door. I open it, and I'm about to just step outside, when I turn.

'Is everything okay? You seem a bit off.'

'Yeah, fine. Just hungover.'

'Come on, it's more than that.'

I cross my arms.

'To be honest,' he says, after another unpleasant pause. 'I feel a bit weird.'

'Weird, how?'

'You know, what we did last night.'

'Why weird? Do you mean you feel guilty? It's fine. More than fine.'

'No, I just, you know, can't get my head around the fact I slept with a man last night.'

I have no words. I manage to close my mouth. I think of my self-respect.

'Right, well, there you go,' I manage to calmly say. 'I'll see you at work next week, then.'

I stride down the gravel drive, slipping slightly on the loose stones in my haste to get away. Half of me is imploring

Scott to shout out my name, the other half wants to go back and knee him in the groin. I feel tears building as I try to walk casually out of view, but it's tough. This really is the walk of shame. For the first time, I really understand why Angelica felt the way she did.

I get around the corner, sink to my haunches, put my hands over my eyes, and ugly cry.

CHAPTER 66

I decide to walk home in the hope of clearing my head, but I'm soon regretting it because of my weakened state. My mouth is budgie cage dry, or should that be canary?

I think of Angelica and how her hopes and dreams went up in smoke. She reckoned she was making a statement by taking her life in prison. She hoped that it would be front page news, but I asked the guys on the site. If it was, none of them noticed, and Stevie and Chris always have a newspaper on their van's dash. Maybe it just didn't register, as our plight often doesn't.

Losing Angelica like that is such a tragedy, and she's not the first. Vicky Thompson, Joanne Latham, Tara Hudson, Jenny Swift and Jade Eatough all took their own lives in prison. Why will nobody in charge connect the dots?

It makes you wonder if anyone's watching, but they must be. One day, the chorus will be deafening. It makes me remember events in the prison. I pull my phone out of my handbag and do a search. I find an article:

Samuel James Mainwaring was found dead in prison yesterday. Mainwaring told the judge at sentencing that he was taking hormones bought over the internet before the trial and wanted to be called Samantha, but he had no other proof of transition. Prison authorities stated they had supported him, but he was inconsistent in his claims. They confirmed that HRT hadn't been issued to the inmate who refused to attend doctor's appointments.

A family friend informed this paper that Samantha felt unsafe out of her cell due to intense bullying and was desperate to be moved to a female prison. He said she was devastated at no longer being on HRT drugs and told him shortly before her death that she was starting to turn back into a man. Mainwaring, of no fixed abode, was serving a year for aggravated burglary. He said he committed the offence because he was hungry.

The date was two weeks after Samantha was removed from our wing after attempting to hang herself. The article has so much wrong. The system took her liberty, her dignity, and, even in death, stole her identity.

I now fully understand Angelica's wish for me to be a canary because others must pick up the baton that women like her have laid down.

Every trans person and their allies, if they are able, should try to break down barriers. Although, for some, the world they live in is simply too hostile. Like when I first went to jail, they must keep to the skirting board in their worlds.

It's up to people like me to put ourselves out there and be seen, and be proud to do so. Together we can make it safer, so others can live as they wish.

Perhaps if Scott had any understanding of trans issues beforehand, all this wouldn't have been such a shock. He would have known that misgendering me like that was incredibly hurtful. It strikes at my very core.

I'm a gasping and sweaty mess by the time I get home. I open the door and look in the hall mirror. My make-up is a disaster zone, and my hair looks like I had amazing sex last night and didn't brush it this morning, which I suppose is the truth. It's my eyes that are the real shock. They stare back like a wild animal does when it's found cowering next to the body of their mother who has been killed by poachers.

There's a gentle hum coming from the lounge. I wander in there to find Trevor snoozing in an armchair with a newspaper folded on his lap. It's reassuring seeing him. I'm lucky to have such a solid presence in my life when the rest of it appears to be balancing on shite. His glasses are low on his nose, and he looks smaller in the big chair. Time eventually catches up with everyone. Even The Whirlwind.

I take a quick shower to wash the smell of Scott's aftershave off me and contemplate bed. My stomach rumbles, so I go downstairs and find Trevor cooking again in the kitchen.

'I'm just doing some eggs. Fancy some?'

'Sure.'

I slide into a seat at the kitchen table and try not to look hungover. Trevor joins me a few minutes later after sliding a couple of plates of scrambled egg on toast onto the table. He must have used twelve eggs. He starts shovelling his in, and, for a brief moment, I envy him his simple black and white life. Then I remember what he's lost.

'How was the date last night?' he asks.

'Fantastic. It was this morning that sucked.'

'How so?'

'Buyer's regret.'

Trevor puts his fork down.

'Everything all right?'

'Not particularly, but it will be.'

I think of Angelica and taking that cocaine. If I had some now, I'd have my nose buried in it.

'You sure?'

I nod, even though I'm not sure. I feel unstable again, like I don't fit in here. Life can be so volatile. Yesterday, I was on top of the world, now I'm under it.

'Trevor, why don't we get out of here? Let's go and work abroad. Forget all these bad memories.'

Trevor takes another bite, then chews slowly. He swallows it as though it's a struggle.

'The memories of my family and our lives together are in this house and garden, and in these streets and roads. They're all that I have left. I can't leave, darlin'.'

Trevor continues eating, but he takes his time, while keeping an eye on me. I push the plate away only half-finished. I can't remember the last time I didn't finish a meal since I first

started working for him. He taps my plate with his knife.
'Don't you dare do anything stupid.'
'Don't worry.'
But he should worry. I've no idea what I'm going to do.

CHAPTER 67

The following week at work is different. Scott turns up, and it's as though we were never an item before. The site is subdued. It's like in the prison when the atmosphere shifts. People are wary of change.

I'm paranoid when I see him talking to others. I keep thinking he's discussing our night with everyone else, which is daft, when he's obviously ashamed of what he did. Samson is acting weirder than normal. He's looking at me more often, but he's not so obvious with it. Although he is quick to glance away, he's not fast enough. It's a different kind of look to the one I used to catch Scott giving me.

Stevie and Chris find me mid-afternoon while I'm tidying the site. Stevie has a present for me. I pull off the wrapping paper. It's a lovely tool belt.

'What's this for?'

'We were discussing you last weekend,' says Chris.

'Oh, great.'

'No, in a good way. This has been one of the best jobs we've ever been on. There's been very little trouble, amazingly nothing's got pinched, and we've had a great laugh. You've changed the atmosphere on here so much it's not really felt like work. Even Trevor singing the wrong words badly to Smooth FM has been tolerable.'

I give them both a hug and put the present around my hips.

'And this is from me, says Stevie. 'Your first one for the belt.'

He hands me a heavy hammer-shaped package, which

once unwrapped drops nicely into one of the loops on the belt.

A thick black cloud arrives over the site around three and starts to lash the workers with torrential rain. Trevor's nipped off somewhere, so I can't get home. Scott offers, but I can be doing without that. Samson says he'll give me a lift, so I accept. Scott looks a little put out, which makes me want to smile at him, but I manage to restrain myself.

Samson's car, a rusting black Vauxhall Astra hatchback, is disgusting. He swipes all manner of rubbish off the passenger seat onto the floor so I can sit down. I crush the drink cartons and food boxes in the footwell with my boots. The back seat is full of clothes, shoes, coats and boxes, and the boot, which is missing the parcel shelf, has a duvet in it. After we've set off, I can't help asking.

'Samson, do you live in this car?'

'Have done, few times.'

'How come?'

'I was homeless.'

'Yeah, I get that, but why were you homeless?'

'I grew up in foster care, which was okay, but you kind of have to leave when you're eighteen. My last foster parents were cool, but we weren't that close. They didn't have me long because I had a few issues when I was younger. The council put you in bedsits afterwards on your own, which is quite a shock.'

'They just leave you?'

'No, there's support, but most teenagers aren't ready to live on their own, or with strangers in a shared house. I ended up arguing with the other tenants because I wasn't sure how to behave. Arguments got out of hand. Instead of apologising for playing my music too loud, and turning it down, I'd tell people to mind their own fucking business and turn it up. I ended up moving around a lot. The first time I became homeless was when I lost my job and couldn't make the rent, so they evicted me. It was summer, so that was fine.'

'It's not really fine, is it?'

He shrugs.

'No, but it's cheap and at least you don't freeze to death.'

'Go on.'

'The second time I was working on a site. It was something to do with Landsman, but he reckoned he wasn't the one paying us. We did the work, then the guy who was supposed to settle up did a runner with all our wages. I was screwed and it was December.'

'Bastard. Did you have to sleep in your car at Christmas?'

'No, my landlord threw me out in the New year. Building sites don't do much in mid-winter, so I was back in my car. It's the cold that gets you, then the damp. I got ill.'

'Why didn't you go to the council?'

'I don't know. They open up the churches if it's below zero, but I felt embarrassed.'

'Are you homeless now?'

'No, I've got a nice little bedsit. It's perfect.'

'How did you get back on your feet?'

Samson smiles. 'How do you think?'

I pause, but only for a second.

'Trevor?'

'Yeah. He wasn't on that job, but he was looking for a couple of brickies for some work in April when the weather was better. He tried to get hold of me and Scott, but Scott was abroad. My phone had been cut off, and there was someone else living in my flat, so Trevor went to see Landsman. Apparently, they had a right barney. Almost came to blows. Trev called him a rich prick and said he should pay the wages, but Landsman refused. They squared up, but Trevor left in the end. Landsman has a rep as a fighter, and Jacko and Eduardo were there. Smart call. That Jacko is nuts.'

'How did Trevor find you then?'

'He knew I'd been homeless before. He knows the places in the city where we sleep. Years ago, him and Jim rescued a fifteen-year-old from under the town bridge. Trevor found me down by the river. It used to be free parking next to the Nene Valley Railway. There were a few of us living there. Trevor knows everyone and every piece of gossip, so I woke up one morning and he was staring through my car's back window.'

'Wow. Did Trevor pay you for the job?'

Samson laughs.

'No, he's a mate, not a charity. He just let me stay at his house for free until I got sorted. I tell you, man. That first night, inside, safe, in a warm bed, it was amazing.'

He reminds me of how it felt that first night out of jail at the Thistles'.

'I hear you.'

'Yeah, I was there for three months. His son was going through some changes, so Trevor was a bit quiet. His wife was struggling with it all too. I moved out because of the weird atmosphere. Don't get me wrong, he probably saved my life, and I'll never be able to pay him back, but it felt a bit like living in a foster home again.'

I'm not sure what to say to all that, so I move the conversation along.

'I might have known Landsman would be involved again.'

'Too right. I was surprised when Trevor took this job, but he insisted on us all getting paid up front, so there was no risk.'

We're halfway to Trevor's house when I make an instant decision.

'Can you drop me somewhere else? It's only five minutes away.'

'Sure. Where is it?'

'I'll direct you.'

I send him back onto the parkway, and we're soon outside a huge house on Thorpe Road.

'Pull over here, please.'

Samson slows down, but then he twigs.

'Why do you want to stop at this place?'

'I need to sort something out.'

'Are you sure that's a good idea on your own?'

'Yes, no problem.'

'I'll wait here for you.'

'No, it's okay. Thanks for the lift, but I'll get a cab back.'

I get out of the car and slam the door. I crouch down and wave to Samson. He leans over the passenger seat so he can see my face. His is full of concern.

I feel his eyes on my back as I walk up Landsman's long drive.

CHAPTER 68

When I arrive at the porch, which is about as big as our house was back in Ecuador, I stop. It's a beautiful property with gabled windows. I remember Angelica telling me about it when she first started seeing him. There are three cars parked outside a triple garage. One has a Ferrari badge on the front, the others are a big Range Rover and a Ford Ranger truck.

Turning around, I notice that the slight slope of the drive stops me seeing to the road. Thick fir trees at the perimeter of the garden make me think of the high sides to a football ground, or the Colosseum.

I find myself tiptoeing to the door. I'm just about to knock when I hear raised voices. They're coming from somewhere deep within the house. It's hard to tell if it's an argument or something else. I notice there's a doorbell, so I press it. Chimes sound from inside. I'm expecting a butler, so it's quite a surprise when Jacko opens the door in another tight T-shirt. Red for a change.

Aggression rolls off him in waves.

'What are you doing here?'

'I'm here to see Landsman.'

He steps outside the house, biceps bunching as he closes the door behind him.

'Do you have an appointment?'

'No. I want to talk to him.'

He scowls at me. I haven't been up this close to Jacko before. He exudes strength.

'You'll bugger off, little boy, if you know what's good for you.'

'Screw you. I'm here for the manager, not the player.'

'I said go,' he growls. 'It's not safe for you here.' His hot breath buffets me.

He puts a big hand on my shoulder and spins me around as if I'm weightless. I feel the hand move to the small of my back. I put out my arms, knowing I'm going to fly off the porch, but the door opens behind us.

'Is that you, Robbie?'

I turn and push Jacko's meaty arm away.

'Yes, I'd like a word.'

'Of course. It's good to see you. Bring her in, Jacko.'

I follow Landsman into a huge hall. He keeps walking, so I follow. Any confidence I have quickly evaporates as we move further into the house. He pushes open some double doors and continues into a dingy room. The lights are on, but it's gloomy. There's a full-size snooker table nestled in the dark in the right corner. Landsman, who is dressed more casually than I've seen him, jeans and a loose white shirt, walks behind a bar.

'What would you like?' he asks with a cold grin.

'Nothing for me. I'm here about Angelica.'

'Okay, bear with me.' He takes a glass from under the counter and puts it under an optic in the neck of an ornate bottle of a brown liquid from the row of many behind him. He gives it a small push, then places the drink on the bar in front of him.

'Take a seat.'

'No, thanks. I won't be staying.'

'Fair enough. I hope that hammer's not for me.'

He gestures at my new belt and the hanging tool. I forgot I had it on.

'No, but you deserve it.'

He looks over at Jacko who must have followed us. Jacko stands to my left with his hands linked behind his head. Landsman laughs a slow laugh. It echoes around the room. Jacko doesn't respond.

'Why's that?' asks Landsman.

'She told me what you did to her.'

'Oh, and what am I supposed to have done to her?'

'Angelica said you exploited her, made her take drugs, and filmed her. Then blackmailed her afterwards to make her do it again by saying if she mentioned it to anyone, the video would be released onto the internet where it would stay forever.'

'Did she now?'

'Yes, you're disgusting. Why would you do something like that?'

My voice tails off as I realise how pathetic I sound. While he takes his time to respond, it sinks in how vulnerable I am. Landsman is used to doing anything he likes. He lifts his drink and takes the tiniest of sips, reminding me of that time in the hotel when I first met him. He puts the glass down, then casually wanders around to my side of the bar.

He puts his hand ever so gently under my chin and lifts my head so I'm staring up into his hard eyes. I feel like knocking his hand away like I did Jacko's, but I dare not.

'Did Angelica really need anyone to force her to take drugs? Hmm?'

I don't say anything.

'Did Angelica not like to party? My recollection is that we had to calm her down. She loved it. A little too much in the end, so we had to part ways. I'm sure you understand that. You seem more together, though, which is nice to see. Do you like to party, Robbie?'

'No. I don't believe you. I trust her.'

His hand is still under my chin.

'Trusted. She's gone now.'

I slowly raise my hand and push his to the side away from my face, then I take a step back.

'And that's mostly your fault.'

Landsman looks over at Jacko, then cruelly smiles down at me.

'Did she tell you about stealing my cocaine? Took about

ten grams from me. Very naughty. I think the only person she has to blame for killing that policeman is herself. Or did you have a hand in it?'

I notice a shift in his demeanour as he steps forwards again. His voice is commanding.

'Maybe we should have a party now? What do you reckon, Jacko?'

This time he doesn't take his eyes from my face. I feel under a snake's mesmerising gaze, not able to move. The sound of slamming doors ruins his moment. Trevor bursts into the room.

'Get the fuck away from her,' he snarls.

Landsman shifts his gaze onto Trevor. He returns back behind the bar and leans on it with his hands out of sight.

'Trevor. It's customary to knock when you come unannounced. You seem to be making a habit of this.'

'That's okay. I was in a rush, and we aren't staying.'

'I think Robbie wants to stay.'

'Come on, Robbie. Let's get going.'

'I don't think so. Jacko, educate Trevor.'

Jacko looks over at Landsman for a few seconds, then nods. He's cautious as he walks towards Trevor. He stretches his neck. Trevor turns to greet him, rocking slightly on his heels. It feels like oxygen is in short supply.

They circle each other. I'm expecting them to box, but Jacko lunges forward at the same time as Trevor and they grapple. At first, it seems they are equally matched. They twist together. I notice the strain on Trevor's face. He stumbles. Jacko yanks an arm out of the embrace. His punch into Trevor's stomach has the power and speed of a piston. Trevor takes the first two blows, but the third makes him bare his teeth. He shoves Jacko away, then backhands him across the face, sending him spinning.

Jacko puts a hand to his mouth. It comes away bloody. He smiles. The men circle each other. Again, Jacko lunges, but this tussle is short lived. Trevor is thrown out of sight over some chairs. Jacko walks behind the chairs and puts the boot in. Again, and again. The spell is broken.

'No!' I scream.

I run around the chairs and find Trevor curled up in a ball. Jacko steps away, smiling. Trevor's teeth are gritted, his face contorted.

'Both of you, get out of my house, now,' says Landsman slowly and without emotion.

I manage to help Trevor to his feet. He's bent over on the side that Jacko punched him. Trevor shuffles and lurches towards the door looking as though something inside him is broken. When we reach the door, I turn to Landsman and shake my head. It's all I have left. I help Trevor down the corridor, although I'm too small to be of much use.

'Make sure they get the message not to come back,' says Landsman to Jacko loudly. I hear slow footsteps heading in our direction.

'Come on, Trevor. Please, be faster. We need to get out of here,' I urge him in a whisper.

We've stumbled to the open front door by the time Jacko catches up with us. Jacko grabs Trevor and roughly moves him through the doorway. Outside on the porch step is Samson, with his car behind him.

'Get him in the car,' snaps Jacko.

I expect Jacko to hurl Trevor off the property, but he helps him down the steps, and, with Samson's help, pushes him into the front passenger seat. Jacko closes the car door, then looks at me. For a moment, I detect a hint of humanity, but it vanishes. He roars in my face.

'Now, fuck off!'

CHAPTER 69

After I leap in the back, I expect Samson to burn rubber down the drive, but he's cooler than that, knowing Trevor's ribs wouldn't enjoy a fast ride. He drives slowly in low gears. No one makes a noise apart from the odd grunt from Trevor when we corner. We're soon back at Trevor's, where Samson helps him into the house while I open the doors in front of them.

'Run me a bath, please, Robbie,' mumbles Trevor.

I run up the stairs, worried sick that he should go to the hospital but knowing he'd be angry if I mention it. I hear the murmur of talking downstairs, so perhaps he's not too bad. I lob in one of my soothing bath bombs that I treated myself to when I first started labouring. Trevor has used one before, but afterwards reckoned he got grit up his arse.

When the bath is three-quarters full, I turn off the tap. Trevor is already gingerly climbing the stairs and staggers into the bathroom. I fetch two big towels while he strips. I can see his tan lines as he steps into the bath. The side of his body that I can see is red and blotchy. I place the towels on the floor and go downstairs.

Samson has found Trevor's brandy. He hands me a glass, but I wave it away.

'No, I'm fine. I just feel useless. Thank you for fetching Trevor.'

'That's okay. When in doubt, eh?'

'Yes, but it didn't turn out so well this time.'

'I don't know. Trevor's plan was to get you away from that house in one piece, so you could say he was successful. He'll live to fight another day.'

I let out a small laugh as I realise something. Samson has been watching me ever since he started.

'Trevor told you to look out for me when he wasn't there, didn't he?'

Samson blushes a little.

'Bloody Trevor.'

'He's a good man, Robbie.'

I nod. I suppose he is, which makes me more furious about what just happened to him.

'I'm so sick of the bad people winning. Why is it always like that?'

Samson takes a sip of his drink and runs his hand through his hair.

'I suppose it's just the way it is. But what can you do?'

I take the glass of brandy off him and knock the rest of it back. The harsh liquid burns on the way down.

I welcome it.

CHAPTER 70

Trevor returned to work on Monday with a slight limp which was gone by lunchtime. I offered to strap his ribs, but he declined. You really have to marvel at the man.

The first house is completely ready. It's weird to think of a family living there soon. I can't stop smiling when I look over the impressive features. It's a wonderful feeling that I can come back here in the future and know I played a little part in it all.

By Thursday, it's time to do the foundations for the last house. Trevor lets me use the digger. It's still fairly tough doing it with a juddering machine. Hard to believe Trevor dug the grounds for that extension by hand. As with most of the building jobs, I settle into a natural rhythm and time passes quickly. I phase out the noise and make a decision. I'm going to quit when these houses are finished.

It seems to be the right time to move on. I feel I've been true to Angelica's requests. I've tried with both Trevor and Landsman, with varying degrees of success. The building game is not what I expected, but I've really enjoyed it. The people in particular have been a pleasant surprise. I turn the engine off and look around the site.

The Albanians are working and laughing as usual. I hear Trevor shout something at them. They all wave back, pretending they can't understand him. Trevor throws his hands in the air, but he's smiling too. The travellers and the roofers are hard at it. Johnny Chan and his dad are outside the second house with their bandsaw going.

I feel a warm connection to these people. They're from

all walks of life. Folk doing manual work to put food on their families' tables. They're often exhausted as they leave the site at the end of the day. Accidents happen, arguments rage, but they do their best. They do what they can.

Trevor and I are having a cup of tea when a car with a strangely big aerial arrives. I stand up.

'Sit down, Robbie.'

Two men in suits leave the car and talk to Johnny. He points in our direction and the men walk over.

'Are you in charge?'

'Kind of,' replies Trevor. 'I'm keeping the job on track, but I'm not involved in any more detail than that.'

'I'm DS Brittain. Can you tell me who the site manager is?'

'That would be Jacko and Eduardo.'

'Are they about?'

Trevor pauses for a moment, and I wonder if he's going to answer.

'I haven't seen Eduardo this week, but Jacko was here yesterday with the wage slips.'

That was true. Jacko handed them out to Trevor without a word. I asked him if that wasn't a bit weird, but Trevor says that's how it goes with men like Jacko. You have a barney, then it's over. It was the same in prison.

'It's Eduardo we're looking for. Nobody can find him.'

Trevor shrugs. 'I'm not sure what they're up to. Looks like they're both on easy money to me, but it ain't my position to question that. Fancy a cuppa? You're welcome to wait.'

The two detectives share a glance. The one who's done all the speaking hands Trevor a business card.

'Will you ring us if you see him?'

'Sure,' says Trevor, taking the card.

When they've driven away, Trevor rips the card up and throws it on the floor.

'What do you think all that was about?' I ask.

'God knows. Could be anything if it's to do with Eduardo.

Never talk to the Old Bill, Robbie. Nothing good comes from it for people like us.'

CHAPTER 71

On Friday, Trevor lets us knock off work a bit early. We leave our cars at the site and go down the pub to celebrate finishing the second house. We meet in The Yard of Ale, a fifteen-minute walk down Oundle Road. We're an interesting crew, walking past the commuters.

The pub is full of men in overalls and work boots. There's a bunch of painters judging by their paint speckled hands and faces. I spot four postal workers in the far corner. Everyone knows Trevor.

After three hours, we're all steaming. A big arm drops down on my shoulder while I'm waiting to be served to get what I hope is the last round in.

'How you doing, darlin'?' says Trevor.

'Good. How are you?'

'Drunk. I could do with a lie in tomorrow, so no hooverin'.'

'Deal. Trevor, I haven't really had chance to properly thank you for coming to get me.'

'I told you I'd look after you. He's a strong lad, that Jacko.'

'Yes, maybe you should hang up your gloves.'

He gives me a smile. 'Men like me go out on our shields.'

'You almost did.'

'I'm not afraid to die, Robbie. I've lived, and I've loved, and I've lost. Fate hasn't been kind, and I've made mistakes, but at least I've tried. It'll be time for me to clock off soon.'

I look into his eyes to see what he means.

'Don't talk like that.'

'I rang that Stephanie.'

'Nice, you old hound.'

'She gave me her number after I gave her the tour.'

'Are you going to take her out?'

'Maybe. If it'll get you off my back.'

'No chance. Look, there's something I need to tell you. When we're finished on this job, I'm going to do something else. Maybe return to the restaurant game. Perhaps something else. I might move to London.'

'That's brilliant news.'

'Trevor! You're supposed to be devastated.'

'Why? You don't belong on a building site. You belong on a billboard. Get out in the world and spread the word. Find something that you love.'

'I think I'd like to have my own restaurant one day. Maybe go back home and run one with my mum. She's a great cook.'

'You could do a fast-food place. Call it Trans Express.'

'Very catchy. You'll have to come and visit, although God only knows what my mum would think of you.'

'Women love me. I'm a gentleman.'

I can't help laughing, because it's true.

Trevor and the Albanians soon stagger out of the pub, singing, on their way to the kebab shop next door. Apparently, Stevie and Chris sneaked out an hour ago. Johnny Chan wanders over. We had a chat earlier. His dad came for one drink, which Johnny says is a good sign of him being almost back to normal.

Johnny has full make-up on today which got a few funny looks when we arrived, but everyone soon got used to it when they realised it wasn't a big deal. He leans against the pillar next to me and smiles.

'I'm off, Robbie. Are you at the site next week?'

'Yep. Trevor and I have about a month left. Then I'm going to go back to waitressing, or maybe I'll see if I can get a job in a restaurant kitchen for experience. There seems to be plenty of that kind of work about at the moment.'

'Tired of getting your hands dirty?'

"No, it's been fun, but I imagine it might not be so fantastic in the winter. What about you?'

'You inspired me with your enthusiasm about my clothes designing, so I'm going back to college. There's a course in Brighton that I want to do. Fashion and Textiles. Then I'm going to pitch my ideas to some companies and see what happens. I've been working on my portfolio at night. I can't wait.'

'Good for you. I'll miss our talks.'

As I say it, I realise I really will. Johnny gives me a big smile.

'I'm not going for a month, so we'll be finishing about the same time. I'll install the woodwork for the third house, then my dad said he'll do the last one on his own. Trevor said if I let him know, he'll find someone to help if my dad needs a hand with carrying and lifting.'

I raise my almost empty drink, then I stop. The memory hits me like a sledgehammer. Johnny Chan was on the same wing as me.

'Oh my God! You're a jailbird, too!'

He grins.

'Yes, I was. Cool, aren't we? But I was only there for two days, so I'm not sure it really counts. I was wondering if you'd twig. I remembered you.'

'Why didn't you say?'

'I kind of hoped I was unforgettable, but it was a toned-down version of me. I didn't mention it again because I thought you might think it weird with me not mentioning it the first time.'

'No way, you were just hoping to maintain your clean image! How come you remembered me if you were only there for a few days?'

His smile drops to be replaced by something else. Something serious.

'Trevor's not the only legend that I work with.'

I frown.

'What do you mean?'

'Our community knows all about you and Angelica. Especially her. You both had to put up with so much. We often talked about you after you were sentenced. Stories got told. Especially Angelica's. She didn't die in vain. It's not right that you had to go on that wing. I think the adults in charge are finally beginning to realise how unacceptable that is. Hopefully, she will be the last one to die.'

I remember that the wing we were on was mostly for sex offenders. It's hard to believe Johnny is one.

'Why were you inside, if you don't mind asking?'

'I was living with my boyfriend, who was a bit of a nightmare. His work wasn't very supportive of gay people, and he drank a lot. We used to argue, but one day we had fisticuffs.'

'You *did*?'

'Yes, hard to believe, isn't it?'

'It is.'

'He cut his arm on a broken wine glass. When the police turned up, he said I stabbed him with it deliberately.'

'Ooh, that's not good.'

'They viewed it as domestic abuse. We lived together, and I couldn't prove to the court that I had anywhere else to live. So, for his safety, as he was the victim, they charged me with ABH, of all things, and remanded me in custody.'

'Why couldn't you live with your dad?'

'He was in hospital being treated for his cancer. My mum's English is poor, so I didn't want her to get involved.'

'Wow, tough luck! What happened?'

'When I got to prison, another friend rang my solicitor and said I could stay with him in Huntingdon, so my solicitor went back to court, and they bailed me. My ex sobered up and was mortified at what he'd done. He told the police he was mistaken, but they weren't having it. I suppose they get a lot of ex partners pressured into dropping charges, but the case collapsed when he gave a full statement. He almost got charged with wasting police time.'

'Wait. I don't get it. Why were you with the VPs?'

He poses, Marilyn Monroe style.

'They didn't know what to do with me. I was in full make-up when I arrived. I washed it off the first night, but they still said that wing was the safest place for me to be.'

I shake my head. Poor guy, but it goes to show there needs to be many changes for those who don't tick neat boxes.

'Must have been a horrible shock for you.'

'It was, but I learned something important. From now on, I'll always be thankful for what I have.'

'Here's to a future out of jail,' I reply.

'To whatever it might bring,' he replies, then gestures to the side. 'You have an admirer still.'

I look to my left and spot Scott sitting on his own at a table. He smiles and gives me a little wave. I shrug.

'I'm not so sure about him,' I say, not as quietly as I intended, to Johnny.

'Really? I bet it's not easy putting a catch like that back.'

'No, but I'm not sure he quite gets me. Part of him will always see me as a man.'

Johnny smiles.

'Maybe, but there's nothing to stop you having some fun while you find out if that's the case.'

He bends over and softly kisses my cheek, leaving a clean citric fragrance behind. When he's left the pub, Scott leaves his table and wanders over. He looks about as steady as I feel. I put my elbows on the bar behind me, to look relaxed and for a bit of needed support, and I raise an eyebrow.

'Evening, Boyband.'

'Hi, Robbie.'

The little shit does his cheeky little smirk, and my heart melts.

'My parents aren't back until tomorrow.'

'That's rather presumptuous of you.'

'I can't stop thinking of you, about that night in

particular.'

    I take his hand and drag him towards the exit.

CHAPTER 72

I wake up in Scott's bed. I'm absolutely hanging, again! With a grunt, I roll over and smile. He's still next to me. I'm exhausted. We had more to drink, and we were still rolling around in bed at three a.m. I can remember everything but it's all kind of hazy. My shorts are next to the bed, so I slide my phone out of the back pocket. It takes a while to focus on the screen.

'What time is it?' croaks Scott.

'Ten-thirty.'

'No way!'

Scott leaps out of bed and nearly falls through the bedroom window.

'My parents are back at eleven!'

'Ahh, poor diddums. Nasty for them to find golden boy still in bed with an evil transexual.'

'Exactly, come on, up you get.'

'Are you ashamed of me?'

'No, I just can't be doing discussing it with them in my current state.'

'Am I not worth it?'

'No, it's not that. They're...'

'Horrible? Narrow minded?'

'They aren't modern thinkers.'

I chuckle.

'Nice phrase. That's okay. It's your job to educate them.'

'Robbie, please.'

I get out of bed, stark naked, and stride into his en suite. I turn the shower on. I'm under it before he realises what I'm doing. He runs over.

'Robbie!'

I try to pull him into the cubicle, but he's not having it. I'm a reasonable person, so I only take five minutes. I use his toothbrush, though. After what we did last night, his germs are mine and vice versa.

I pull yesterday's T-shirt on which is minging. My boots and socks are muddy. He gives me a small carton of juice and virtually throws me out of the front door and, again, I start the walk of shame. I'm halfway down the street and just about to ring for a taxi, when I realise I've forgotten my tool belt. As I'm returning, a massive Mercedes saloon cruises past. It bumps up onto Scott's driveway.

Scott opens the front door and notices me in the distance. His parents get out of the car. His dad starts pulling suitcases from the boot, while his mum rushes over and gives him a hug. Scott steps out of the way, so she can enter the house. After a final glance at me, he walks after her and closes the door.

His dad spots me then and gives me a quizzical look, as though it's not a sight he sees every day. He shrugs and probably assumes I'm lost. I agree with him. I don't belong here. He vanishes down the side passage.

I stand in the sunshine and shake my head. Then the door opens, and Scott appears again. He smiles and waves, then drops my tool belt outside, steps back, and slams the door shut.

CHAPTER 73

We have a few days of rough weather. The bricklayers, Scott included, go off site. There's no point in laying bricks in the driving rain. The roofers continue until even they're blown away. Only Johnny and his dad can continue at the same pace because they're inside finishing their job in the second house.

Jacko spends more time on the site, mostly arguing with Trevor. I occasionally see them deep in conversation, though, so maybe they're like a bickering couple.

By Friday lunchtime, we've all had enough. My hands are cold and chapped despite wearing gloves most of the time. Trevor spends ages in the bath each night trying to unlock his back and knees. It's a different job when it's not sunny.

Landsman's wife, Esther, arrives with the pay slips for next week. She seems really stressed. The weather puts the job back. If more rain arrives, they'll have lost an entire week. I know that the brickies have another job lined up as soon as this is finished, so any more than a week and they might not be able to finish the job.

Stan Thistle turns up at the site with a carrier bag. He's smartly dressed in a light brown suit. He makes the point of saying hello to Johnny and his dad. The bag contains a couple of packets of chocolate biscuits and a big flask full of hot coffee, but there aren't many people here to enjoy it.

'We got your text saying you're finishing soon,' he says to me.

'I know. You replied to it.'

'Will you be staying local? You've always got a room at ours.'

'That's lovely, and very reassuring, but I've saved loads of money doing this. It's funny how much you can save when you don't have any bills, so I'm going to have a few weeks off. Then I'm going to do some serious job hunting. My mum reckons I should go and live in London to see what all the fuss is about before I return to Ecuador.'

'Are you going to go home at some point permanently?'

'Probably. I might go back for a holiday first. The flights aren't too expensive at the moment. Probation said that's fine as long as I tell them when I leave and when I'll be back. To be honest, she said they wouldn't care if I left for good if I've only got a few months left, but I might stay after my licence finishes.'

'Come for dinner. We've got a card and letter for your mother.'

'Of course.'

'You look great, Robbie. Very healthy and confident. It's lovely to see. I've got some post for you in the car, too. Hang on.'

He ambles back to his car, taking his time as though it's a summers day instead of a squally grey one. Esther, who arrived a few minutes ago, and Trevor walk over to him, and I watch the three of them chatting. Trevor and Stan seem to be talking at her. They are serious but relatively relaxed. Esther on the other hand, isn't talking. She puts a hand to her mouth and shakes her head.

Esther returns to her car. She opens the driver's side door but shouts something back at Trevor before she climbs in. She spins the car in the mud in her haste to get away. I walk over to the guys.

'What was that about?'

'That asshole, Landsman,' says Trevor. 'He's getting twitchy about the job. He reckons he won't pay us if we don't catch up with what we've missed this week.'

'Won't everyone just leave?'

'That's what I just said. Usually you get paid in arrears, but he's messed people about, so he's screwed. We've been paid this week already, so he can't do anything about it. If we don't get paid Monday morning as usual, we all down tools. Then he has the nightmare of trying to find new teams, and he'll probably have to pay them up front anyway. He's over a barrel. I bet it's driving him chicken jalfrezi.'

Stan hands me another carrier bag.

'That's your post.'

He seems quiet all of a sudden. I get a little smile and a peck on the cheek.

'I'd better be off. See if you can come to ours on Saturday night, Robbie.'

I give him a quick hug, but he doesn't leave straight away. He and Trevor shake hands. There are no smiles.

'Good luck, Trevor. I hope it works out for you.'

'What was that about?' I ask after Stan has left.

'Just reminiscing. Did you know Stan's son, Ellis, worked on the sites?'

'Yeah, Stan said his boy laboured for a bit after university to get some pin money.'

'He worked for Landsman.'

My brain clamours as it tries to process the implications of that. I've seen the pictures of the Thistles' son. He's slim and average looking, but he looks gentle. What if Landsman got to him as well? Maybe that's the reason why he left Peterborough and never wanted to come back? Is his another life ruined by Landsman? And how does Stan know Esther? They were talking like they had some kind of shared history.

'Trevor, what was Esther so angry about? She must know her husband has a history of poor payment, and you lot won't risk not getting paid.'

'He would have spun her a tale about cashflow or some other bullshit. As I said, she's not daft. She's East End. There's a code. Anyway, she's probably getting it in the neck from him at home. There were a few other things that annoyed her. A couple of bits of drainage have gone missing as well, which normally wouldn't be the end of the world, but with all these supply chain issues, she can't get the parts for a couple of weeks.'

'Are they for the conservatory for the fourth house?'

'Yes, it's stopping us filling in the last bit of footing, so that could delay us. I told her not to worry. I'll sort it.'

I shrug. It seems a reasonable explanation, but she did seem incredibly upset for someone who was just missing a bit of plastic pipe.

CHAPTER 74

Saturday morning arrives to bright sunshine. I get up early feeling great. The slower pace all week has helped, and I've slept and eaten well. I'm going around the Thistles' tonight for what Edna calls Italian night. Lasagne and chips. Bless them. I'm going to walk into town and do some shopping this afternoon.

My crazy mother asked me to email her some possible holiday dates and to give her all the news. She's decided she prefers emails to telephone calls because she can re-read them. I spend an hour tapping away on the computer, then take a shower and get ready for a mammoth impulse buying expedition when the doorbell rings. Trev hollers up the stairs.

'Harry Styles is here.'

I trot downstairs.

'Where is he?'

'Outside.'

'Why didn't you ask him in?

'You can't be too careful with these rock 'n' rollers.'

Trevor gives me what he thinks is a prissy old person's look. Even in his pinny, which he has on again, he still looks menacing.

I open the door and step outside. It's a gorgeous day. There's the odd high, white cloud racing across the blue sky and a gentle breeze to take the edge off a strong sun. Scott is leaning against his car with his chin up, basking like some kind of lizard. I go and stand next to him.

'Didn't you hear me coming out, or are you striking a boyband pose?'

'The latter.'

'Thought so.'

I raise my face to the sun for a moment.

'Can we talk?' he says.

'About what?'

'Us.'

'I'm not sure there is any us?'

Scott scratches his head.

'Robbie, I'm getting there. My parents are old school, that's all.'

'Seems like you are as well.'

'Let's go out for a bit, just the two of us and not tell anyone. Then, when we're cool, I'll tell my parents.'

'That's very brave of you.'

'I'm trying, Robbie.'

Not hard enough, I think, but I don't say it. He waits for me to talk.

'Let's just be friends for the moment,' I reply. 'I just want to get next week done and finish the job, then I can plan my future. There's no point in us being together if I'm moving away.'

'I thought you were going to London, not New Zealand.'

I smile, but my head was getting around the thought of going to parades and clubs, and getting myself out there. I'm not sure bringing a trans-embarrassed bricklayer along is the look I'm after.

'Friends for the moment,' I say.

I push away from his car and offer him my hand, which he shakes. Then I reach up to his face and squeeze his cheeks together.

'It's lucky you're so good looking, because you're a bit of an arsehole. You can give me a lift into town, though. I was going to walk but my make-up will run in this heat.'

I nip inside to tell Trevor.

'Okay, darlin', no worries. I'm off to the site in a bit. I managed to lay my hands on that drainage material. Someone had moved it into the first house for some reason.'

'Perhaps they did it when we were trying to get everything out of the rain.'

'Maybe. You still going out for dinner tonight?'

'Yeah.'

'Okay, cool. I might be late. I've managed to get a bit of concrete for late this afternoon, so I'll stick the pipe in the ground, then fill in the last bit of footing and the base. The brickies will be able to get going on the conservatory first thing Monday, and we might get finished in time.'

'Do you want me to give you a hand?'

'Nah, it's only a bit of pipe work. No problem at all.'

Trevor doesn't quite seem his normal self. I can't quite put my finger on it. He was shifty last night as well. He was on the phone for a long time on different calls. When I went in the kitchen to make a coffee, he went out the back door and talked in the garden.

'Okay,' I say. 'I'll see you tomorrow if not later. We could maybe go bowling again, if we aren't banned.'

'Yeah, definitely.'

I step out of the house and get in Scott's car. He notices I'm quiet.

'Everything all right?' he asks.

I nod my head, but I'm not sure.

CHAPTER 75

I wander around Queensgate Shopping Centre for the first hour with enthusiasm. I have tight jeans and Roman sandals on with a skimpy tight crop top. Many a glance comes my way. I've practised my walk for many years, but I put some extra swish into it. I feel like I could stop trains.

I'm hungry by eleven. I want a McDonald's, but my jeans buttons won't thank me for it. If I stop manual labouring, I'll need to be careful what I eat, or I'll be the size of one of the houses we've been building. I also fancy a beer, which is weird. To think I barely drank beforehand. As Trevor says, it goes with the game.

I order just a hamburger meal with a diet coke as a compromise and sit upstairs with all my bags around me. The shopping over here is insane compared to back home. Shops like Primark and Peacock are so reasonable for nice things, but it does make you wonder how they're so cheap. It makes me think of Ecuadorians working for peanuts in banana plantations. I hope these clothes companies pay decent wages in their sweatshops.

Even though I've only had a small fries, I still feel a bit sleepy afterwards. Trevor keeps sneaking from the back of my mind to the front. I push my worries aside and carry on with my acquisitions. After finding some fabulous reduced-to-clear lipstick and eyeliner in Boots, I head to a specialist shoe shop that's recently opened. There's a pair of yellow high heel strap stiletto sandals that have been calling my name since they emailed me about them a month ago.

I walk in and spot them straight away. They are sirens.

The shop assistant is a young bored-looking Asian woman. I look at her name badge.

'Hi, Seema. Do you have the other one of these?'

Her eyes light up.

'Nice choice,' she says.

I sit down and slide my feet into them and stand up. They feel so good and look so great that I want to squeal. Seema lets out a little one for me.

'Wow, killer!'

I stride around the store feeling like a princess.

'I don't suppose by some miracle these are in the sale?' I ask Seema.

'No,' she says with a mischievous grin, 'Although, the sole on this right shoe has a little scuff on it. It's probably just from people trying them on in the shop, but I might be able to get the manager to give you a discount.'

Ten minutes later, I wave to See as she prefers to be called and leave the shop with my hundred-pound shoes. That's even with the twenty percent off that she got me. I'm tempted to go mad and buy a dress to go with them, but Trevor bursts into my mind again. I'll kick myself if something strange is happening.

I head towards the taxi rank but spot the bus arriving which goes down Oundle Road, so I race through the bus station with my bags clattering around me and just make it. I stick my shopping on the seat next to me and blow out a big breath. God, I love those shoes! A woman with a small baby on her lap opposite me smiles at my happiness.

The stop isn't too far from the site, which is unlocked, so I'm soon wandering up the long drive. It's quiet. The fourth house is the far corner plot. I expect to hear hammering or, at the very least, swearing, but there's nothing. A pigeon coos from one of the tall surrounding trees. Goosebumps rise on my arms. Has he done something stupid?

'Trevor!'

His van's parked up, but there's no response.

'Trevor!'

I hear a toilet flush, then the sound of a door opening and closing. The handle of the front door of house three moves. Then Trevor appears two seconds later. I wave at him with relief, but the expression on his face is one of horror.

CHAPTER 76

Trevor races towards me.

'What the hell are you doing here?'

'I was worried about you.'

'Why?'

'You were flighty this morning.'

'What the hell does that mean?'

'You weren't yourself.'

'I'm fine. Now get out of here.'

The familiar sound of a powerful car moving up the drive has us both looking to our left.

'Shit,' says Trevor. 'Robbie. Whatever happens now, do not get involved. This is for me and him to resolve.'

'What's going on?'

The car comes into view. It's Landsman's Range Rover. He stops at the end of the drive next to house one and the engine dies. For at least a minute, nothing happens. I can see there are two people in the car, but not who they are due to the visors being down and the sun glinting on the windscreen. The doors open on both sides at the same time. Landsman gets out the driver's side, Esther the passenger side.

Landsman is his usual cocky self, although he has shorts and a T-shirt on like he's come from the gym. He has wraparound sunglasses, but they're resting on his head.

Big shades cover half of Esther's face, but her head movements are jerky and unnatural, as though she doesn't know what to do with herself. She stands in front of the car. Landsman strides towards us, but stops halfway. He's only twenty-five metres from us, but there are piles of bricks and tiles and the cement mixer in the way.

'Trevor,' he says. 'What's she doing here? I said to come alone.'

'I did come alone. She's just popped in on the way home to get a lift with her shopping. I thought you were arriving solo.'

Landsman's eyes narrow. He glances around, seemingly with time to burn.

'Well, we both have a lady present, so that equals things up.'

'What do you want, Landsman? I'm busy. Are you going to pay us next week or not?'

Landsman looks down and seems to be listening for something, or someone. Then it comes to me. He's playing for time. Landsman is expecting someone else to turn up, and that person will tilt the scales in his favour.

'I'm going to pay the others, but not you.'

Trevor takes his baseball cap off.

'No problem. I'll call it a day then.'

Landsman curses under his breath as he checks the drive, but we still hear him.

'Expecting Jacko?'

Landsman's head shoots around to face Trevor.

'Yes, he said he might pop over. I thought it would be good to have the foreman here, too.'

'Right.'

'I'm sure he'll arrive soon.'

'He won't be making it I'm afraid. In fact, it's unlikely you'll see him again.'

Landsman's cheek twitches.

'What have you done with him?'

'If you believe in the afterlife, you might meet him in the bowels of the netherworld.'

'What's that supposed to mean?'

'The game's up, Fabian. It's over. You've abused your last person.'

'You can't threaten me. You've got no proof of anything.'

'I've seen everything I need to. There's a video of my girl, Angelica, and your pal, Eduardo. Deeply disturbing it is.'

'You can't pin that on me.'

'It was taken in your house.'

'You can't prove that.'

'I can now I've been in your gaff. Your bar is in the movie, even the snooker table has a starring role.'

'I'll sue you.'

'For what? You've already taken everything I ever truly valued. The only pleasure I've got left is to watch you suffer. I want to see the walls of your life fall in on you.'

Landsman pauses to think. I force myself to breathe properly.

'How can I make amends?' he asks.

'You can leave Peterborough for good.'

Landsman barks his cold dry laugh.

'All my businesses are here. My home is here.'

Trevor nods twice, but doesn't comment.

'That's enough of this bullshit.' Landsman turns his back on us, but we both clearly hear what he says.

'Esther. Fetch it now.'

CHAPTER 77

I catch my breath. Nothing feels real. I watch, seemingly in slow motion, as Esther's head turns towards her husband, then back at us, then at him again. Her oversized sunglasses give her a fly-like appearance. She glances back at their vehicle. The car doors are still open. She walks to the driver's side, sits in the seat and looks down. I take a step forward, but Trevor grabs my arm at the wrist.

'Get ready to run, Robbie,' he says.

Landsman's focus is purely on Trevor. His victorious smile is cruel. He is clearly a man who isn't happy purely with winning. Everyone else must also lose.

His vehicle's engine starting startles him. I can make out Esther leaning over and pulling the passenger door shut, then the driver door clunks into place. The big car creeps forward. I think for one happy minute she's going to mow her husband down, but the wheels cut into the gravelled surface and the car turns in a tight arc. Esther floors the engine and she's out of sight in seconds. The smell of burnt diesel makes my nostrils flare.

To his credit, Landsman doesn't panic. He strolls forward as relaxed as if he was walking towards an ice cream van. I moisten my lips. He's so confident, perhaps he has a weapon. Landsman takes his sunglasses from his head and rests them on the cement mixer. I'm so close I can read the words Ray-Ban on them.

'In a way, I like you, Trevor. But I've been hearing stories. They tell me that you've been poking your nose where it shouldn't be. They say you've been stirring up bad feelings.'

'You know what, Fabian? I used to know everything that happened in the building game in this city, but I decided that I'd had enough of other people's problems.'

'Yes, I remember you used to think of yourself as Peterborough's Godfather. That's me now, sunshine. You're yesterday's news. Nothing more than a piece of gritty nostalgia.'

'I heard stories about your antics years ago. But I thought, it's the 21st century. What people get up to with other people is their business.'

'Too right. You should look the other way.'

'I did, and that was my mistake. In our close-knit community, one person's problems can soon become your own. That's why we look out for each other. It becomes my business when some of those people don't consent.'

'They all consented.'

'You drugged them.'

'They took those drugs willingly.'

'Then you filmed them.'

'They didn't mind.'

'Then you blackmailed them.'

'Enough of this shite, Trevor. Let's have it out. Man to man. Then I'll have it out in a different way with your beautiful little ladyboy friend.'

Trevor steps around the bricks and the cement mixer and stands two metres away from Landsman. They gauge each other. Trevor's left arm is close to his ribs, protecting the area which Jacko pounded. His right fist is suspended at waist height, ready to come forward like a battering ram.

Landsman is light on his feet. There's a natural grace to his movement. Even his fists which are in front of his chest wave like flowers in the wind. Theirs is a deadly dance.

Trevor chuckles

'Jacko's not coming to save you, Fabian.'

'I don't need Jacko to beat you, Trevor. You looked like an

old man when he put you in your place. I bet those ribs are still sore.'

'Jacko's dead.'

'Good. He was getting above his position.'

'So is Eduardo.'

'That's not a surprise.'

'Do you know how I got this job?'

'Yeah, because McPherson left me in the lurch.'

'He didn't leave you. I ran him over. Accidentally, of course.'

'I don't remember hearing about that.'

'No, I didn't tell anyone. I put his body in my greenhouse afterwards.'

That's a surprise to Landsman. It shocks him into action. With animal speed, he moves forward, and a fist snaps out straight into Trevor's nose. Trevor's head jerks back, but the blow was solid. Another fist flies towards Trevor's face, but he manages to move so it's only a glancing blow on the side of his head.

Trevor pumps his own fist forward, but it's slow and telegraphed. Landsman, smiling, sidesteps it and flicks another hit at Trevor's mouth. Trevor manages to turn his head away, but he still takes the brunt of the shot on his cheek, which causes him to stagger. When he turns, that cheek is red.

Trevor spits out blood onto the floor between them. More blood is beginning to drip from his nose. They circle again. Trevor is now crouched so there is little difference in their height. He lunges forward a huge step which takes Landsman by surprise. Trevor's arms are freakishly long and his blow hits Landsman in the gut. Landsman sneers, but I heard the whoosh of air as the blow landed.

I've inched closer, but I have no idea what to do. Should I run? I almost trip over something silver on the floor. It's a thick metal spanner. Did Trevor put it there for a purpose? Landsman has his back to me now. I could brain him, and it would all be over. But I can't. I just don't have that level of violence within me. Perhaps if I was being attacked, but not like this.

Landsman moves swiftly forward and slightly sideways. He throws out a right, but it's fairly obvious, enabling Trevor to slip to his right and dodge the blow. I realise it was a deliberate feint by Landsman only as he pivots and sends a stinging left at incredible speed into Trevor's injured ribs.

Trevor grimaces and gasps, his tongue lolling. He looks tired now, maybe even already accepting his imminent defeat. Landsman flashes another fist at Trevor's face, but this time there's another movement in the air. Trevor's big hard calloused hand grabs Landsman's fist and seizes it tight. He pulls Landsman forward and headbutts him in the face. There's an audible crack, and Landsman hits the deck.

Again, Landsman is brave. He climbs to his feet, but his smile has gone. He hits out at Trevor's face, with the blow landing on his brow, but Trevor takes it, lunges forward, and grabs Landsman's throat with one hand. He steps to the side, and his other paw grabs the scruff of Landsman's neck from behind.

The dong sounds exactly like a single, solitary church bell as Trevor bangs Landsman's head onto the cement mixer. Trevor lets him fall from his hands. Landsman slumps to the floor. He scrabbles in the sand, noticing the spanner near him in the dust. My hand goes to where my tool belt would normally be.

He grabs the spanner and wearily climbs to his feet. I shuffle backwards with my arms raised. Trevor steps forward, snatches the spanner from Landsman's limp grip, and, in a wide swinging arc, cracks Landsman around the head with it. Landsman's eyes roll back, his arms drop down, and he topples forward like a felled tree. He smashes face first into the dirt and blood sprays out from between his lips.

CHAPTER 78

I move my hand over my mouth. I've never seen anything as savage, and that includes the many fights I saw in prison. Trevor sniffs, then spits more blood on the floor.

'Grab his legs. We've got to move him.'

'Are you okay?'

'I'm the Whirlwind, darlin'. No man can hurt me.'

'Jacko did.'

'That was staged.'

'What do you mean?'

'I'd already got to Jacko and told him what was going down. We agreed that if there was ever a fight between us at Landsman's house, I'd let him win.'

'You were in pain afterwards.'

'Yes, I had to straighten Jacko out afterwards about what pulling your punches means.'

'Why did you kill him, then?'

'I didn't. Jacko's returned to Lithuania. I told him Old Bill said Eduardo had been seen at the central bus station in Vilnius. Jacko's gone back to find him.'

'The police didn't say that.'

'I know. I knew that Jacko would return to look for Eduardo if I told him where his brother had been seen, so I made it up.'

'Then you didn't kill Eduardo either.'

'Eduardo was a piece of shit. He abused my child. I buried him in the foundations of plot three.'

CHAPTER 79

I glance over at the now built house and try to imagine Eduardo encased underneath it. Then I remember the other men that Trevor mentioned.

'Was that McPherson's trainer which I saw in your greenhouse that morning?

'No, I told you that was Marcus's, my previous labourer. The other one was in my van.'

'McPherson isn't still in the greenhouse?'

'No, he was, but now he's under the extension we built in Ramsey Forty Foot.'

I can feel my eyes bulging.

'What?'

'I buried him in the ground that Tuesday you took off.'

'Jesus, Trevor. You can't go around killing people.'

'They were worthless scum. McPherson was in the videos too. All of them had blood on their hands. They fucked with the wrong guy. I've taken care of business. It's what I do.'

'There are laws, Trevor.'

'In my world, there are rules. Those men knew what they were, and they still broke them.'

I watch Trevor put his hands under Landsman's shoulders and lift them up.

'Pick up the legs,' he says.

I only pause for a moment, then grab the ankles. We carry the body towards plot four. He isn't that heavy, although I suspect Trevor's taking most of the weight. When we reach the plot, Trevor guides us around the back. The trench has the missing shiny black plastic drainage pipes inside it. Next to it is a base, which has been dug out deeper than normal. There's an indent about six feet long and two feet wide.

'Drop the legs,' says Trevor.

I do, and Trevor drags Landsman into the indent. He fits neatly, like it was made to order, or more likely, dug to fit. I know who hid the piping now so all this couldn't be finished.

Trevor picks up a long shovel. There's a gasp next to us, then a groan. I stand over the body and see that Landsman's eyes have opened. His chest rises, but only a little. He grits his teeth and gasps through them.

'Ring for an ambulance,' he whispers. 'I'll say I fell.'

I hear a scraping sound. Trevor shoves the spade under the pile of sand to the left of the hole.

'You have fallen, Fabian,' says Trevor. 'But not far enough. You're going all the way. You were too cocky. I know Jacko's and Eduardo's stories. Their father was a monster who abused the whole family. It made Jacko violent and angry, but for Eduardo it was learned behaviour. He got off on controlling and abusing people. It was a power thing. He met you, and you were as twisted as he was.'

Trevor drops a shovelful of sand on Landsman's chest. Landsman feebly pushes some away with his right hand. His left side seems unresponsive.

'I got the video of my poor kid. Then I saw a couple of others as well. You even got my bloody labourer, Marcus, and his girlfriend involved, you sick bastard. I showed Jacko those videos. He wasn't happy. He wanted to kill his brother for repeating the abuse their father inflicted on them, but Eduardo was his blood, and he couldn't do it. I told Jacko you were going down, and he could choose which side to be on. He chose to live.'

Landsman tries to talk again, but it's an incomprehensive gurgle.

'I've been planning this a while, as you can see by your grave.'

Trevor shovels eight more piles on top of Landsman, so

only his head is completely visible. I watch, feeling strangely emotionless. Does he deserve to die for what he's done?

'The hard one to persuade was Esther,' continues Trevor. 'You had a real good one there. Loyal to the bitter end. She wouldn't believe me or Jacko. It was Stan Thistle who persuaded her. His son, Ellis Thistle, worked on a job at your house ages ago. You got his girlfriend hooked on drugs and both of them involved in your film making. You blackmailed those kids so they couldn't stop. Ellis fled to Cumbria to escape your perversions, but he had to leave his girlfriend. She took her own life shortly after.'

Landsman's mouth moves, but no sound comes out.

'That,' says Trevor, 'makes you a murderer in my book.'

We hear beeping behind us. A cement lorry is reversing up the drive with its mixer tank slowly revolving. Trevor loads up his shovel one last time.

'I was sand before, but now I'm concrete. And so will you be.'

He covers Landsman's face with the shovel load, then does two more for good measure.

'Are we running the concrete?' I ask

Trevor smiles and nods. I don't smile back.

'I'll get the barrow.'

CHAPTER 80

The lorry driver, who has thick, snow-white hair, greets Trevor warmly.

'How's it going, Trev?'

'Good, Chalky, mustn't grumble.'

It's chilling watching Trevor chat so easily after what he's done. He tells Chalky we're ready and walks back behind the house. The driver pulls down the shoot and climbs up the side of the lorry to operate the release mechanism.

I find the trainers that I keep onsite so I don't trudge mud through the finished houses and pull them on, then put the barrow under the chute and concrete pours down it. I fill the first barrow two-thirds full, then wheel it around the rear. It's much easier than a full load, but that isn't important this time. I put the barrow down in front of Trevor, then return to the front and fill the second barrow. By the time I get back to Trevor, Landsman is half covered. Ten loads later, he's out of sight. By the time we're finished, the footing has been filled in and so has the base. It's completely flat and smooth.

Trevor stands next to me and waves to Chalky as he drives away.

'Let's go for a pint. I should probably explain.'

CHAPTER 81

We walk down the drive and turn right towards the Gordon Arms. Trevor doesn't bother locking the gate. I suppose he doesn't care now.

My shoulders sag. What we've done is beginning to sink in. I shiver despite the heat and feel my McDonald's hamburger rising from its resting place. I stop and swallow, then have to jog to catch up with Trevor.

He strides to the bar when we reach the pub and orders two pints of Stella. I follow him to a table in the corner. We sip our drinks in silence. It looks like Angelica got her way, and she was granted her second promise. Today, we took a life.

I can believe the others Trevor buried not being missed, but not Landsman himself. I say as much to Trevor. He wipes froth from his moustache.

'That's why it was important to get Esther on board. I told her that he was going down. Silly loyal mare begged me not to. Said she'd have a word and put an end to it. She even wavered after I showed her the recordings. At the end of the day, he was still the father of their child. Then Stan told her about his son and dead ex-girlfriend. It was Stan who hinted that it was possible that Esther's husband had been up to no good with their own child. Maybe Landsman blackmailed their daughter into not saying anything and that screwed her up. That was enough for Esther.

I think of Ellis fleeing to Cumbria to escape the extortion. The poor Thistles couldn't work out why he'd detached himself from them and his hometown. The memories for Ellis must have been too raw. For the first time,

I'm not looking forward to seeing them later.

'What's Esther going to say when people come looking for Landsman?'

'He goes abroad and travels a lot. She's just going to say he never came home. The police won't have a clue. They won't suspect him of being under his own houses.'

'Can't the police scan for bodies?'

'Yeah, but only if they know where to look. They'd have to drill through the floor in the right spot to find them. I shouldn't think they'll care too much. He's had no end of close shaves over the years with stolen materials, beating up workers, and general complaints about shoddy workmanship. The police only seriously get involved when the family start banging on about someone being missing and only then if it's suspicious.'

'What if she folds and tells them he was killed?'

'She won't. She's East End. It wasn't uncommon for nonces and rapists to go missing down our streets. Besides, her focus is their young daughter. Her care must be really expensive.'

'What if he's hidden his money?'

'Nah, she does the accounts anyway, so I'm sure she'll find a way around it. The last thing Esther wants is Old Bill digging around where she has most of her eggs in the same basket. Those four houses will be rented out, the people under them will be forgotten.'

'How did you know that the meeting with Landsman today wasn't genuine?'

'Esther was on her guard after I told her Fabian was up to no good. She overheard him yesterday ordering Jacko to get rid of me today at the site. Fabian had already arranged the meet with me. Esther called me this morning to say I was going there under false pretences, but Jacko had told me anyway. That was why Fabian was surprised to see me there and still breathing.'

'And if someone decides to build another level over

where Landsman is buried?'

'Don't you remember? The reason the footings are dug so deep the first time around is to make it so you can put a second floor on later without digging again. If, somehow, it came out there were hidden bodies, I'll take the blame. I don't mind going down.'

I contemplate his answer.

'What about all this revenge and digging two graves?'

'It's true. Maybe someone will come looking for me, but I'm old now. Your life hasn't started yet, whereas mine is almost over.'

I finish my pint quickly. It gurgles in my stomach. Being sick quickly becomes a matter of when not if, so I go to the ladies which are thankfully clean and empty. I quietly empty the contents of my stomach into the sink.

What do I do now?

CHAPTER 82

Trevor drove me home without saying much more. My mind was running through the past few months. I recalled Trevor often going out on his own. Was he doing jobs, or preparing graves? He lied to me on many occasions, or had at least been economical with the truth.

Yet, I strongly believe he was doing it for the right reasons, or to protect me. It's what he does. He looks after people.

As I expected, the meal with the Thistles that night was a bit awkward. I didn't want to mention what had occurred earlier, and Stan didn't comment on seeing me at the site the day before. I suspected Edna might have been protected from all this, but she hugged me when I arrived like she never expected to see me again. I suspect Stan received a call from Trevor at some point saying it was over.

Edna and Stan were pleased when I told them I was leaving for London the following week. I found a house-share on Gumtree in South Ealing, which has two rooms available, rentable on a six-monthly basis, so I bagged one.

Stan came over the next day. When he kissed me goodbye, he passed me an envelope. He said it's probably for the best that I get out of Dodge for a while, if I knew what he meant. Not so naïve after all. There was a cheque inside for £700, which will almost pay the first month's rent. I'm guessing they looked on Google to see how much things like that were. In many ways, I've been so lucky.

It's my last day at work. We've caught up a bit of the time we lost last week. Only the bricklayers are struggling. Both teams work harder for Esther, who paid everyone on Monday including Trevor, but theirs is not a job you can rush. With no sign of her husband, Eduardo or Jacko, it's as if everyone knows they are working for her now.

We're all going out for a ruby tonight at the Bombay Brasserie, so there weren't any big goodbyes when everyone left for the day. Trevor drives me home as usual. We haven't broached the subject of last weekend since it happened. It's as though we're both processing it, but I can't leave without a few final questions. One is a horrible thought which came to me last night.

'Trev, what happened to your old labourer? Was it that guy you pointed out with the ginger ponytail, because something doesn't add up?'

'Marcus? We fell out. I told you.'

'Why did you fall out?'

'Do we have to talk about this?'

'Yes, did you kill him, too?'

'He wouldn't tell me what Landsman had made him do, so I had to get physical with him. I overdid it.'

'Is he up north like you said, or is he dead?'

'I'll show you where I put him.'

Trevor indicates left and races down Thorpe Road towards Netherton. Halfway along Audley Gate he pulls over next to a house which has a brand new two-storey extension attached to it. There's a team of Asians digging up the old drive with a stack of block paving on pallets. They wave when they recognise Trevor. A slim mixed-race youth appears through a side gate. He tenses his fists when he recognises Trevor's van. He gives Trevor a rude gesture.

'Wait here,' says Trevor.

Trevor gets out of the car, slides open the side door of the van, then slams it shut. He walks over to who I assume is Marcus. He starts to take small steps backward.

I watch Trevor hand over the trainers. One from his greenhouse, one from the back of the van. Marcus isn't dead after all, just transient. Trevor talks to the lad for a moment, then offers his hand. The youth reluctantly takes it. Trevor has a quick word with the other men, then returns to the van. He's whistling when he gets back in the driver's seat.

'Not murdered, then.'

'Nope. I knew he'd got tangled up with Landsman. I had to scare him to get the information out of him. He didn't like it. He was embarrassed more than anything.'

'How did you get him to talk?'

'I shook him. Physically.'

'I'm not surprised he didn't like it. You do know it was his choice whether to talk.'

'Yeah, whatever. Better out in the open. I knew I was going to be working for Landsman soon, so I got him this job here, so he was well out of it. I didn't tell you in case you let it slip at work. The Pakistanis looked after him. This crew are real solid. They're almost finished here, so Marcus might come back to my loving embrace for his next job, as long as I promise not to manhandle him.'

'You're a violent man, Trevor.'

'Aye. It's a violent world.'

'Don't you feel guilty about Jacko spending the rest of his life looking for a brother he'll never find?'

'No. Don't lose any sleep over that wanker. He's been doing Landsman's dirty work for years. He beat a plasterer up once, and the poor guy never worked again.'

'It's horrible to think there are people like Jacko in the world, but it still seems tough to think he'll never find his brother.'

'What do you think would have happened if I hadn't beaten Landsman in that fight? Jacko would have flipped sides like an acrobat. If I'd lost, it'd be me wearing a concrete overcoat, and Jacko would probably have been the one to put me in it.'

'I don't feel bad for Landsman.'

'Good. Men like him don't get nicer as they get older, they

sicken. If I'd lost, your fate would probably have been much worse than mine.'

I feel a bit down as we near Trevor's house. All this has soured the end of my time here. The decision to leave is the right one. Generally, I've made some great memories, so I don't want to forget all the positives. I'm a stronger person now, but like the Thistles' son, Ellis, I don't want to be constantly reminded of the bad stuff either.

I think of poor Angelica, pacing her cell, thinking she was a burden to everyone. It's a strange thing to be so lonely when you're surrounded by over a thousand other people.

Trevor slows as we near his house.

'Look, Robbie. I had all this planned for months, but I wanted to get away with it. That's why I had to bide my time. I wobbled. Killing someone is not something you do easy. I'd already seen the video of Angelica and Eduardo, and McPherson was the one who'd taken advantage of Marcus. I tell you, they were tough viewing. But when you told me exactly what Angelica said, then my mind was set.'

I don't want to think about any of that anymore, so I fold my arms and look out the window. When we park up, I realise I do have one final question.

'Do you reckon you could have beaten Jacko in a fair fight?'

Trevor laughs his slow, deep laugh.

'Of course, darlin'. He can't beat nature. I'm the whirlwind.'

CHAPTER 83

A month later

I've moved to London as planned, but I'm not enjoying it. There are so many people, that I feel like an insignificant ant. There are five others in my house share, but I rarely see any of them. I've done some shifts at a restaurant in the centre that serves South American food. They love that I know Spanish, and I love speaking it again, but it's not home.

I had a call from Trevor. I asked about Stephanie, and he said she was a good shag. I could tell he was lying. Trevor only ever loved one person in that way and Stephanie can't compete. It's a shame, for both of them, probably.

I hope this city grows on me, but the worrying thing is that I feel alone again. When I was on that site building those four houses, I was part of a family. I didn't realise how secure that made me. I feel exposed here.

I got an email from Johnny Chan saying I'd love Brighton. He's having a ball down there. The course he's doing is exactly what he wants, and he loves the LGBTQIA+ scene, which he admits is a bit of a mouthful. He reckons they should just call it Liquid, because humans don't fit into categories and their forms can change.

I'm re-reading Johnny's email lying on my bed when my phone rings. It's Scott.

'Robbie. Nice of you to pick up.'

'I was at work when you rang before.'

'All three times?'

'At least two of them.'

We chat and get on easily as usual, but I get a sense

there's something he wants to tell me.

'You remember the female plasterer with all the tattoos?'

'Yes.'

'Two drunken idiots walked past her van and took the piss out of her. They didn't realise that Trev was watching.'

'Oh, no. What did he do?'

'It was hilarious. He called them a pair of phobic cunts. He said if they didn't apologise, he was going to educate them with his fists.'

'I take it they apologised.'

'Profusely. Trevor said to tell you that he's *woke* now.'

I smile. He's only sent me the odd text. I think we probably needed some space. I'll give him a ring in a bit.

'I can come and visit you if you like?' says Scott.

'Yeah, that'd be good. We'll sort something out.'

I finish the call wondering whether it's wise to carry on with Scott, but I'm distracted by thoughts of Trevor. Looks like he's back to being a Godfather. I think of what he said when he had his confrontation with Landsman. That when he stopped bothering about other people's problems, they soon became his own. The world should take note of that.

Angelica knew that was how this world worked. She wanted me to step up and be seen. She told me to get involved.

Maybe Trevor, her father, in his own special way, is a canary.

CHAPTER 84

A month later

I decided to move to Brighton shortly after talking to Scott. Maybe London is something I can tackle in the future, but I just feel swamped here at the moment. A room came up in Johnny's house-share, so he's picking me up shortly to move my things down. I've lost a few quid on rent by moving out so quick, but I'm making the right decision. And I get to live by the sea!

I can't help smiling at Johnny when he turns up in his dark-blue estate car. Luckily there's a space out the front. He parks up, winds down the window, and sticks his head out.

'Not taking the mick out of my efficient and spacious vehicle now, eh?'

'Nope. Who'd have known that utility was so sexy.'

'You're looking hot,' he says, lifting his sunglasses.

I look down at my spray on jeans and yellow trainers. A few too many buttons have come undone on my baggy, white shirt, so my sports bra is on show.

'Dirty little removal piglets shouldn't be checking out their customers.'

Johnny sticks his tongue out.

I haven't got loads of things, but I've picked up a few framed pictures from various thrift shops since I've been here, which would make public transport a nightmare. The property owner arrives to check the room and take back the key. I explained my predicament to him, and he's been great in letting me leave my six-month contract early.

'See you in a couple of years, Robbie,' he smiles. 'London will be waiting.'

My phone rings as I get in the car. I answer it.

'Robbie,' says a serious voice, which I only just recognise as Scott's.

'Morning, Boyband. Don't you know when to quit?'

Scott doesn't sound his usual self. I can tell he's upset straight away.

'Hang on,' I say to him, and turn the radio down.

'Can you wait a min?' I ask Johnny.

He nods.

'Go on, Scott. What is it?'

'It's Trevor. He's dead.'

CHAPTER 85

It doesn't sink in at all. The sound of Trevor's laugh bursts into my head. If ever there was a person who was going to live forever, it was him. I almost don't want to hear the specifics, but if Trevor taught me anything it was to deal with things head on.

'What happened?'

'I haven't got the exact details. Stevie just rang me. He knew you'd want to hear as soon as possible, but he didn't have your number. Stevie said that he was up a roof while Trevor was preparing for the plasterers inside. Stevie dropped his hammer and almost hit Trevor on the head. Trevor obviously called him some choice names, but he said he'd come up the ladder to save Stevie's old legs.

I smile, knowing Stevie was seven years younger than Trevor.

'He climbed up and passed Stevie the hammer, then Trevor noticed Chris had returned from getting more lead. Trevor shouted down to Chris, asking him if he'd had a nice kip in the van while the real men were grafting. Chris looked up, and Trevor's expression changed. Chris reckoned that for a moment, Trevor smiled, then his eyes closed. He fell five metres to the floor.'

'A heart attack,' I say, thinking of another of my mother's sayings, which is that big hearts don't last.

'Yes, although it sounds like he landed on his head, which wouldn't have helped. The ambulance was there in minutes, but they were too late.'

'Okay, Scott. Look, I'm going to go. I'll ring you in a bit.'

I put my phone down on my lap and put my head in my hands. After a few seconds, I look out of the window and shake my head as people go about their lives. Johnny reaches over and puts his hand on my arm. I expect it to be coarse from his work, but it's soft and warm.'

'I'm sorry, Robbie.'

'I can't believe it.'

'What do you want to do?'

'What do you mean?'

'Do you want to head back to Peterborough and sort things out? There isn't going to be anyone else.'

'I never thought of that. Yes, drop me at the tube, and I'll get the train up.'

'I'll drive you.'

'It'll take two hours, then about three back to Brighton.'

'That's okay. We've got lots to talk about. I've got the day blanked out anyway. I sorted my grandfather's affairs when he passed, so I'll help.'

The M25 is moving freely, so we make good progress to the A1 and back to Peterborough. Johnny lets out a chuckle halfway there.

'So, Trevor's an angel now. That's hard to imagine.'

I can't help laughing. 'Not hard. Impossible.'

Johnny grins.

'I can imagine the scene when Trev arrives at heaven.'

I can't stop myself picking up the story.

'Yes, I can see him eyeballing St Peter as he opens the book of life. St Peter frowns when he reads about Trevor's antics.'

'Trev puts a reassuring arm around St Peter's shoulders.'

'Yeah, then Trevor casts an appraising eye over the Pearly Gates.'

Johnny looks over at me before he replies.

'Looks like you've had the cowboys in here, guvnor.'

We grin at each other, both knowing that St Peter would have liked him immediately, too.

We shout the words, which surely should be on Trevor's tombstone.

'No worries, Pete. I'll look after ya.'

CHAPTER 86

Two weeks later

I stand at the door of the Woodman pub and greet the mourners. The funeral was a good one, as much as these things can be. Thin Jim did a very funny speech, or whatever they're called at funerals. There wasn't enough room at the chapel, so some had to stand outside. Nearly all those who came have shown their faces at the pub, which is nice, although Trevor did leave money for a free bar in his will.

I wander around the tables, thanking everyone for coming. Stevie and Chris sit quietly with their wives. The lads stand and hug and kiss me. After a minute in the company of their partners, I feel like I've known them for decades. Stevie has tears in his eyes.

As I walk around, I hear stories galore, many of which start with, "Do you remember when Trevor…?"

I wave at the Thistles and their son, Ellis, who has come home for the first time in years. Stan waves back at me. Edna doesn't notice, she's still beaming at her boy.

Just before I arrived in Peterborough with Johnny on the day I heard, I received a call from Stan, who somehow already knew. He said to go around their house when I got back. When I called around, he told me Trevor had given him an envelope. It had turned into a cool but bright day, so I took the cup of coffee Edna had made me and sat outside on a bench in their front garden to read the contents of his letter. It was one of those days where it feels like the sky could fall on you.

There was a copy of his last will and testament, which was dated a few months ago. He'd left everything to me.

Trevor had a big pension which he'd stopped paying into the month after Angelica died. His house was also mortgage free. Combined, they made me a wealthy woman.

There's something called probate to sort out, but his affairs were simple. I sorted all his bills out and let everyone know who needed to. When I checked his bank statements, he had five direct debits to various charities for ten pounds a month each. One of which he'd only just started to the LGBT Foundation. That made me smile. He said I would know what to do with his remains.

Another wave of sadness comes over me as it hits me that I won't see him again. I walk outside to get some fresh air and stand against the mesh fence. The final hole of the golf course next door rises up in front of me. It's like a green path to the heavens. Tears trickle leisurely down my cheeks. I hear steps as someone walks towards me. Scott appears at my side with two glasses of wine.

He hands me one, then reaches up and gently wipes a tear from my chin.

'Nice funeral,' he says.

'Yeah, good turnout and all that. I wonder if he knew how many lives he had an impact on.'

'I hope so. I doubt we'll meet anyone like him again.'

I shake my head.

'You can come back to mine if you like afterwards, if you don't want to be alone.'

I raise both eyebrows at him.

'Oh, I see. That's rather sneaky, and at a funeral. You slope over saying how unforgettable and influential Trevor was, yet you're really just horny. Parents away, are they?'

'No, they're both at home.'

I smile but don't commit, although it's been a tough year. Perhaps I deserve a treat. I hold my glass up.

'To The Whirlwind!'

'The Whirlwind.'

So, it's goodbye to Trevor. Was he a man or a monster,

hero or villain? I guess that depends on your point of view. This wouldn't have been a sad day for Trevor, though. He'll be pleased to be back with his family. The tears pouring down my face are for me.

    I simply loved him.

CHAPTER 87

Four months later

Heathrow is heaving. We've checked in and dropped our baggage, so we're able to shop and people watch. There are loads of people checking us out, too. I've come to realise that airports are special places. All of our emotions and lifestyles are on display in one place. There's hope, excitement, sadness and joy written on the faces of every type of person dressed in every type of way.

It was the one-year anniversary of my release from prison yesterday. My licence has been completed, and I'm a free woman. I'm also a happy one. Brighton welcomed me like a returning daughter. It's been easy to build a life there.

I remember watching the TikTok videos and Instagram posts of others like me who were happy and surrounded by love and friendship. I wondered where they lived. They must be in places like Brighton, where you can be yourself. I'm so glad the world is slowly awakening to the truth. We are not all the same, and nor should we have to be.

I can't wait to see my mum, but my future is in England for the moment, so I'm only going home for two weeks. That said, I've been researching the pesticide industry in Ecuador, and that's something I'm going to look into whenever I have the time.

Right now, the cause I'm most interested in is my own, and that of people like me. It won't be easy. It never is when different groups' rights overlap, but we're all in this together. If we can remember that, then we should all have hope.

My boyfriend walks out of WHSmith. I watch him,

smiling as he looks around to see where I am. I receive a theatrical wave when he sees me. The smile turns into a grin. Johnny Chan. I even love the name.

You'd think someone like me wouldn't make mistakes around stereotypes, but I did with Johnny. Trevor called him the queer carpenter. I assumed it was just his homophobic terminology, but not in this case.

Johnny doesn't know how to describe himself most of the time. Sometimes he feels female, other times male, the rest of the time he isn't quite sure. He says he only has one certainty, and it's a wonderful one.

Johnny knew that he was in love the moment he met me. He joked to me that he'd swung both ways in the past, but he says he'll only swing my way in the future! What an absolute mush ball.

Not long before he died, Trevor had a chat with Johnny about pronouns, in particular the 'they' one. Johnny explained it to him, but said he preferred to be just called Johnny. He said that Trevor listened attentively, then said it sounded like a load of old bollocks. Johnny thinks he was joking.

When I picked up Trevor's ashes, I took them to his house and scattered them under that old yew tree. It was the same spot June and Trevor had put Felix, and the same place Trevor placed the remains of June and Angelica. They are together now. I imagine the little plastic seat was June's to start with, but then Trevor took up the mantle. I've sat there since myself. I cried and cried the first time, but I often think of their laughter now. Their spirits live on in me.

I did have a last night of passion with Scott after the funeral, but our relationship was never quite right. Part of me would have always suspected that he would never have seen me exactly as I am. Whereas Johnny doesn't think like that. He doesn't know what he is most of the time. So, what I am is of no consequence to him. He ticks non-binary on official forms if they have that option. It's becoming more common.

I told Scott that I was dating Johnny and it was serious.

He didn't beg me or anything. All he said was that, for a moment, it felt as though he was holding starlight. Like a fool, he let it go.

More talk like that and he might have had a chance!

Johnny says he loves it when we're together more than anything else in the world. Should it be any more complicated than that?

Right now, he swaggers towards me, looking like a cross between a hell's angel and a flamingo.

'They've called boarding, Robbie. Are you ready?'

I am ready. For everything. We stride through the airport together, sharing the occasional glance. It's great to be part of a team. I am not alone.

I have my outrageously expensive, high heel, strappy sandals on and a dress of Johnny's creation. It's short and figure hugging with a slit up to my hip on the right-hand side. People stop and watch as we pass. An older couple stare at me in surprise. No doubt because as well as the dress and heels, I'm made up to the nines. My hair is pure Cleopatra.

In black sequins across my chest is the word TRANS. It's part of a new range from a hopefully up and coming new designer, Johnny Chan. He called the range *Chan from Within*.

The face of the female of the older couple changes from a tired frown into a huge smile, and she slowly claps her hands. That's right, baby. Others gawp at us as I swish by. Today, *we* are whirlwinds.

They'll love the back of my dress, where it has the words, "LOVIN 'IT" written on my builder's arse.

And the colour of my dress? There can only be one. Canary yellow.

It's time to educate the world. I'd love you to help. Ask yourself the question. Will you be a canary, too?

The End

AUTHOR'S NOTE

Thank you for reading this novel. The initial inspiration came from two sources. The first was my sister. She had the most luscious thick long chestnut hair. When she was about thirty-years-old, it started to fall out. Alopecia Universalis. Strangely, it grew back when she had her first child. Just as it reached a length where she was considering what hairstyles would suit, it vanished again, never to return.

At the time it made me consider society's norms, or expected norms. She felt obliged to wear a wig to fit in. They are hot, sweaty and uncomfortable, never mind the expense for a good one. Going without one often results in unwanted stares as though a Martian has landed. It's tough for people like her to endure, especially if great hair was something they identified with.

To take control, she got her head tattooed. After an unpleasant divorce, she began internet dating. That's tough enough considering that it's very much based on looks. Imagine the scenario. You've had a few dates with someone, and you begin to connect. At some point, fairly quickly, you need to explain to them, actually, I'm bald.

How do you say it? When do you say it? Sex on the fourth date, and follicular revelations on the fifth? Sometimes the person has been admiringly stroking her hair while kissing her before she manages to pluck up the courage to tell them it isn't real.

It made me appreciate how lives can be so unexpectedly difficult. Cancer patients often go through similar experiences, but their 'secret' has an extra more devastating barb in the tail.

Put simply, at a very challenging time, it's an extra unwanted challenge.

The second motivation was from when I first started as a prison officer at HMP Peterborough, which is the only prison in the UK to have male and female inmates at the same location but who are kept separately in their own jails.

I was working on the male side, escorting the prisoners from the Vulnerable Prisoner unit to their visits. At the time, I used to escort them next to me if there was only one or two to move, while the rest of the prison was still operating normally. Later, after too many assaults, the route had to be cleared for their safety.

The VPs were regularly subjected to abuse from the other inmates, who would shout paedo and worse at them as they passed by. Rightfully so, some would say, for what they'd done.

Yet the VP unit wasn't only a sex offenders wing, it was the place where we put the people who were vulnerable to being exploited or attacked by mainstream inmates. This of course was mostly sex offenders. Rapists and child abusers get fiercely assaulted in prison. It's one of those things. But the wing also included those who had impairments of any kind. That might be those with autism or other learning difficulties, or folk who simply couldn't mentally handle the vicious atmosphere of a mainstream wing.

Not long after I started, I returned a prisoner to the VP wing and found a young, slim, mixed-race woman in civilian clothing standing on the other side of the gate. She had very tight light-blue jeans on, a white cotton shirt that was tied at the waist, and little black prison pumps. In that moment in time on that wing, leaving a woman on there alone would have been akin to tethering a goat inside the T-Rex enclosure.

'Hi, sir,' she said to me with a wink.

How the prison system processed transgender people hadn't even occurred to me. Going to prison shakes your foundations. Imagine arriving with all the worries that entails. That's without thinking about gender. Imagine if you were a trans woman, dressed that way, and you were placed on a male wing which was occupied by those who'd abused children with the odd violent rapist dotted around.

Saying that, the vast majority of the inmates, whilst curious to start with, accepted trans people quickly. Even behind high walls covered in razor wire, most people are human. Being behind bars is a great equaliser. Everyone in prison has enough of their own serious troubles for them to worry too much about others.

This woman became one of my favourite prisoners. Permanently upbeat, despite what challenges were thrown her way, she regularly made me laugh. Although, I often wondered if the mask slipped when her cell door closed.

She was one of the few prisoners on my landing for whom I didn't check why they were in prison. I didn't want to know, even though the length of her sentence would mean it wasn't a minor offence.

Another motivation for this tale, which came much later, was the builder. We had some building work done over the last year. As with such things, it was a bit of a nightmare going over budget and time. The Trevor in this story does exist. Perhaps not quite as exaggerated as I've made him, but not too far off. I bet most readers know people like him. I bet most of you like them.

His lad quit just before he started my job, so I laboured for him. It was tough work and a real eye-opener. Like Robbie, I spilled the concrete, struggled with jack hammers, filled skips, shovelled, lifted, and felt the peace that an honest day's labour provides.

I just thought Trevor was a fabulous contrast to the more woke element of our society. How Trevor changes in this book is how the rest of society is beginning to change. It's how we are all awakening.

It's not easy for a lot of people. If you've grown up and lived your life in a binary world, seeing it as any different is hard. For some, their God is a higher power than their parliament. This change is coming though. It's being largely driven by generation Z and those younger. They are the future.

If you're thinking, I don't get it, then you aren't alone. Luckily, as Angelica said in the book, we have the internet. www.healthline.com/health/transgender is a great place to start.

Authors tend to get an idea in their heads, and it grows. The characters come alive, and it's almost as though they want their stories to be told. Even so, I decided that perhaps I wasn't the right person to write a book like this. Cancel culture is alive and kicking, even though those affected by the issues in this book understand that shutting the conversation down is usually more damaging than getting it wrong.

What changed my mind is a very sad tale. In February last year, I hadn't heard from my friend Sharyn for a while, and I felt the urge to ring her. We'd known each other nearly thirty years with her best friend being the girlfriend of a guy I lived with when I was twenty-one.

She got married fairly young and had two children, setting up home in Peterborough while I moved away, but we often bumped into each other at the local pub on Christmas Day. We also caught up a few times when I finally grew up and returned to my hometown to raise a young family.

That day, I messaged her on Facebook. She replied that she'd just arrived at the hospital on her own due to Covid restrictions. It was to have a scan after being very ill over New Year. She was frightened and in a lot of pain. She was only forty-six.

Her funeral was on a warm day the following August. It was sad and uplifting, as those services for the young often are. Sharyn was more into science than religion. In life she had been a busy ball of determination and enthusiasm. She was full of energy. She believed that the energy in the world is never lost, it merely moves elsewhere. She hoped that each one of us would receive some of her energy now that she'd left us, and we would use it to do something positive.

Kae, who spoke these words on Sharyn's behalf, had lost her teenage daughter, Abby, to cancer the year before, and she was inspirational in managing to finish that speech. You may remember the dedication at the start of this book. At the wake, many people came across to tell Kae they had taken something from the reading, and to thank her for being so strong and brave. I detected real purpose when they said they would act on Sharyn's words.

The next day, I received a message from one of Sharyn's friends.

She said that Sharyn's seventeen-year-old daughter had taken the decision to share that he wished to actively live as a male and be referred to as he/him. He asked that his mum's friends be contacted to inform them. He would like to be known as Darren going forward and appreciated our understanding and acceptance of this.

I got in touch with Darren to offer support and encouragement, saying I had some knowledge of the topic. We got chatting and I mentioned the idea for the book and that I wasn't going to write it. Darren helped change my mind. He said that what their community needs right now is a better awareness from the public about the struggles they're going through.

Gender dysphoria dramatically affects those who suffer with it from the moment they wake up in the morning and look in the mirror. Each new day often starts with a feeling of suffocation. At this point in time, very few people have any understanding of what they're going through. Some think they decide to be trans on a whim.

Through Darren, I received plenty of help and guidance as I wrote this book, both from him and others in the trans community. I've even had trans inmates read it whilst on the wrong side of the bars.

Years ago, when I had the idea, I thought it would be a different book about different people. But the hopeful reality is that one day, it won't be a big deal. It will just be a normal book about normal people. Apart from all the killing, of course.

It took a while for me to get my head around what it's like to be trans. Darren, in particular, has been so kind with his time at a moment in his life that is hard to comprehend. His school haven't found accommodating him easy, mostly due to centuries of tradition, but like Trevor, they're getting there. Darren is breaking down barriers and making it safer for those who come after him. Darren is a canary.

The world is full of them if you know where to look. You could even argue that the migrants taking incredible risks to cross seas and mountains are canaries. How many more must die before we take notice that more barbed wire and soldiers with guns won't stop the waves? It merely makes it more dangerous. As our planet warms, heavily populated parts of our planet will cease to be habitable. A great migration will begin. The tide is coming in.

Those who go on ahead, the brave, the reckless, the desperate, will surely make it safer for those who follow. Now is the time to decide a way forward that works. It is a trickle now, but a tsunami will follow. How many more children do we need to collect from our beaches before we say enough?

So, thank you for reading my story, and that's all it is. Some of these views are my own, others are just the characters'. I wished to create debate because only that starts the process of change. Consideration, acceptance and kindness are the engines that drive it.

I imagined right at the beginning that the twist would be the trans element. But perhaps the real twist is that after the obvious surprises due to our assumptions, the story just carries on. You are already invested in Robbie and Trevor, and perhaps Johnny if you saw that coming. The gender of the people becomes unimportant. It's just a crime story about people like you and me, with all our flaws and strengths, and all our hopes and dreams.

One of my older beta readers described this novel as like

reaching a doorway. She felt like she was stepping through that door into the world she actually lived in, as opposed to remaining in the world she thought she lived in. It's a choice for everyone. Enter, or walk on by. Please, give it some thought because people are suffering.

My local prison was kind enough to let me return and visit the female side of the jail where they had three trans men on the enhanced wing. We had a chat for an hour about their experiences within those walls and before their sentences. They helped immensely with the terminology and feelings in the book. Again, I was struck by their empathy. They've been through many tough experiences, yet they are still aware of others struggles.

Funnily enough, the publisher for my detective novels turned down this novel saying it was too negative a view. The three men in prison said I'd sugar-coated it a little. As with all things, people's experiences will differ, with how and where they grew up, and factors like money and family make a big difference.

Those inmates had all suffered hardships. One was in prison because he was waiting for space at a psychiatric hospital. Another had been living as a man for a long time and his friends were unaware he was AFAB. So how could they visit, if he was being held in a female jail? Even his arrest warrant and court paperwork were in his dead name.

The three guys were still hopeful for the future. They can see change is coming. It's clear to them that by remaining positive and maintaining respectful dialogue, it will be easier for those who follow.

In fact, the whole concept of being a canary is an interesting one. Throughout history, people have taken incredible risks with their own happiness and safety to make the world a better place for those who tread their path afterwards. Many have lost their lives.

That applies to lots of different causes. Some were persecuted, others were ignored or made to live as second-class citizens. The most inspiring people on our planet have already paid, or are paying, a high price to help others. Martin Luther King Jr, the students in Tiananmen Square, Belarus, Mother Teresa, Uighurs, Karl Heinrich Ulrichs, Emmeline Pankhurst, Judith Heumann, the founders of many religions, the list goes on and on. We can now add Ukraine to it.

Many others do incredible things, but society ignores them, then history forgets them.

One of the most inspirational people in the history of the world is Nelson Mandela. He spent thirty years in dreadful conditions, some of which were spent actually breaking rocks in an arid courtyard with a small hammer. His story is so inspiring because if ever there was a man who should have been angry and vengeful when he was released from his lengthy incarceration, it was him. But he wasn't. His was a message of love and tolerance, and that's why he was so successful.

In a way, whatever your cause, be it gay rights, women's rights, disabled rights, or another, Mandela's message is important. It's sometimes difficult not to affect other people's rights in pursuit of your own, so be tolerant, understanding and forgiving as he was, even though it may take practice.

Human nature dictates that you don't make progress, or change people's minds, by shouting in their faces or insulting them. Blocking roads so people can't reach their sick children or spitting at the police polarises people. It stops the conversation, or people stop listening.

Having said that, you can understand the fury of climate change protesters when governments and big industry don't listen. Cash rich companies continue to make bigger profits while the poor pay the price. Meanwhile, the earth burns.

At the end of the day, all of these causes are noble. Let's shine a light on them. It's time for some real progress.

I have a final observation. How come it's the suffering party who always have to be the better person to achieve change? It's the curse of the repressed. When will they inherit the earth?

After a discussion, we thought it would be a good idea to finish the novel with Darren having a few pages to say something for himself. It's time for people like him to be heard. His message follows on from here.

Read his words with an open heart. My book is fiction.

His life is not.

DARREN'S MESSAGE TO THE WORLD

Aged eighteen

Being trans isn't easy as you may now understand having read this book. It's an extremely challenging thing for anyone to have to go through. It doesn't happen overnight, as many seem to think. There are years of confusion beforehand.

I couldn't understand why I felt different to everyone else. An on-going sense of loneliness developed as I struggled to see myself fitting in anywhere. I sometimes wondered if that feeling would ever leave me. It is absolutely not a choice. I think I speak for most trans people when I say that if it were a choice, we wouldn't pick it.

Why would you choose to be hated by so many people? Why opt to pay thousands of pounds for operations that have serious risks involved? Waiting years to access treatment on an underfunded NHS is bad enough without all the hate we receive for simply trying our best to be happy.

I hope that reading this book may give you an insight into the struggles of being transgender and maybe even change some people's views on us. We are just trying to live our lives.

I hope that in the future more and more people begin to acknowledge this lack of choice. We go through turmoil, both mentally and physically, and any support from kind people goes a long way. A sympathetic word, showing interest, or just asking how we are, helps me feel alive.

For many of us, the most important opinion is that of an adult we are close with. It could be a parent, an aunt, or a family friend. You'd hope that all these people would offer support, but that is often far from the case. The support of the adults in my life has definitely made me feel more seen. This makes me feel happier, and perhaps more importantly, it helps me feel safe.

People like my mum's friend Ross offering support and understanding, and chatting to me about football like two dudes together reassures me that I am normal, because that is so hurtful, when people imply that I'm not. They forget that we are human. I have feelings, too.

Although it's an incredibly difficult journey to go through, it is character building. If you meet trans people, you will invariably find us empathetic. We understand how it feels not to fit in, or to know that you aren't respected, because I've regularly felt that way my whole life. It has made me way more considerate of how people might be feeling in certain situations. It has given me the confidence to speak out for them, even though it has taken me many years to find my own voice. Going through this allows me to see who's struggling in a room, and I will try to help.

I hope you'll treat trans people with respect. Our lives can be extremely difficult. We are just humans who've been given the wrong body and have no idea why.

Hopefully this book will allow you to consider the concept. Perhaps you will talk to your friends about it which would be fabulous. For many people out there, the conversation hasn't even started.

The UK has made progress over recent years, but it still feels like they are discussing our rights, as opposed to actively protecting them. For some people, as soon as we mention we are trans, our rights and feelings fly out of the window.

Trans people understand that for those who've grown up in a binary world, it can be a difficult concept to get your head around. We don't mind if you make mistakes and get our pronouns muddled up, because we sometimes do it too. Making mistakes is part of learning, and that brings us closer.

We don't care if you say that you don't get it because for many people, that's the start of their journey to finally understanding who we are.

That we are here. That I am me. And I am real.

Photos below: Ross and Trevor. Beautiful.

CANARIES IN THE COAL MINE

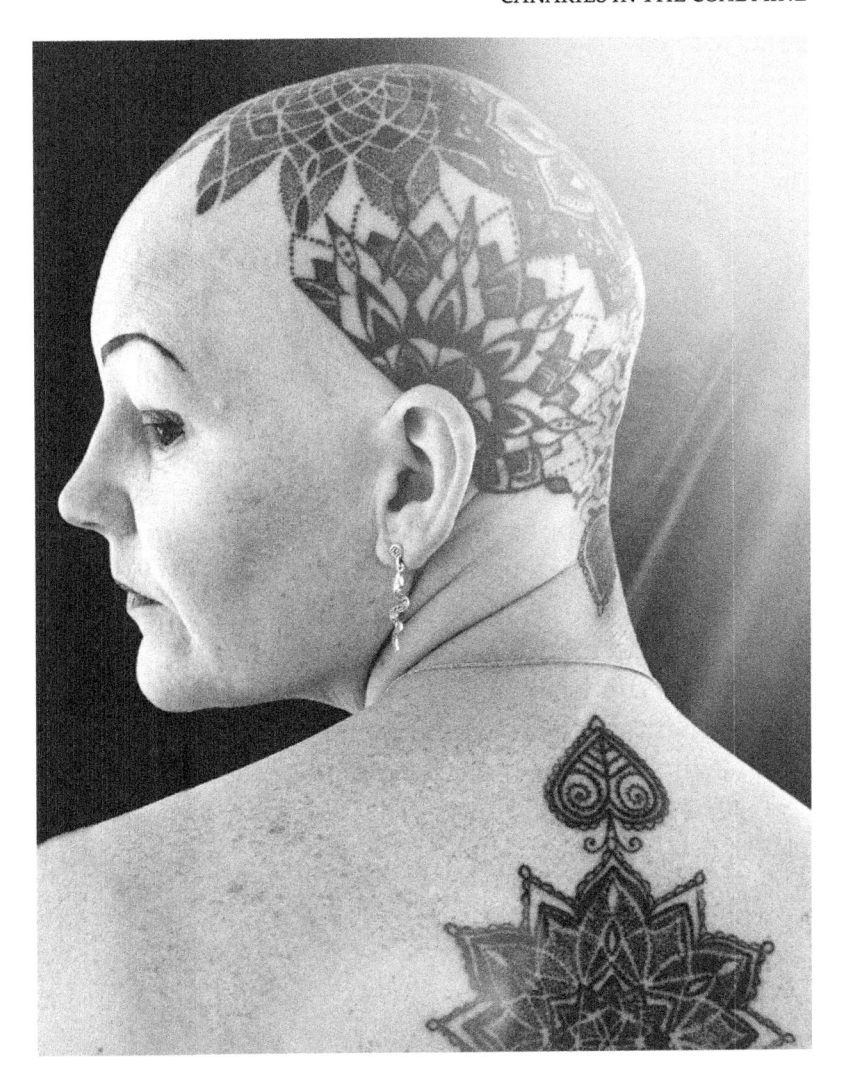

THANKS TO

It's hard to know where to start. Over a hundred people read this book through its incarnation. Everyone gave helpful feedback. There were only a few indifferent reviews. Some loved the prison part, and others the personal struggle of the main characters, but everyone learned something.

So I'd just like to thank those who've been involved for their honest and personal feedback. Every single reader had someone in their family or in their friends' circle who has been affected by the issues that have been covered. Whether it be prison, mental health struggles or their identity.

A lot of progress has been made, but more can be done.

Have your say and write a review on Amazon, and, please, tell others about it.

Printed in Great Britain
by Amazon